ON THE CASE
EDWARD MCKEOWN

THE
LAIR OF THE LESBIAN
Love Goddess
FILES

Cover Art by Pat Ventura

MoonDream
PRESS

AN IMPRINT OF COPPER DOG PUBLISHING, LLC

On The Case
The Lair of The Lesbian Love Goddess Files

Copyright ©2015 Edward McKeown

Published by Moondream Press, an imprint of Copper Dog Publishing, LLC
537 Leader Circle
Louisville, CO 80027

Visit our Web site: www.copperdogpublishing.com

Credits:
On The Case written by Edward McKeown
Cover and Interior Design: Helen Harrison

Cover art: Pat Ventura

Library of Congress Control Number: 2015919004

ISBN: 978-1-943690-07-7 Print

ISBN: 978-1-943690-05-3 Kindle

First Edition: November 2015

Printed in the United States of America

Stories previously published in other magazines or anthologies:
Lair of the Lesbian Love Goddess first published in *Lowport* 2003
Into the Robot Harem first published 2003 *Far Sector*
Al Clone Capone first published in *Futures Mysterious Magazine* 2005
Geeks from the Stratosphere first published 2003 *Far Sector*
Bloodsucking Gourmets from Outer Space first published in *Bloodlust* 2002
Bone to Pick first published in *Goremet Cuisine* 2005
Mars needs Men! first published in *Hellfire publications* 2009
The Robot not Taken First Place *Crosstime* SF contest and first published in the *Crosstime Anthology Vol VII* (nominated for New Mexcio Book Award 2008)

DEDICATION

Dedicated to all my friends who have helped

me with my dream of writing

CONTENTS

FOREWORD

By Tim McLoughlin

EVER SINCE ISAAC ASIMOV SMACKED DOWN EDITOR JOHN W. Campbell's assertion that science fiction and mystery tales couldn't be successfully combined, by writing the classic *Caves of Steel* in 1954, the floodgates have been open to writers eager to try their hand at the sub-genre. All of the permutations of crime fiction can now be found in science fiction and fantasy stories, from cozy amateur detectives to dystopian noirish thrillers.

The stories in *On the Case* are private eye tales with characters firmly grounded in investigative methods of the police procedural, which, for me, and you, is the best of both worlds. Oh yeah, and they're a hell of a lot of fun.

What Edward McKeown does in the stories collected here, as he does with all of his writing, is a marriage of classic structure to absolutely contemporary detail. When he goes serious he's as good as Larry Niven's Gil Hamilton, when he goes light he's like Eric Frank Russell, and either way he is constantly reinventing the sub-genre. McKeown's 24th century Port Authority may be frequented by a knockaround guy who cracks wise like Bogie, but he has a female coworker who is every bit as brave and resourceful as he, if not more so. She's a partner in the truest sense of the word, not an assistant or a sidekick. And when we *are* introduced to the sidekick, a sexy office vamp named Freddie Bouvier, she comes equipped with a few factory extras, being a transgendered drag queen. See, this is McKeown's gift: he tells tales like Heinlein, and he makes them brand new. In *The Robot Not Taken*, a tip of the hat to Asimov's robot stories, he introduces a highly functioning artificial intelligence to poetry, and the result is a beautiful rumination on what it means to be human. But he is by no means a guy locked in the Golden Age, he's a cultural omnivore. One of my favorite pieces, *Drowning in the Past*, is inspired by Ed's love of Japanese Anime.

If you have read any of these stories when they were first published you'll be thrilled to see how they are integrated into a – dare I say it – novelistic story arc. And if you haven't, well then I really envy you the ride. Enjoy!

Tim McLoughlin—Editor of *Brooklyn Noir* and author of *Heart of the Old Country*

INTRODUCTION

by Edward McKeown

SOME BOOKS START AS A LABOR OF LOVE, THIS ONE STARTED as a labor of laughs. One night my writing group was wondering about a missing member. This person was something of a character and prone to disappear for considerable intervals. One friend observed that she had probably disappeared into "the Lair of the Lesbian Love Goddess." I immediately wanted to know where that was! Suffice to say, I know now but am sworn to secrecy. Don't ask.

The sound of it though kept going around and around in my ears. It had the pulp-noir ring to it, like a 1930 serial gone horribly wrong and kinky. And so was born the Lair series with Brian McManus, everyman cop, Regina Del Mar his attractive and ambitious new partner and best of all and originally not appreciated, Freddie Bouvier, transgender informant and later Gal Friday. In earlier versions of these stories I sometimes referred to Freddie as a transvestite, which was largely out of ignorance, live and learn. Freddie was originally a minor character, almost a throw in as I wanted a street hooker to serve as an informant, but the usual characters seemed too stock and flat (Freddie is anything but flat) and I decided to reach for something more.

Horror of horrors, I almost killed off my Elvira-looking Freddie in the second story before my group staged an intervention to save Freddie. As they pointed out he had the best lines and since I wanted my everyman character to be faithful to his wife, Freddie generated a weird little substitute for sexual tension.

The original Lair story gave me my introduction to respectability being published in Lowport, a hardcover anthology actually sold in major bookstores. Most of these stories have been printed, some multiple times in multiple formats. However there are two stories seen here for the first time, *Seachange* and the dear to my heart, *Drowning in the Past*. This last one is something of an homage to my anime and horror roots, honoring an episode of Princess Resurrection and several movies about drowned cities and towns.

I am not through with these characters and there has been talk of a book but for now, enjoy the stories.

CHAPTER ONE

THE ONE, THE ONLY, THE ORIGINAL
LAIR OF THE LESBIAN LOVE GODDESS

I STRAINED TO READ THE MOVIE HOLO-MARQUEE THROUGH the rain-smeared windows of our unmarked aircar. The sonics weren't doing a very good job of keeping the windscreen clear from the driving gusts. Sometimes I think we were better off with the old-style solid wipers. A gust blew a clear spot on the windscreen. "*Lair of the Lesbian Love Goddess,*" I read aloud.

"Yeah, great," said my new partner, Regina Delmar. "You sure he went in there? It's a duplex. What's the other movie?"

"*Countdown to Cannibalism,*" I said. "Hey, I've heard of that one. A bunch of writers get stuck in a turbovator and end up eating each other. The survivor writes a book and wins a Pulitzer."

"Maybe he went in there?"

I looked at her. "Reg, he may be Arcturian, but he's male. He went into *Lair of the Lesbian Love Goddess.*"

"What is it with men always wanting to watch two women have sex?" she said, obviously disgusted with males of all species. "And I prefer Regina."

Rather than debate the basic psyche of the male gender, I changed the subject. "Do you want to catch this bozo or what?"

"Did Command have any idea what the Arcturians are smuggling?"

"Nope–just a buzz that there's something new, hot and illicit driving Arcturians wild and this Toldas Harkarian is the Arcturian at the bottom of it. Don't know if it's tech, drugs or biologicals. Just that there's a lot of money flowing all of a sudden. Who knows, maybe it's some new version of cyber-feelies for the movies."

"Like we don't have enough of that now," Regina sniffed. "Seems like there's another of these porno cyber-feelie palaces every week in the offport. Just more sleazy films."

"Hey, are you a Port Authority Cop or a movie critic?"

"Okay, okay. Let's nail this creep. And no watching the movie."

"Yes, ma'am," I grumbled.

We exited the unmarked into the cold, wet streets of what used to be Red Hook, Brooklyn. New York City in the late 21nd century burst its old bounds, adding artificial reefs and islands. Red Hook was no longer the shoreline; it was part of the off-port. In the distance we could hear the gathering rumble of a climbing starship as it took off from what used to be part of the Atlantic Ocean.

Regina was out front, as usual, hot-dogging again. Young, ambitious and just out of uniform into the detective ranks, she was grimly determined to be the youngest NYPA captain on the force. I'm only three years away from getting my twenty in and retiring. The last thing I needed was a hotshot bucking for rank.

The Lieutenant stuck me with her after Frank retired as punishment for one of my periodic dust-ups with Command. I never could learn to keep my mouth shut, so I inherited Regina. She had all the hallmarks for success: she was young, pretty, fearless, and tough. My wife hated her with the dispassionate hatred wives reserve for good-looking women who spend all day with their husbands. Me? I was just afraid she was going to get me killed.

We flashed our tin at the old guy in the ticket booth. Regina leaned into his box as we walked in. "You give any alarm and they'll be washing what's left of you off the walls."

The old man gulped and dove back into his newspaper. I groaned inwardly and thought of Internal Affairs.

We started looking for our Harkarian. Arcturians were common in this area of the Port of New York, but I didn't think we'd see many in here. Like most of his species, our boy would be about eight feet tall, with gray pebbly skin. Fortunately, he also had a big patch of white scarring on the dorsal fin that rose from the crest of his head.

Regina stopped and I almost ran into her. Silently, she pointed at a small mirror over the long-unused concession stand. The Arcturian stood around the corner from us, wrapped in a heavy, gray travel cloak. He was handing a package to someone we couldn't see.

"Come on Brian, let's get him," she whispered.

"Wait," I replied, "stun settings don't work on Arcturians. We better call for back…" too late, Regina was off and running.

"Halt, police," she yelled.

"Oh, hell," I said.

The Arcturian bolted. Whoever had been with him was gone already. All eight feet of the alien sped for the entrance to the movie theatre.

Just as I started running, the door to the john opened. I slammed into it full tilt. "Hey," yelled a bearded man as we both crashed to the ground.

"Police," I snarled, struggling to my feet. I looked around frantically for Regina. She was closing with the Arcturian when he turned, throwing a glass sphere that hit her in the chest and shattered. Immediately, smoke started to rise from her clothes.

"Reg," I yelled, running toward her. "Molecular acid! Get out of your armor before it eats through." I pulled my service pistol, but my partner was jumping up and down, frantically stripping right in my line of fire.

I reached Regina's side. Her jacket and the body armor on her shoulders and chest protected her from having her skin dissolved immediately, but the acid worked fast. She dropped the big chest panel as holes began to appear in it. I kicked open a door to find what I desperately hoped for, a janitor's bucket full of water. Regina had stripped down to a bra, but a dot must have hit the bra's bridge strap. It parted and the bra practically blew off. I upended the big bucket of cold, filthy water over her, the best chemical base handy to counter any acid left. She let out a howl as the water hit her back.

"That should do it," I said, looking over my now topless partner for any sign of acid burning. I couldn't help noticing that she kept a spectacular pair concealed under her armor. God bless body armor.

"I'll kill him," yelled Regina, pulling her sidearm. Before I could stop her, she plunged through the doors into the *Lair of the Lesbian Love Goddess*. This time I was only a few steps behind my track-star partner.

The Arcturian was battering down the exit door diagonal from us when I came in. Regina hurdled over the rows of seats and the occasional moviegoer. Not being a gazelle, I ran down the long way. I cheated on Regina's early admonition and looked up at the screen. At least three women writhed in an erotic tangle, doing something very unusual. I ran into a seat. Concentrate, I thought to myself. The moviegoers with their visual and sensory helmets were either too distracted by the agile minxes on screen, or they assumed the topless Regina and the Arcturian were part of the film. *Well*, I thought, *porno is usually short on plot anyway.*

Regina tripped and landed on one guy. He promptly grabbed her breasts. "Man, this is some great simulation," he said to his friend. Regina whacked him over the head with her pistol. He slid out of sight, disappearing into the general ick that coated the floor. I ran past Regina, for once in the lead, and dashed out what was left of the door. The Arcturian was gone, its two-meter stride having taken it out of sight.

Regina dashed up behind me and looked both ways.

"Shit," she said, breathing hard.

"Did you see the other guy?" I asked.

"No," she said, "just a foot as he went though the other door."

I looked at her. "Your magnificent bosom is heaving," I observed.

Glare.

I slipped out of my jacket and handed it to her.

"Thanks," she growled.

"I'm never telling my wife about this little chase," I said, "and neither are you."

Unexpectedly, Regina gave a rueful laugh. "I guess I went a little gung-ho."

"Just a bit," I replied. "You spooked a big tough alien that our stunners can't stop. That means we either had to use deadly force or take him down by hand. The former is undesirable, as he's our only lead, and the latter was probably impossible."

"Plus, God damn it," I added, "you almost got the aforementioned magnificent bosom, which I now have to forget I ever saw, chewed up by an anti-personnel acid-ball."

"Boy, I sure don't sound too smart," she replied. She gave me a rather enigmatic look. "So why do you have to forget my magnificent bosom, having saved it?"

"I got involved with a woman partner twenty years ago when I was single. It redefined utter, complete disaster. Now that I am married it would be utter, complete disaster squared."

Reg grinned at me. Sometimes I really had to work at staying mad at her. "I'll bear that in mind," she said. "Thanks anyway."

"Back to business," she continued. "How do we find our guy now? There are a thousand Arcturians or better in their section of the port."

"Well, we're not going to get anything else done tonight. It'll be sunrise in a few hours. Start of shift tomorrow night we'll go talk to Fredericka."

"Who's she?"

"Funny you should ask," I said, holstering my gun.

We found Freddie, or Fredericka, as he preferred, trolling for spacers around some of the wilder off-port bars in what used to be Governor's Island. Freddie did an astonishing job of passing for a good-looking girl: with glossy black hair, a splendid surgically-enhanced rack, and nice legs. Freddie had the brains to do other things, but his soul had turned dark early. Or as he put it, 'I like the night life.'

We cruised over to the curb. Freddie spotted the unmarked and smiled a lop-sided smile after he saw it was me. We got out of the car. It was still raining, always seemed to be lately.

"McManus," said Freddie, looking out from under an umbrella at me. "You finally come to your senses and leave your wife for me?" The husky voice didn't quite give Freddie away. A whisky voice my dad would have called it.

"Sorry, Freddie," I replied, "not that you don't look good."

Freddie did a mocking pirouette, his dress swirling up around legs that were unfairly feminine. "So what can I do for you Flatfoot?" he asked, using my street name while glancing down at my size twelve brogans.

"Knock off the crap," Reg snapped.

Freddie raised an eyebrow at Regina. "Ooohhh, she's a cutey. New girlfriend, Brian?"

"Freddie, meet Detective Regina Delmar. Reg meet Freddie."

"That's Regina," she said archly, then, looking at Freddie, added, "and to you it's Detective Delmar."

Freddie extended a hand. Reg ignored it, so Freddie turned it into a curtsey. I could see Regina going into a slow burn.

"Come on, ladies, there's a coffee shop across the street. We can get out of the rain. I'll even buy."

"See," said Freddie with a wicked grin. "Brian thinks I'm a lady."

Reg muttered something obscene under her breath.

Hoping gunfire wouldn't break out behind me, I led the way to a little Greek shop. We slipped in out of the rain and grabbed a table by the window. Gusts of errant wind scrubbed rain into the gutters outside. The waiter, a Rigellian, looked like a cross between an old man and a goat. He smelled like the goat. He brought us coffee and danishes. I triggered the booth's sonic curtain for privacy.

"So, Freddie," I said, "what do you know about Arcturians?"

"Bad people," Freddie said with a delicate shudder. "Got a lot of weight and like throwing it around."

"Lately there's one who seems to be moving into the smuggling racket," I said. I sipped the coffee, savoring its warmth and smell. The danish was good too.

"Heard that," Freddie said.

"What else have you heard?" Regina asked.

Freddie gave me an expectant look.

I slipped a small envelope across the table to Freddie. He took it without looking inside. It was the usual. Not much, but it was a ritual. It insulated us from any thought that our relationship was anything other than business.

"There's an Arcturian named Toldas Harkarian," Freddie said, "trying to set up a network to move something past a few corrupt customs guys over in Area 88. Haven't heard what it is. You tangled with him last night, I hear."

"How do you know that?" Reg asked.

"Oh, honey," Freddie said. "When a beautiful female cop goes running topless through a feelie-porno, whacking people on the head...well...word gets around. You've got a street handle now: Topless."

I could hear Regina's teeth grinding.

Freddie continued, "The Arcturian is working with Rat-face Moestel. He owns the theatre. Say, did you catch any of *Lair of the Lesbian Love Goddess*?"

"I was too busy to watch," I lied, not daring to look at Regina.

"Film's got artistic merit," Freddie said, "especially the scenes where the Love Goddess ties up—"

"Freddie," I said, exasperated.

"Oh, all right. You know Moestel?"

"Yeah, I know him," I replied. "Never heard of him being mixed up in anything other than sleazy movies."

"He moves a lot of stuff out the back of the theatre," Freddie said. "Fenced goods, contraband, things that fall off the truck when the union boys are loading."

"The uniforms should have picked up on that," Reg said.

"Unless they are being paid to look the other way," I replied.

"The theatre is the drop-point for the stuff, whatever it is. That's all I know."

"Thanks, Freddie," I said.

Freddie drained the last of his coffee. "See you around Flatfoot. Thanks for the coffee. Nice to meet you, Topless. I'm sure I'll be seeing more of you too." Freddie sashayed out into the dark and rain.

Regina started to say something but caught my eye and subsided.

After a minute, we got up and headed for the car. The rain awaited us. It fit my mood. Seeing Freddie always made me feel sad. His was a wasted life and nothing would change it. We got back into the car.

"How do you know that...that person?" asked Reg

"Freddie was getting the crap beat out of him by some spacers. False advertising."

"What?"

"Goods delivered were not goods bargained for. Some of those Free Traders get kind of picky about that sort of stuff."

She looked at me.

"You know, our work day would feel a lot shorter if you'd develop a sense of humor."

"Ha-ha," she replied.

"Okay, that was gruesome," I said. "Anyway, they had poor Freddie beat half to death when I stopped them. Took him to the hospital, made sure he was okay."

"What are you a cop, or a social worker?" Reg asked.

I started the car and put it in gear. The turbines whined. "All creatures great and small," I quoted, "the Lord God made them all."

An hour later we crept into the alley behind the theatre. This time we both had our weapons drawn. I was wondering why I let Regina talk me into doing this without back-up. Again. Her pride, I suppose. Slowly, we made our way to a window outside what the city computer said was a storage room. We crouched below it. The glass was partially cracked and a chunk was gone from one pane.

I started to rise for a look when a voice sounded from inside the room.

"Do you have the cargo, Human?" rumbled a deep, heavily accented voice.

I quickly sat down on my haunches and looked at Regina.

The Arcturian, she mouthed silently. I wet my lips and nodded. The S.O.B must be just on the other side of the glass.

"Yeah, it's all here," said a recognizably human voice. "And I told you, the name's Moestel. The customs guys are covered and everything is ready to go."

I looked at Reg and nodded. We hit the back door side by side, crashing through.

"Freeze! Police," I yelled.

Rat-face squeaked as he dropped to the floor. The Arcturian turned toward us and lurched forward, a gray-skinned tower of muscle. His hands were empty, so I couldn't shoot him. I leaned to the right and kicked his knee. Hard. He made a booming sound and began hopping on one leg. His hand whooshed over my head as I ducked. Regina leaped with a "*ki-yah*" and kicked him full in the chest. The Arcturian crashed into some crates behind him with a howl.

Three of the large crates broke and cats exploded into the room. Lots of cats. All colors and shapes. They ran frantically in all directions. Most of them ran over the Arcturian. His arms and legs jerked spasmodically, he gave a loud cry, then collapsed.

Rat-face looked at me from the floor. "I ain't saying nothing till I see my lawyer."

Ambulances came and took the comatose Arcturian away. Rat-face left in the paddy wagon. Animal control arrived, called for reinforcements, and gathered up the cats as evidence. There was much hissing and scratching. Some of it was from Regina. "Cats," she kept repeating, "they were smuggling cats."

After several hours of writing reports, the Lieutenant called us down to the hospital where the unconscious Arcturian had been taken. The Precinct Captain had been and gone by the time we arrived. The Lieutenant was staring at two Arcturians as we walked into the ward. One wore a doctor's coat, carrying a medical scanner.

The Lieutenant looked over at us sourly. "So you're here finally. Detectives McManus and Delmar, meet Dr. Verhoo and Mr. Sandanvah of the Arcturian Legation."

Diplomats, I thought. *Crap.*

"How's the prisoner?" Regina asked crisply.

"His condition is serious," replied Dr. Verhoo. "While he is no longer in danger of dying, the coma may be indefinite, a side effect of extreme sexual stimulation in our species."

"Excuse me?" Regina said.

"This brings up a delicate subject," Mr. Sandanvah said. "It is only recently that we've learned that the presence of *Felis catus* causes a state of almost manic sexual arousal in the Arcturian species. Harkarian accidentally discovered this on his last voyage. He brought home a few felines and sold them for fabulous sums."

"Cats," I said.

"Yes," replied the doctor with a hint of defensiveness. "Does not petting a cat generate a feeling of euphoria in your own species?"

"Usually only in women of a certain age and marital status," I replied.

"The effect is many hundred times greater in one of our species," the doctor stated.

"So, when he fell into crates full of them..." Regina began.

"Essentially a lifetime of sexual pleasure crammed into a few seconds before his nervous system simply shut down," finished the doctor.

Hysterical laughter lurked at the back of my throat. "Couldn't handle a little—"

"Don't say it!" interrupted Regina.

"Our species would find it most embarrassing if this were to become generally known. We must keep this entirely quiet. Your President has assured us of your cooperation."

"Of course," I said, trying desperately to keep a straight face. The Lieutenant looked daggers at me.

The two aliens bowed and walked off, deep in conversation.

I looked at the Lieutenant. "Don't say it," he ordered.

I pressed my lips together firmly.

"So," began our Lieutenant, "thanks to you two, we got Arcturian brass talking to Earth brass, who are talking to the Chief, who is talking to the Captain, who told me that it was a good thing that we had all this spare time on our hands from chasing tech, drugs, and illegal aliens, so we could now chase pussycats!

"And all I wanted," mourned the Lieutenant, "was a quiet shift where nothing happened." He looked at us darkly. "Back to the streets for you two. Try not to stir up any more trouble and, for God's sake, avoid reporters."

"Yeah," I said. Regina followed me out silently. I made it all the way to the parking deck before I collapsed against a wall, laughing my ass off.

"It's not funny," Regina snapped. "We aren't even going to get credit for the bust."

"The case of *Lust in the Lair of the Lesbian Love Goddess*," I laughed in a mock British accent. "After all, it was all about kinky sex. Or maybe we should call it, *"Looking for some Earth..."*

"Don't say it," she yelled.

I looked at her and laughed harder as tears came to my eyes. After a moment, she couldn't help it and started laughing too. We both ended up sitting on our butts, incapacitated.

After we laughed ourselves out, I turned to her. "Well, Topless, wanna go fight some crime?"

She sighed. "Why not, Flatfoot. I don't think I'll be sitting for the Lieutenant's exam anytime soon."

We hopped in the cruiser and headed out of the parking lot. Overhead, thunder rumbled through the sky. It seemed it was always raining lately.

CHAPTER TWO

INTO THE ROBOT HAREM

"**M**Y FEET ARE KILLING ME," I GROANED. ACROSS THE RIVER, the UN President's hovercade sped under the Brooklyn Bridge on its way to a meeting with the Snorge Premier at the UN building. We stood atop the South Street Seaport Museum overlooking the old sailing ships and primitive subs making up the exhibits.

Detective Regina Delmar sat on an air-conditioning unit and looked down her aquiline nose at me. Trim, dark-haired, and striking, my partner seemed an unlikely Port Authority cop. Her feet clearly didn't hurt, but then she was half my age and one of those nuts who run even when nothing is chasing them. "Grumbling again, McManus?"

"What are we doing here anyway? Isn't there enough uniformed security for the VIPs? We're detectives; we should be detecting stuff in nice, comfy donut shops."

"Yeah," she replied, hopping off the a/c unit. "Let's check in at the station."

I followed my partner down to the street and we rode over to the Port Authority building at the New World Trade Center. Like most cophouses, the interior walls bore the two-tone scheme of cream and institutional green that's greeted generations of unionized government workers. Uniformed cops herded hoods and skells this way and that. I reached my desk and logged onto my computer. An incoming audio message popped on the screen.

"McManus, come over to the *Red Witch* as soon as you can. It's urgent. You know who it is, Sweetie." The caller didn't leave a visual, but I didn't need one. My informant, Freddie, had a distinctive Southern accent. Freddie looked more like a girl then some girls do. Why he hadn't gone all the way and just changed gender I couldn't figure. Freddie's mind worked in its own bizarre fashion. I'd saved his silk-clad ass from being stomped by a couple of dock workers after their little party got out of hand. Since then he often came up with useful information.

Freddie frequently hung out at the *Red Witch* while working his trade. In the three years I'd known him he'd never called the station. It gave me a sinking feeling. Something wicked this way came.

Regina arrived with a cup of coffee and the last of the variety of half-dozen donuts I'd bought her. "These things are evil incarnate. Each one is a sugar-coated cardiac arrest."

"Come on, Reg, we're off to Red Hook. Freddie called."

"That's Regina. And if Freddie says anything about my hair again, I'm going to beat his ass."

"I think he charges for that sort of thing."

We headed out. The summit meeting put every law enforcement agency in NYC on government-mandated union overtime. It doesn't get better than that. I said hello to a few veterans like myself, who were also getting close to retirement and an escape from the near constant bullshit of being a Port Authority cop in New York. The unions had preserved "twenty years and out," even though the human life span had nearly doubled since the contract was first negotiated. With the Snorge delegation safely tucked into their embassy on the Lower East Side, things might get back to normal.

I took our aircar up to the police express altitude. Skyscrapers still towered over us; some stretched into the thousands of meters. The sun never reached Wall Street anymore. Maybe it never had. Overhead a huge starship rumbled into a landing pattern, heading the same direction we were.

We dropped down beside the old four-story that contained the *Red Witch* and parked the unmarked cruiser in the nearby alley. Just as we stepped out, Freddie came flying up the alley. Nice trick in heels.

He skidded to a stop, long, black hair in disarray. "Let's get out of here!" He grabbed open the door to the back seat and dove in. Reg had her weapon out and watched the alley with narrow eyes. I threw the aircar into gear and hit the boost. Our car headed into the normal traffic pattern.

"OK, Freddie," I said. "What the hell's going on?"

"I got picked up for a party last night," he said, collapsing back against the seat cushions. "Special party for a client with very exotic tastes. Turned out that they needed ten girls on short notice, could only find nine and figured I'm close enough since the client was a Snorge. They snuck us in blindfolded through a secret entrance. I don't know where, but I heard commercial garage door open—"

"You hooked for an alien?" I said in disgust. The Snorge might be humanoid, but they certainly didn't look human to me. Black-eyed from lid to lid with short bandy legs and broad foreheads, they looked kind of Neanderthal. I couldn't imagine wanting to score with one of their females.

Freddie looked defiant. "Hey, a guy's got to eat."

"Get a fucking job," I growled.

"I have a *fucking* job," Freddie shot back with a lazy smile and a wink.

"So who's chasing you?" asked Regina, clearly impatient with the two of us.

"The head of Snorge Security, Akkul Pertabular, threw the party. He has a real thing for human women."

"So he figured you for a guy—" began Regina.

"No, nothing like that, I just told him I was a different type of girl. What does he know?"

"What indeed?" I added.

"Late in the evening, everybody crashed. I fell asleep behind a couch, trying to get away from the horny bastard. When I woke, I heard Pertabular talking to one of his people. He was drunk. Maybe he didn't figure anybody would be wearing a translator disk, but anyway, McManus, he's planning to assassinate both the UN president and the Snorge Premier!"

"What!?!"

"I was terrified," Freddie said. "I laid there out of sight. I couldn't hear any of the other girls. The guards came and took Pertabular off to bed. Thank God, they didn't see me. Security let me out the embassy door. Somebody must have become suspicious about my leaving alone and called upstairs. But by the time they realized their mistake, I had enough of a lead to get away, but they've been looking for me ever since. You've got to help me!"

"Secret Service?" Reg asked.

"Yeah," I said, looking at Freddie. "This is too big for us, Freddie. We're just PA cops. We've got to take you to the Feds."

"Ok," Freddie whispered, "I guess I don't have much choice."

We raced for UN Plaza where the Feds had set up their headquarters.

Two hours later Federal Agent Desai Servatius showed us the door. "Thanks for the tip," he said, glaring at all three of us. "Our security didn't show any troops of hookers being shown to the embassy. Snorge Security assured us that no non-Snorge entered the grounds last night."

"I told you we didn't come in through the front door," Freddie huffed. "They have a secret entrance. I can't tell you where. We were all blindfolded."

"Yeah," Desai said. "I think your pigeon thought this story would be good for some more birdseed."

"Freddie's been reliable-" I began.

"A transgender hooker?" he barked. "Use some damn sense. You think that I'm going to create an interstellar incident with just that," he pointed at Freddie, "as a witness?"

"Oooh," Freddie said, turning away.

"Get out of here," Servatius said, slamming the door.

We trooped to the car in defeat. In a few seconds, we were out in the traffic stream.

"McManus," Freddie said, "if I go back on the street, I'm dead."

I sighed and dialed up my brother on the car comp. His homely Irish face filled the screen. Mother always said I got the looks in the family.

"Hey, Sean," I said, "how you doing?"

"Brian," said Sean, "I'm doing well."

"Sean, I need a favor."

"Let me guess, you need to stash somebody out here. Remember the rules, no druggies and nobody violent."

"Ah, this one's not dangerous. But don't let...her...date either of my nephews."

Freddie sniffed. "They should be so lucky."

"Working girl, huh?" Sean said.

"Something like that," I said. "I don't think that anyone would ever think to look for Freddie in a small museum, but take precautions."

"Oh, God," Freddie said.

"I'll keep an eye out," Sean said. "How hot is this?"

"Don't know yet. Could be big."

"Got it, kid-brother. Well, this could work out. Is she cute? I could use a new docent."

"Docent?" Freddie whispered.

"Sure," I said, "Fredericka has a knack with clothes. I'll bet she'd look very fetching in an apron and cap. I'll call you back with the flight number later."

"Okay, give my love to Toni."

"Same to Pam," I said.

Freddie gave me a stricken look. "You're sending me to the sticks?"

"Staunton, Virginia isn't the sticks," I said. "They've got indoor plumbing and everything."

"Just shoot me now."

"It'll be good for you," I smiled. "My brother runs the Museum of Frontier Culture there, farms through the ages. Yep, real pigs to slop, chickens to round up, stalls to muck out."

Freddie closed his impeccably made-up eyes and shuddered. "What," he said weakly, "is a docent?"

"Oh, that's the best part," I replied. "You'll have to work for your supper, Freddie. You'll give tours in period costume: long skirts, aprons, sensible shoes, and white tie-on caps."

Freddie looked as if he might cry.

"McManus," Regina said, "you're kicking a man while he's down."

"So anyway," I continued, "you'll be safe there. My sister-in-law is a great cook. Put some meat on them bones."

"Great, I'll be size fourteen, when and if I get back."

"We're going straight to LaGuardia," I said. "You'll get everything you need at Sean's place."

"McManus, thanks. I owe you."

"Pay me back by seeing a counselor while you're down there and try to get your life straightened out. I don't care who you sleep with or what you wear. I just don't see why you should be peddling your ass on the street."

Freddie looked down at the floorboards. We drove the rest of the way to LaGuardia in silence.

After Freddie departed, Regina and I stopped in the airport pizza parlor. All difficulties are lessened by pizza. Reg left her salad untouched. I couldn't blame her. I leave salads untouched all the time.

"How can you sit there calmly stuffing your face?" she demanded.

"Starving won't help anything," I said. "What can we do with just Freddie's word? Servatius isn't a fool. He'll beef up security as much as he can."

"What good will that do if the head of Snorge Security is a terrorist?"

She had me there. Assassinations are hard enough to prevent with everybody on the same team.

"Assuming Freddie is telling the truth," I mused, "there has to be a way for the Snorge to get in and out of the embassy unseen. If we could find that secret way, it might make Servatius think again."

"Wonderful," she said, smiling as if she were proud of me. "It can't be far. Freddie said they weren't blindfolded long. I think we need to take a look at the area around the embassy." She jumped to her feet, salad forsaken. "McManus. Come on!"

I snarfed my pizza and raced after Reg, gulping Coke and trying not to choke.

A half-hour later we cruised the area by the Snorge Embassy. Houston Street had once been a haven for bums a century ago. It'd become a commercial and political hub for the lesser embassies. Security walls surrounded the embassy, an unlovely structure with a bunker air about it that squatted in the middle of a grassy lawn surrounded by office towers.

We flashed our tin at the NYPD and Feds on the street barrier and drove into the secured area.

"What do we know about this Pertabular?" Reg asked.

"Just what was in the briefing," I replied. "He's a member of the Snorge Royal family but went over to the Republic. The Premier made a big deal of his defection, given that he's fifth in line for the throne."

"He seems to be an undisciplined idiot," she replied, "hookers and parties in the middle of a covert op?"

"Comes from too many generations of marrying your cousins," I replied. "Look at the Hapsburgs."

We circled the block as nothing facing the embassy itself looked suspicious.

"Pull over," Reg said and pointed to a small alley to the right. "See that garage door? Back the car up so the carcomp can't see down there. We don't need any record of this."

We walked down the alley. I checked my watch: 3 p.m. Few office workers would be out. We came up on the garage door. Next to it was a small door with a wire glass window. I couldn't see anything through it.

Reg pulled a hand comp out. "Computer says it's a warehouse owned by Redlich Enterprises."

"Cross-check with the name Ingerbretsen," I said.

Reg looked at me. "The Swedish mob?"

I nodded. After the Italian Mafia petered out, the Colombians were exterminated, and the Russian mob went legit, organized crime fell into the hands of the Swedes. It only seemed strange until you remembered the Vikings.

"Not clear," she said. "There's a bunch of holding companies for Redlich. The Ingerbretsens have some involvement with one of them: Navigator Exports."

"Which, let me guess," I said, "is heavily involved in the Snorge trade."

"Dead on target," said Reg.

I walked up to the door, took out some burglar tools I'd confiscated long ago and went to work. Reg watched the alley.

We slipped inside quickly, crouching in cover behind some crates by the door. Crates and a couple of mid-sized ground-trucks filled the space. Lights shone in the back. We headed toward those.

I peered around a corner and ducked back. "Shit."

Reg looked a question at me.

When nothing happened, I slowly peeked around the corner again. They stood stock still in a gaggle. Glassy eyes reflected the light. Hair gleamed in every color, skin varied from chocolate brown to ivory. Some wore fishnet stockings, others leather and others silk. Clearly they were deactivated.

I stepped out and Reg followed. She gasped at the line of robot joy girls.

"I guess our friend decided that synthetic joy was better than going without," I said. "Deactivated robots tell no tales."

Regina looked at the line of erotic robots with disdain, then turned to me. "Men suck."

"There must be at least twenty of them," I said. "Our friend has quite a thing when it comes to human women."

"This warehouse backs up to the street the embassy is on," Reg mused. "The entrance must be around here somewhere. We've got to get in there and find out what's going on."

"Forget it, Reg," I said. "We couldn't get a search warrant even if we had evidence. It's an embassy, for Crissakes. It'll be enough if we find the entryway."

"McManus, if we don't find out what's going on, it could mean war."

"Reg, we can't go in there. It's invading a foreign planet. It's also an issue for the Secret Service. We're just Port Authority Cops."

"They didn't believe us."

"Then that's their bad call," I snapped.

"Dammit, McManus, I'm not going to stand by and let the President get assassinated."

"Yeah, it would be bad for your shot at a captain's bars. That's what this is all about, isn't it?" The words hung in the air between us, falling in slow motion to the ground.

"I'm sorry you think so little of me," she said.

"Look, Regina, I'm sorry."

"It's OK, McManus. Where I'm going, you can't follow. What I'm going to do, you can't be any part of."

The smell of burning bridges began to clog the air. "Reg, what are you talking about?"

"I'm going to go where no man has gone before."

"What!"

"Into the Robot Harem," she said, unbuttoning her top.

I looked at her for a second, then laughed. "Wow, you had me going there for a second-"

"I'm serious," she replied.

"You can't pose as a sexbot," I hissed at her.

Regina looked miffed. "Look, Buddy, I run four marathons a year."

"Willya look at those things," I said, hoping reason would overcome vanity. "They look like Vegas showgirls with bowling balls for boobs."

Regina pulled off her top and flung her jacket, holstered weapon, and shirt at me. "I believe, during an unfortunate wardrobe malfunction, you once described these as magnificent," she said pointing at her chest.

She wore a lacy black bra and it did look like it was straining some.

"They're machines," I said, trying to keep my eyes on her face. Unfortunately, she began to pull off her pants. The panties matched the brassiere but seemed to have been made from a small cocktail napkin.

"You're going to freeze," I croaked.

"Meet me at the back of the embassy at midnight," she said, throwing me the pants. "Bring my clothes."

"Reg, I'm sorry to use force, but you've obviously lost your mind."

Just as I started for her, the garage doors of the warehouse started to open. I froze. Regina sprinted to the back of the pack of sexbots before I could grab her. If they caught me here, it was the end for sure. Cursing under my breath I snatched her clothes and dove behind a pile of packing crates.

A couple of Snorge came in with a human woman and man. The man had a robo-controller. He activated the comp he held in his hand. Animation flooded into the robots.

"Come on, ladies," he said. "You've got a date with a sex fiend."

The line of overbuilt robos jiggled into motion and headed for the back of the warehouse, evidently the location of the underground entrance to the Snorge embassy. I peered around the crate long enough to see a fake wall slide open and the whole party disappear into the dark beyond, including my black-thonged partner.

New words, I thought. *It will take new words to define the coming disaster.*

"I am out of my effing mind," I said as I had at least once every five minutes since I stashed the unmarked in the nearby alley. My cop ID allowed me to get close to the embassy. I was, after all, part of the detail supposedly guarding the place. I'd carefully bashed my car-cam against a fireplug and reported it to the garage earlier. I wanted to disable the car computer, but it would trigger alarms back at the station.

I could only marvel at how bad Snorge security was. I hadn't even seen a foot patrol. Pertabular seemed to be a complete incompetent. Avoiding the security cameras, I found a secure spot by the decorative silver maples, thankful that the mayor made a gift of the trees to the Snorge. Rumor said it was to block the view of their hideous architecture. The trees had fully leafed out and the shimmering leaves provided nice cover. I overturned a garbage can and climbed up to look into the grounds.

I am out of my—

Alarms and lights wailed. Cries and yells sounded, followed by the sound of breaking glass. I spotted Reg. The sight of a young, beautiful, athletic, and mostly naked woman running should have been more enjoyable.

"This way," I yelled.

She heard and cut in my direction. Behind her Snorge poured into the courtyard. Stunners buzzed.

I reached inside my jacket, grabbed a military surplus flash bomb and hurled. It landed behind her and flashed, ruining the Snorge's night sight and causing most of them to hit the deck.

Reg reached the wall and leapt. Just as she cleared the top, a stunner hit her. The nearness of the beam made my teeth ache. I jumped off the trashcan and managed to catch her. We tumbled to the ground. I let her lie long enough to fling two more flash bombs and two sonic stunner riot grenades.

I snatched Reg off the ground. My back complained bitterly. Reg stood five foot eight inches tall and her license said she weighed 135. It felt like more. I got her up on my shoulder just as the bombs went off. Crack-crack-fwoosh, fwoosh.

Firing my stunner wildly behind me, I hotfooted it to the car. I opened the back door, pitched Reg in, and leapt into the driver's side, flooring it.

"Dammit, dammit, dammit," I said. The net would know where my car was and in a few seconds the embassy alarm would be out.

"Five-Lima-12 to base," I announced activating the car-com. "Shots fired in the vicinity of the Snorge embassy. In pursuit of a late-model aircar on Houston Street, heading for the FDR Drive."

"Five Lima-12, this is Dispatch. We just got the embassy call from Snorge security. We are scrambling units to the embassy area. Do you require assistance?"

I turned onto the FDR; there was hardly any traffic.

"Five Lima-12 to Dispatch. Do we have any units on the Brooklyn side of the River?"

"Negative. I'll put you through to NYPD."

Great, I thought. The link to the city cops worked only about half the time. I steered for the area under the Brooklyn Bridge Museum with the car in hover, racing over the murk of the East River. It was a well-known dead spot. Sure enough my comp began to sputter into the unintelligible. I blessed the bureaucrats who'd stalled putting signal boosters in the area for the last twenty years. New York resisted modernization at every turn. I flew across the river, dashing up the Gowanis Canal, halfway to Bay Ridge already.

"Five Lima-12 to Dispatch. Where's the damn NYPD? I just lost my tail."

"Five Lima-12. We put you on their frequency. Didn't they pick up?"

"Negative, Dispatch. I don't have anything for them either. I didn't get a tag. My cameras are still down from that accident earlier. Vehicle is dark, might have been a Taiko, Caddy, or any large, dark, air sedan."

"Not good, Five Lima."

"Hey, Dispatch, I'm most of the way toward home. Delmar and I are going to stop at my place for a ten-minute."

"Roger Five Lima. The embassy is secure. The staff says they think it was a prank by some NYU kids."

Yeah, I thought. They don't want any attention either.

I looked at Reg. She sprawled in a most unladylike fashion, her brassiere finally expiring against its exertions. I thought about trying to make it to her apartment, but there'd be no way to get her inside unobserved. No, it had to be my place. I couldn't even call ahead for fear dispatch would overhear.

"Oh God," I groaned. "How am I going to explain this to Toni?"

I landed the car on our street and slid the cruiser into my garage, hitting the automatic on the door. Wrestling her into her clothes in the car's back seat wasn't practical. I tried refastening the bra, but it's easier to get those things off than on, so I just picked her up.

"McManus," I huffed at the house comp. "Door open," I stepped into the kitchen.

My wife, Toni, waited on the other side. She wore a red sweater and black skirt. I remembered tonight was her night out with the girls from the hospital. Tony came up to my shoulder, with a buxom figure that always had her counting calories. The welcoming smile froze on her face as she saw Reg. I had 2.3 seconds before the torrent of abusive Italian began, possibly followed by an attack with a sharpened crucifix.

"Help," I demanded, "I'm in trouble."

"You may well be, buster," she said. "That looks like a naked woman."

"Oh, for crying out loud, honey," I said. "Do you think I'm bringing home bimbos to stash in the basement? It's my partner, Regina Delmar."

She looked at Reg. "I love the new uniforms."

"She's been stunned," I said.

"At an orgy?" Toni demanded.

"Toni, there's a perfectly good explanation. I'll give it to you later; she's not getting any lighter."

"Yeah," said my wife, "must be that big butt of hers."

I got Reg to the couch.

"Would you look her over?" I asked. "Make sure she's not hurt."

My wife sat next to Reg, checked her briskly, finally putting her head on Reg's chest. "This is as close as you're getting to a threesome, buddy."

"Is she all right?"

"Yeah, she seems fine," Toni said, covering Reg with the afghan. "Was she hit at close range?"

"No."

"Military stunner then. We used to get these from the 69th Street Armory every St. Patrick's Day. She'll be out for hours yet."

"I'm going to have to get back on the street, gotta pretend she's with me."

"I thought you told me she was homely?"

"I never said that," I replied. "Right now she's a pain in my ass and a threat to my retirement. Can I leave her with you?"

Toni looked at me. "You are goddamn lucky I love you."

"Never more clear to me than at this moment."

"Brian, what's going on?"

"Honey, if you don't know..."

"Do I have to get the sharpened crucifix?"

I sighed. "I'll explain later. I swear."

She stood and kissed me. "Get back out there. I'll take care of your...partner."

I dashed out to the car and began four hours of fake messages and dodges with the station. When I finally got home, it was to find my wife and a very sheepish Regina Delmar at the kitchen table, sipping coffee. Reg wore my son's robe. She looked puffy and bruised but intact enough for me to yell at. I started winding up for a line drive when my wife interrupted.

"Now, Brian, none of your Irish right now. The poor girl has had a bad enough night."

I stopped in mid-swing, caught off-guard by the mysteries of female bonding.

40

"No," said a glum Regina. "Let him yell. I've got it coming."

I started my windup again, only to have the missus interrupt again.

"Don't encourage him," she warned. "He has a terrible temper and it just adds stress without solving anything."

"I do not have a terrible temper," I howled.

"See," Toni said. "Brian, honey, go sit in the dining room. I'll bring your favorite breakfast. You can talk to Regina."

Strike three, I thought, and headed for the dugout. Reg trailed me.

"Your wife is very nice," Reg said, "and very understanding."

"We'll see how long that lasts after you leave," I replied. "What did you learn?"

"Not enough," she said. "Pertabular is planning to kill the President and the Premier. The delegations share security functions but not all the time and not in all locations. Pertabular said, 'they'll push the button and get the ride of the end of their lives.' He boasted this to two of his aides while the three of them porked sexbots. There was one live, human female and she became suspicious of me. About the same time Pertabular came for me." She shuddered. "I made a run for it. They were so surprised at my 'malfunction' I don't think they realized what was going on till I was out the door."

I shook my head. "Reg. It's too big. We've got to try Servatius again."

"Yeah," she said without conviction.

I found Special Agent Servatius in a trailer outside the Snorge embassy. "Oh Vishnu," he groaned, "not you again? What? Is the sugar plum fairy issuing warnings again?"

"Very funny," I replied. "Best half-witticism I've heard all day. Take a walk with me, Fed."

His dark face flushed at the crack. "I'm busy."

"You'll be a damn sight busier filling out paperwork after the President and Premier get whacked."

"Still on about that?" he said. "We've checked everything-"

I shook my head.

"McManus," he said, rising and putting on his jacket, "your file shows you to be a nonconformist pain in the ass."

"Then my work is nearly done."

"And the only reason I'm even talking to you is that it also shows you're a good cop. Your rather pneumatic partner-"

"Actually she's Spanish."

He glared at me. "-has the best scores seen recently at the PA academy. For all that she can't keep her mouth shut either."

"Tell me about it."

"All this gets you fifteen minutes of my precious time," he concluded.

"Good. Follow me. The pneumatic Regina Delmar awaits."

We walked out to the heliport down by the East River. Reg, now discreetly clad in a red bolero jacket and black pants waited for us. Cargo choppers took off behind her, protection against any boom-mikes pointed at us.

"Detective," Servatius nodded.

She nodded coolly. "Is he unplugged?"

I pulled out a pocket scanner and proceeded to check.

"What's this crap?" Servatius said.

"We are about to tell you something that could either touch off a war or get us sentenced to hard labor on Pluto," Reg replied. "I see no reason to risk giving evidence against myself."

"He's clean," I said.

"Last night," Reg began, "I infiltrated the Snorge embassy in disguise."

"As what?" Servatius exploded.

"Never mind that," Reg snapped. "Pertabular and his men are actually Royalists pretending to side with the Republic. The Republic couldn't turn down the coup of getting a prince on their team. They made him head of security, probably at his demand. For the political benefit of having him, they'd have paid any price. Although as far as security goes, he's a driveling idiot. Isn't that so?"

Servatius said nothing, but I sensed Reg had scored a point.

"Pertabular is making his move today. I'm betting that the Snorge have exclusive security jurisdiction over part of the meetings. Probably caused considerable argument, Agent Servatius, but the Snorge prevailed. Didn't they?"

Servatius started. "I can't...I can't answer that."

"Meaning she's dead on target," I said.

"So far," Servatius replied, "all I've got out of you two is talk. Take me to see this warehouse. If there is some sort of passage there, I'll intervene with my superiors. But if there isn't, then both of you are under arrest."

"You gonna call for back up?" I asked.

"I don't want any record of this until I have some proof," he said.

Fifteen minutes later we arrived at the warehouse. This time a loading crew labored on the docks. A harassed foreman objected to letting us in until Servatius showed his Fed credentials. We headed toward the back. I didn't like the look of the roughnecks doing the loading. I was watching them so closely that I didn't see the black woman and five blond Swede goons step from behind a truck.

"Hey," said the tall black woman, "that's the one from the embassy last night." She pointed at Reg. All around us people drew hidden weapons. Then the world went black.

I woke with the splitting headache that a stun shot gives you. I recognized it the way you would an old acquaintance whose company you didn't relish, but whose presence was inevitable. Servatius stirred as I looked at him. Reg was already awake. Ah, youth. A couple of Snorge goons watched me with a distinct lack of sympathy as I shifted to a sitting posture before realizing I was cuffed.

We weren't in the warehouse anymore. The linens on a nearby table bore the marking, *The Imperial*. We were in the hotel basement. Snorge Security must have moved us in one of the trucks.

The black woman looked at Reg with a broad smile. "Your friends are back."

"So," Regina asked, "how did you pick me out from the robots last night?"

"Your boobs, honey," the black woman said. "When you lay on your back, they headed for your armpits just like the good Lord intended. So I knew they and you were real. Fool Snorge wouldn't believe me. Like I don't know tits, owning a fine pair myself."

"Damn," Reg muttered.

"Yeah," the woman continued. "I can't understand why a man would want one of them silicon sexbots anyway. Be like trying to lie on top of two big, old bowling balls."

"They're not even good fakes," Reg concurred.

"Men," the black woman said.

"If you ask me," Reg said, "the whole breast thing is overrated. Infantile really."

"You said it."

"I hate to interrupt this," I began, "but would somebody tell me what the hell is going on?"

"Very simple, Detective McManus," said a new voice. "What's going on is my rightful ascension to the position that God and my birthright entitle me."

I shifted and caught sight of a Snorge dressed in a smart business suit.

"Akkul Pertabular," Reg said.

"He thinks he's the king," said the black woman. "He was real disappointed that you left the party so soon."

"Indeed," Pertabular said, "you should have stayed. It would have been an experience for you. I assure you my appetite is quite... prodigious."

"I have a rule against penises below a certain size," Reg replied.

The black woman laughed, only to be smacked by one of the Snorge guards.

"Nice company you're keeping," Reg said.

The woman spat out blood and glared at the unaffected Snorge. "They pay good GalFed credits, redeemable anywhere in known space."

"Silence," Pertabular ordered.

"Pertabular," said Servatius, "it's not too late to get out of whatever trouble you're in."

Pertabular laughed. "I'm not in trouble."

"No," I said, "he's not. Mr. Pertabular is a prince among the old Snorge aristocracy. My bet is that the princes ahead of him in line for the throne have met with accidents recently. You're looking at the new crown prince of the Snorge."

Pertabular gave me a grand bow. "How perceptive of you, Detective McManus."

"It's brilliant really," I said, as sweat ran down my back. "The Republic would never hire the actual crown prince, but one who stands fifth in the accession would be a valuable political tool. How much the better that you joined the presidential security team? I bet you even turned over some monarchists to gain favor with the Republic, proving your loyalty."

"Or so I let them believe," Pertabular said.

"How do you plan to pull it off?" I prompted.

"Simple really. We insisted on providing security for the meeting in the Imperial hotel. I've secured a human-made pulse motor to the underside of the elevator that the president and premier will use. Terran-make, quite powerful, designed to kick a lifepod clear of an exploding starship. As soon as they press the button for the conference room, up the shaft they go at six gravities. If the smash into the roof doesn't suffice, there is a 100-story fall to the basement."

Pertabular giggled. "My kind has governed our world since the beginning of time. Now we must yield to these lowborn pretenders? Democracy's roots are not so deep that we cannot yank them out. The president and premier will die. In the confusion that follows, we Royalists will reclaim our birthright. If it takes a war, so be it."

"*Apres moi, le deluge,*" I muttered.

"What?"

"Something another nut just like you said," I replied.

"McManus," Reg whispered.

I subsided.

"Mr. Servatius and Mr. McManus, you are a bonus, agents of the plot," Pertabular said. "You'll be dead and unable to explain your presence. I'll do so for you."

"As for you, my dear," he said, looking at Reg. "I will enjoy adding you to my collection." He nodded to two of his men. "Take her upstairs and discipline her. I don't feel like wrestling just now."

"You mother-fuc-" I said, trying to get to my feet. A Snorge goon kicked me in the head and I fell heavily. My vision dimmed, but I heard Reg fighting and cursing furiously as they dragged her from the room.

"Finish them at 1:30 p.m. precisely," Pertabular said. "The time of death must be close for the coroner's exam."

"Goodbye, officers."

In a minute my vision came back. Only one goon guarded us, but he held a large-bore slug thrower.

A muffled scream came from upstairs.

I growled and got to my feet.

The Snorge looked at me impassively. "You want it now? Chief says you have twenty minutes more to live. But you could take one in the leg now."

"*Erin go braugh!*" I shouted and charged.

The guard laughed and raised his pistol. I don't know which of us was more surprised by the hole that appeared between his eyes. He dropped over backwards. I stopped and looked at Servatius.

"Thanks for the distraction," he said. He'd wiggled his cuffs out in front of him and held his dark suit by the lapel. A tube projected from it.

"I had the one shot," he added scrambling over to the corpse. "He must have the cuff keys to get these off our dead bodies. Ah, here." In seconds we were uncuffed.

"We've got to get help," Servatius said.

"You go," I said, "they've got my partner." I picked up the Snorge's gun. It was a smartgun, programmed to the owner. Damn.

"Got any more neat gadgets?" I asked.

"No," he said. "Good luck, McManus. I'll return with the cavalry."

I sped up the stairs in the opposite direction. My imagination tormented me with images of my partner being raped by the goons who'd dragged her off. I could hear sounds of a struggle coming from behind a closed door at the top of the stairs. I spotted some construction boards leaning against a wall. I seized one and slammed into the door. It gave under my shoulder, and I stormed into the room, then skidded to a stop. One Snorge lay on the ground, clutching whatever they used for a sex organ. He twitched and emitted deep groans. Reg had the other Snorge in a headlock and was slamming his face into a marble countertop.

"Hey, McManus," Reg said, smiling through a few bruises. She returned her attention to the Snorge who struggled feebly in her grasp. "As I was saying—"

Slam went the Snorge's head.

"—my vagina—"

Slam.

"—is by invitation—"

Slam, slam.

"—only."

"That would look good on a T-shirt," I observed. Trying to make myself useful, I busted my board over the head of the other Snorge as he struggled into a sitting position.

"Wouldn't it just?" Reg returned. "These goons had so little respect for me they uncuffed me before starting in."

Slam.

"Reg, I think he's out."

Slam.

"Not enough," she growled, "and it's Regina."

Slam.

"Got it," I said, "Regina."

Satisfied, she dropped the Snorge.

She spotted the remnants of the board in my hand. "That's sweet of you. Were you worried?"

"Only since the day we met," I replied. "We've got to get moving."

Reg reached for the fallen Snorge's sidearm.

"No good," I said. "It's a smartgun like ours."

Reg picked it up, sighted in on the fallen Snorge and pulled the trigger. The gun did nothing. "Oh, well."

"Servatius went for help," I said. "I don't know if he'll make it in time. We've got to get to the elevator shaft and stop Pertabular or it's war."

Picking up new boards for weapons, we ran down the back stairs.

"Brian," Reg pointed, "this way to the elevator core."

I followed. We came to a door. On the other side, a staircase led down to the machinery room.

"Hey," Reg said, pointing to some plumber's tools in a side room. We exchanged boards for wrenches. We went into the room, creeping down the stairs, hoping the buzz of machinery would cover our approach. I grabbed Reg's arm. Ahead stood Pertabular and two of his people, along with three of the Viking goons. They stood in front of an open elevator. The goons probably had stunners, I doubted the Snorge trusted them with anything deadlier. The Snorge would have more lethal hardware.

"Everything is ready," Pertabular announced. "We'll keep the elevator here under our control until it's time for the presidential party. I don't want anyone else triggering it."

Reg showed me her watch, 1:25 p.m. I gestured to go for the Swedes. Stunguns usually didn't have personal coding on them. We crept up on them as quickly as we dared. I came up behind one Swede and wound up.

"Hey, Ole," yelled another, "look out, willya."

Ole inhaled my wrench. As he dropped, the first Swede yelled, "Sven!"

But Sven had a date with Reg's thrown crescent. It smacked him in the face and he fell into the Snorge, fouling their aim. I shot the third Swede with Ole's stunner. Reg threw her other wrench, connecting with a Snorge whose particle-beam gun banged off a transformer near her.

I shot Sven. Pertabular and his other goon fired at me. The PB cut my jacket sleeve and hot metal from the ducting splashed on me. I howled and ran, firing over my shoulder. I clipped one Snorge, but he only slowed as Pertabular raced past him, chasing me. Reg came out of nowhere, shoulder-rolled, and came up with Sven's stunner. She jammed it into the last Snorge's nuts and fired. He didn't even scream. Hell, I felt like screaming just watching it.

Pertabular fired again. The bolt hit the heel of my shoe and knocked me off my feet. I fell down some stairs. After a few seconds I could hear the snap-crack of a particle beam weapon and the buzzing of a stunner. He must have figured he'd got me and gone after Reg. I struggled to my feet and winced as I put weight on the burned foot. I staggered up the stairs and headed for the shaft. Reg had Pertabular backed against the elevator he intended for the president.

She spotted me and gave covering fire as I raced over to her. As I reached her, she looked at me in dismay. "I'm down to a few shots."

I belatedly realized the palm-tingler in my gun was giving the same warning.

"So, Detectives," Pertabular called. "Care to match your stunners against my particle beams?" He fired a shot into the machinery between us.

"He picked up the other one," Reg said, "and he seems to have reloads."

I popped my head out and nearly got it shot off. Reg took a chance on the other side and fired. "Damn, missed."

We alternately ducked and fired. The Swede I hit earlier began to stir. I shot him again. "Reg," I said, "I'm out."

"Me too," she said, her face white and desperate. She showed me her watch. It said 1:30 p.m.

Pertabular laughed and fired three, quick shots, beginning to cut through the mechanical casing we cowered behind. "You're out of time," he yelled, "and, I bet, out of energy." He stepped into the open, a PB in each hand, and started toward us.

We reversed the grips on our pistols and prepared to rush him.

"It's been good, McManus," she said.

"And I was so close to retirement," I mourned.

The doors to the machinery room flew open and human and Snorge agents flooded in with leveled weapons. Pertabular leapt back into the elevator.

Servatius walked up, his weapon sighted on the elevator. "Drop your weapon, Pertabular. You're under arrest."

"You cannot arrest me," he snarled from inside. "I have diplomatic immunity."

"Your immunity is revoked by order of the premier," announced a Snorge officer in military uniform. "You're under arrest for the attempted murder of the Snorge Premier and UN President."

Pertabular looked like the trapped animal he was. A dangerous light crept into his eyes. "You're the traitors. You shall not take the crown prince alive." He slapped the elevator button.

"Down," Reg screamed, bodychecking me. We collapsed behind a packing crate as everyone scrambled for cover.

The pulse motor under the elevator roared to life. With a maniacal laugh, Pertabular disappeared up the elevator shaft, riding the column of flame he'd intended for the president and premier. Fire spilled out of the shaft, scattering human and Snorge officers.

A few seconds later we heard a crash as the elevator, having accelerated to six gravities in six seconds, slammed into the roof. Sunlight appeared in the shaftway and debris began to rain down.

"Top of the world, Ma," I muttered.

Servatius stood up, brushing off his dark suit. "It will be a low orbit," he predicted, "with a messy landing."

"Very amusing," the Snorge soldier said. "We wanted the crown prince alive to reveal the other conspirators."

At that moment, it clicked for me. Of course, it was so obvious.

"Brian," said Reg. "Are you all right? Can you get up?"

"You're not going to knock me down again?"

"No," she promised.

I stood, staring thoughtfully at the Snorge officer.

"McManus, Delmar," Servatius said, "thank Vishnu you are alive. Fortunately, I ran into Major Duis and his SWAT team nearby."

I smiled at the major. He did not return it. "How very fortunate," I said. Reg picked up on something in my voice and gave me a questioning look. I shook my head. She nodded almost imperceptibly.

Servatius looked around and sighed. "I don't know how I am ever going to get this to make sense in a report."

"Cop's life is a bitch," I said.

Reg kicked my ankle.

"It's hell," I amended, "pure hell."

An hour later we stood in the presidential suite of the Imperial with President Rumsen, Premier Lynvig, and their staffs.

"The Snorge People owe you a debt of gratitude for your service," Premier Lynvig said, his cold eyes looked out of a face like an old saddle.

"Which service was that?" I asked, knowing I shouldn't. "Saving your life or helping your plot to destroy the Monarchists?"

President Rumsen looked faint, but before he could interject the premier forestalled him with a raised hand. "What do you mean?"

"It's rather amazing that Prince Pertabular could rise so high, so quickly, in the new Republic."

"He was a pillar of the Republic," the premier said, "a monarchist gone over to our side."

"He was an imbecile," I replied. "A sex addict, pervert, and his knowledge of security couldn't have protected a Space Scout Jamboree. You knew he was a plant. You gave him enough rope to hang himself and the Monarchist movement. Dangerous, perhaps, but maybe less so than a civil war between Monarchists and Republicans in a world suddenly facing bad economic times."

President Rumsen looked at the Premier.

Servatius stared at me as if I'd sprouted a horn and said, "Sir, Detective McManus was struck in the head..."

"Of course," said the premier, his thin lips compressed.

"The moral of the story," I continued undeterred, "is that even idiots get lucky. If that pulse motor had gone off under you and the President, you'd both be a fine, red mist and there'd be a war."

"Fortunately, you and Detective Delmar were there to forestall the villain," the premier said. "I am sure you will be decorated by your services and that the Snorge Republic will add to that."

"You can take your decoration—"

Reg seized me by the arm. "As Mr. Servatius said, my partner was stunned and beaten. I think I should take him home."

"And we should get back to the table," the president said. The predatory gleam in his eye did not bode well for the Snorge Premier who now had something to hide.

"The Snorge people will not soon forget you," the premier said, looking daggers at me.

"Mr. Servatius," President Rumsen said. "Please see to it that Detectives McManus and Delmar reach their homes and are comfortably looked after. They're very important people now."

"Yes, sir."

"Good day, detectives," the President said, smiling broadly.

The Secret Service took us home and staked out both our places in a clear warning to the Snorge. Reg dropped me off with a promise to meet her for breakfast on Monday. I went in and embraced Toni, reassuring her that everything was all right.

Toni plunked me in front of the house comp with a beer and tousled my hair. She'd already heard the official story on the news. Reg and I were heroes, perhaps our best insurance against Snorge revenge. Mercifully, the Secret Service was keeping reporters at bay for now. Servatius had made it very clear to me that I would toe the official line, or bad things would follow. Tired of fighting, I agreed. The mines of Pluto didn't appeal to me.

I decided to tie up a loose end before dinner and called my brother. Sean picked up.

"Brian, my famous brother," Sean said. "You're all over the news."

"Yeah. I'll fill you in later. I'm kinda beat." I leaned back, starting to relax and took a long sip from the cold Amstel. "Where's Freddie? The Big Crapple's safe for working girls again."

"Oh, Aidan and Pierce took her to a square-dance in Waynesboro."

I spit my beer across the tabletop.

CHAPTER THREE

AL "CLONE" CAPONE

"**M**CMANUS," VINNIE HORSE-KILLER SAID, "YOU DON'T KNOW what's going on." He leaned forward against the bare metal table of the interrogation room, wringing his hands.

I stared at Vinnie with interest. Not that he was much to look at. Vincenzo Deluca was part of a resurgence of the old Mafia. The Swedish mob had fallen on hard times after being linked to an assassination plot on the UN President. Nature abhors a vacuum, and the Swede's misfortune proved fair wind for the old mob.

Deluca served as a leg-breaker for Boss Agosta, the current capo du capo. Vinnie stood six-feet tall, with a nose like mashed potatoes and a bit of gut. He'd been christened Vinnie the Horse-Killer after he took a ride at a New Jersey stable. The horse ran away with Vinnie. Unable to control it, he reared up and whapped it on the head. The nag piled into the ground, stone dead.

"I asked him to whoa," he'd told the stable manager. "I said, whoa, horsey, whoa. He wouldn't listen. I hadda kill him." The stable manager hid in a stall and told Vinnie just to leave the saddle and go.

That wasn't half as interesting to me as knowing that Vinnie had appeared at the Port Authority front desk an hour ago, nervous and shaking, asking to be arrested. Insisting on it. In addition to that particular bit of weirdness, Vinnie wore a peculiar suit about two centuries out of date: black, pinstriped, with large lapels. He topped it all with a gray fedora. The desk sergeant decided it was a matter for detectives.

I looked over at Regina. She sat on another steel chair in the interrogation room, her athletic legs crossed. She cocked an elegant eyebrow at me, but otherwise her oval Spanish face gave no hints.

"Well then," I said to Vinnie, "how about you tell me what's going on?"

"You know Boss Agosta."

"Yeah," I replied, "that cockroach has been on the streets almost as long as I've been. Me, at least I'm thinking of retiring. I hear he gets nuttier every year."

The sheen of sweat on Vinnie's forehead reflected the glow from the interrogation lamp. "Easy for you to say. You've got a badge, a gun and about 80,000 other cops just in New York. Agosta doesn't take kindly to that kind of talk, even from cops."

"I'm shaking," I said, taking a sip of coffee.

"Like I said, copper," Vinnie retorted, "easy for you to say."

"Vinnie, now you're talking funny too. What's with the lingo and the getup? You auditioning for something?"

Vinnie stared at me for a few seconds, took a deep breath and said, "It's all on account of Little Napoleon."

My eyebrows shot up. "Bonaparte?" I asked.

"No. Jeez, how can even a cop be so ignorant? Capone, Al Capone."

"Capone," I mused. Then it clicked. "Yeah, a skell from back in the Twentieth Century. He used to rob banks or something when this was the United States."

"Capone wasn't an operative," Vinnie said. "He was a mob boss, like Franchesca Bidon, only worse."

"Interesting," Reg said in a tone that suggested otherwise. "Why the history lesson?"

Vinnie leaned forward his eyes intent and pleading. "He's alive."

"Who's alive, dammit?" I'd become cranky, remembering that I'd left my donut back in the car. Coffee without a donut is only half the experience.

"Capone," Vinnie whispered, eyes darting about the room.

"Oh crap," I said looking at Regina. "Didn't they check him for happy juice before they dumped him in here?"

Reg shrugged.

"No, no," Vinnie insisted. "He's alive again. Agosta had a sample of Capone's DNA stolen from somewhere. He gave the DNA to an illegal genetics lab and had him grown. The doctors even cut scars on his face so the clone would look more like the original."

I looked at Vinnie. "What the hell for? A clone isn't the same person as the original, it just looks like them."

"Agosta has always worshipped Capone, claims he's descended from him. He's had programming tapes made with everything that's known about Capone and then had it RNA encoded into the clone's brain." Vinnie's voice began to rise and wildness grew in his eyes. "You haven't seen it. The thing thinks it is Capone—the real Capone, escaped from hell back to Earth. He says he's here to bring back the original mob: Bonnie and Clyde, Pretty Boy Floyd, Machine Gun Kelly, Ma Barker, all of them. He makes everybody dress and talk like they did two centuries ago."

I put my head back and howled with laughter.

"You wouldn't laugh if you'd seen him take a baseball bat to a guy's head," Vinnie shrilled.

I sat up. "You telling me this clone killed somebody?"

"I ain't telling you nothing, copper," Vinnie rapped.

"You want to spend some time 'lost' in the system, Vinnie?" Reg asked.

He looked at her, sitting half in light and half in shadow at the end of the table. "Yes," he said. "I would very much like to be lost in the system, preferably for a couple of weeks."

He turned back to me. "McManus, you know me. I'm a hood, but I've never offed anybody. I don't mess with drugs or prostitutes. I'm a bad guy, but I'm not *bad*. Give me a break. Lock me up on something."

I stared at Vinnie in disbelief. "I'll see what I can do," I finally muttered.

Relief washed over Vinnie's face, and he collapsed back into the chair. "Thanks, I'll owe you."

Reg stood up and opened the door. A uniformed officer stood just outside. "We're through with him," she said.

Vinnie stood as the uniform took him in tow. "Lose me please," he said as the door closed.

Reg walked over and sat at the edge of the table. My partner was about twenty years younger than I and should have taken up a career in modeling. For reasons I had yet to figure, she'd opted to *'serve and protect'* instead. Despite her promising Academy scores they'd teamed her with me. Everyone had to admit that the old dog and the new gun had set quite a record, breaking up Arcturian kitty smuggling, presidential assassination attempts and vampire cults. Unfortunately, it also meant that we got everything weird.

"He's cracked," she said.

I shook my head. "Deluca is scared, and he isn't the type that scares easily."

"You don't believe this?" Regina laughed.

"Well, something's going on," I growled. "We have a respectable criminal dressing and talking like an escapee from an ancient, whaddya call em's?"

"Films," Reg said, "the old 2D style."

"Yeah. Anyway something is going on, and no one in the department has a clue."

She looked at me, slowly shaking her dark-brown hair back and forth, a small smile on her face. "Ok, McManus. Let's go. I want to hear you tell the lieutenant, no, the captain, that we believe Al Capone is behind the latest crime wave."

"The clone of Al Capone," I corrected.

"Even better," she said.

"Yeah," I grimaced. "How about we knock around on our own for a bit before taking this to Command?"

"Probably a good idea," she responded. "What do you want to try?"

"Let's go see Freddie. He usually knows what's going on in that side of town."

"Ooooh," said Reg. "This gets even better. We get to go hang with your transgender girlfriend."

"I don't make enough money to have a girlfriend," I said, stretching. "Besides, I'm reasonably sure I'd need a note from my wife first.

"It's not all bad," I continued, reaching for the door. "You could use some of Freddie's fashion tips."

Reg stood. "Cold, McManus, very cold."

We cruised over to Queens in an aircar at the government altitude to avoid rush hour traffic. I love June evenings in NYC. The bridges, still used by most vehicles and heavy trucks, glittered like diadems. Hovercars cut across the East River like bejeweled bugs skittering across a pond. I looked up through the slightly-polarized canopy at the running lights of aircraft, shuttles, and spacecraft rumbling up from Koch Spaceport in what used to be Long Island Sound, before it was drained and inhabited by another 4,000,000 people.

Queens, I noted, as we cruised over the BQE, remained the city of the dead. Acres of monuments gleamed vilely in the necropolises. Enough to make you shudder.

We passed the Elmhurst liquid boron tanks, hoping the shielding was as good as Con Ed claimed. Reg dropped us down to street level, and we drove onto 78th street on our road wheels. She pulled in front of a decent-looking apartment complex.

"This is it," Regina sniffed. "The address on the disability form."

I sighed. Regina was still sore at me for approving Freddie's disability request. It wasn't legitimate, but for however long it lasted, it kept Freddie from hooking in the off-port. It also put off the day when some enraged docker or subjockey cut Freddie into dog food after figuring out his date's true nature.

We tinned the guard robo, which admitted us after it recognized our badges, then walked up to 7B and rang the bell.

The door whipped open and there stood Freddie, resplendent in a flaming red nightgown and looking enough like a pretty girl to make a man insist on doctor's notes for all future dates.

"You're not the pizza delivery boy," Freddie pouted.

"Planning on giving out a big tip?" Regina asked, looking at Freddie's outfit with interest. They were about the same size. Freddie had bigger shoulders and was bustier but had cheated with surgery.

Freddie caught her glance. "It's not your color, honey. I'm a 'winter' and you're an 'autumn'. I have one in gold you'd look fabulous in."

"Really," Regina replied, dropping the air temperature by several degrees.

"Sure, Topless," Freddie said, his Southern accent turning languid. "I'll even model it for you, then we'll see where it goes."

"What, and disappoint the pizza guy?" I asked. Reg merely glared at Freddie for using her street handle, gained after an unfortunate clothing failure during a chase.

"Boys, girls," Freddie shrugged a bare shoulder, "what's the difference?"

"One word would be too many and a thousand too few," I replied.

"Ooohh," said Freddie. "I love it when you talk sophisticated. Come in." He led us into a clean but sparsely furnished living room. Boxes showed he hadn't unpacked yet. Freddie draped himself on a sofa. We found chairs.

"So how's the disability?" Reg asked.

"Oww," Freddie said, "the pain, the pain. Sometimes it's terrible." He rubbed his lower back.

"The only injury you got was from having kinky sex with a female vampire cop in the backseat of our cruiser," Regina growled.

"Is there some other sort of sex you can have with a female vampire cop?" Freddie asked.

Reg blew a breath out through her nose in irritation, then laughed. "You're a bad boy, Freddie."

"Spank me?" Freddie suggested. "Free of charge."

Before Reg's amusement could evaporate I cut to the subject of our visit. I told him about Vinnie Horse-Killer's story.

Freddie looked genuinely puzzled. "Vinnie's a tough bastard. One of Agosta's best. I had heard Agosta set up an illegal lab in Red Hook near the warehouse district. It's somewhere close to the Beard Street subdock entrance. That's all that came my way. I avoid the mob where I can and the Italian mob especially. They aren't hot on cross-gender types. Almost as bad as the Irish."

"Point taken and thanks be to St. Patrick," I retorted. "You heading back that way anytime soon?"

"Subways are bad for back pain," Freddie said.

"Disability won't last forever," I replied. "It's a nice place here. You have to pay rent every month. Well, if you learn anything, call me. Usual rates."

"Sure, McManus," Freddie smiled.

As we left, Freddie tried to talk Regina into a fashion show and pillow fight. I offered to watch, which apparently didn't help. We passed a hopeful-looking pizza guy in the stairwell.

"I can't make up my mind if I like the little trollop or if I want to drown him in the bathtub," Reg said as we got into the car.

I shrugged. "There are a lot worse people than Freddie running around loose."

"He's got a brain; he needs to do something else with his life."

"Freddie can't even make up his mind what gender he wants to be when he grows up," I replied. "He's more confused than Hamlet."

"Maybe getting him DBL wasn't the worst of things," she mused. "He can use the time to get his act together."

"Now who's the social worker?" I teased.

"Yeah. I'm getting soft. You're rubbing off on me."

"So," she added, "where to now?"

"John Jay College in Brooklyn," I said, hit with an inspiration.

An hour later we entered the grounds of John Jay. After a quick check of the faculty room, we learned that my old friend, Carolyn Halford was in the gym. Carolyn was a reserve police officer and taught criminology during the day. She'd never been able to choose between academia and the street.

Reg followed me into the school's small gym and we found Carolyn bench pressing about 150 pounds of free weight. She spotted us and put the weight down. "Brian," she boomed, "you old dog. Good to see you." She hurried over and gave me a friendly thump on the back. Carolyn was about the size and shape of a fireplug. Her salt and pepper hair was irregularly pulled back in a headband.

"You too, Carolyn," I replied. "This is my partner, Regina Delmar."

"Hi, Reg," Carolyn said grabbing Regina's hand and wringing it. Reg winced though I wasn't sure if it was from the much complained of truncation of her first name or the vise grip Carolyn used for a handshake. "Great to meet you."

"Brian," Carolyn said, "doesn't Toni mind your having such a pretty partner?"

"She's too polite to complain," Regina replied.

When you're in hearing range, I thought. Aloud I said, "Carolyn, we have a case where we could use your help."

"What can an old college professor do for you?" Carolyn asked, wrapping a towel around her thick neck.

"I need someone who knows crime history, Al Capone, the old Chicago mob."

"Well!" Carolyn said slapping her hands together in glee. "Now you're talking my meat and taters. Speaking of which," she said, poking me disrespectfully in the mid-section, "are we having too many of those taters these days?"

I sucked in my gut, but before I could defend myself Reg interceded. "More like donuts in his case," she said. "He's even got me eating them."

"Good grief," Carolyn barked, "don't you know what those things can do to her arteries?"

"Carolyn," I said, before she could begin one of her health tirades, "how about we get you some active duty time? Draw your stunner and meet us at the beginning of the morning watch at PA HQ tomorrow."

"Sure, Brian." She looked hopefully at us. "Anybody for a run?"

The next day we picked Carolyn up and headed off to Boss Agosta's territory. Carolyn rattled off facts about Capone and the mob non-stop. Names, nicknames, family, methods and madness. I had to admit she had a knack for making a lecture interesting.

We cruised up to the shabby looking Bay Ridge storefront that Agosta used to move numbers and hold court. We parked right in front so the three bulky guys sitting outside at coffee tables wouldn't get nervous.

"So what are we doing?" Carolyn asked, fingering her stunner hopefully.

"Relax," I said. "We're going to drop in on Agosta's and leave some broad hints about- what did you say his nickname was?"

"Big Al, Scarface, and to his friends, Snorky," Carolyn repeated.

"Right. So we throw some hints, then mention how PA may be doing some spot inspections down in a certain section of the warehouse district later this week. They'll probably get rid of the clone and disassemble the lab."

"And open it somewhere else," Reg grumbled.

"Reg, we don't even have enough for a search warrant," I shrugged. "Sometimes you just do what you can."

"Well," Carolyn flexed her biceps, "let's go beard the miscreant in his den."

I gave her a sidelong glance and hoped bringing her wasn't a mistake.

A couple of toughs watched us warily as we exited the cruiser. I pulled my shield out as we walked up. I knew the oldest one, Giancamo 'Johnny' Dibenedetto, one of Agosta's best men.

The youngest of the toughs looked at it with disdain. "Port Authority. What, are they out of real cops?"

I looked at the oldest hood, who sighed.

"Shut the fuck up, Sal," Johnny said. "Go inside and tell the boss we have company." The young hood grumbled but went inside. "Sorry, asshole kids don't know anything. What can we do for you, officer?"

"I feel like a cup of coffee," I said.

"You got a warrant?" he asked.

"Nope," I said. "We're coming in for a cup of espresso. Ok with you? I mean if you aren't open to the public, we'll have to see about your business license—"

"Okay, okay. You can go in but," he hesitated, "I wouldn't."

"When I want your opinion—" I began.

Johnny shrugged and turned away. "Your funeral."

I pushed open the door with Reg and Carolyn close behind. Curiously, the room was empty, save for one guy behind the lunch counter. Tables with red-checked clothes dotted the floor. At the far end stood a door to the back where the good stuff went on. We took some stools. I looked at the old man behind the counter. His face resembled old carved ivory and held no expression. "Three espressos," I said.

"Decaf for me," Carolyn interjected.

I winced.

"Agosta," came a voice from behind us, "is tied up."

I turned and froze. The door at the back had opened and a short, mean-looking bastard led out a bunch of hoods in weird-looking suits similar to the one Vinnie Deluca had worn. What made me freeze was the lethal-looking hardware they carried. I didn't recognize them, but they were clearly weapons.

"Capone," Carolyn breathed. "God, he looks exactly like the original."

"Ugly sod," I whispered.

"McManus," Carolyn added, "don't do anything. Those are Thompson sub-machine guns, they fire half inch-wide lead balls at 280 meters a second."

I gulped. Illegal particle beam guns occasionally got into criminal hands, but for the most part all you had to fear were stunners. These goddamn things would blow pieces off a man.

Capone gave Carolyn a thick-lipped smile. "Not bad for a dame." Then he turned toward me. "So, Fed," said Capone. "We meet again."

"Huh?" I said. "I'm local, NYPA."

"Don't play dumb, Ness," Capone barked. "You and your Untouchables have dogged me to hell and back. You think this cheesy disguise–these weird threads make a difference? But tell me, Ness–what's with the frails?" he gestured at Carolyn and Regina. "Did I rub out all your boys in that last fight?"

I was still working on 'weird threads'. I looked at Carolyn.

"Actually," Carolyn said with a hint of smugness, "it's a common misconception that Elliot Ness got the original Capone. IRS agent Elmer Irey had more to do—"

"Shaddup you," Capone growled. "You think I don't know my own arch-nemesis? The man who gunned me down with a .45 caliber violin?"

"Hah," Carolyn said. "You died from syphilis while in prison."

The baby-faced mobster glared at her. "Somebody get me a baseball bat," he yelled.

"Can it, Carolyn," I improvised, "it's no good doing a psyche job on Snorky here. He's onto us." I looked at Capone. "Dames," I added, "yakking all the damn time. Can't understand why the Bureau started hiring them."

"All right, that's more like it," said Capone, a broad grin creasing his face, the bat at least temporarily forgotten. "So, Ness, you know what I plan to do?"

"Dastardly evil no doubt," I sneered back.

"Always the blue-nose, huh, Ness?" Capone smiled. He turned to the others. "Scalise, Anselmi, relieve them of their gats."

I looked at the two hoods that came forward, knowing those weren't their names.

"Scalise and Anselmi were Capone's lieutenants," Carolyn whispered as the toughs relieved us of guns, communicators and shields.

Capone looked at our PA stunners with contempt—tossing them into a corner. "Crap," he said, hefting the Thompsons. "Fortunately we found the plans for real guns in a..." he slowed and looked at 'Scalise'.

"Database," filled in the renamed mobster.

"Yeah," said Capone looking pleased.

"So," Reg asked, "where's Agosta?"

"You don't listen so good, dame," Capone answered. "He's tied up." Capone waved and Sal reappeared holding up a bloody, beaten and thoroughly trussed Boss Agosta. He looked at Capone with terror in his face.

"What are you going to do?" Johnny asked. He'd come in through the front. "These are cops here. That's real trouble."

"That's the trouble with you 22nd Century types," Capone said. "No guts."

Johnny looked at me, and I saw desperation in his eyes. "This ain't good. You've gotta let Agosta and the cops go. This is insane."

Capone looked at the rest of the hoods then waved a hand in a grand gesture. "You see, boys, that's loyalty. I prize loyalty above everything else. But only," he finished grimly, "when it's to me." He triggered the enormous gun in his hands. Its roar and flash deafened us. Johnny exploded in a spray of blood and bone.

We looked on in shock. Capone stared at the body. "Damn," he said, "should have done that later. Guess we'll have to relocate down to the lab."

"What about these?" asked 'Anselmi,' pointing at us.

He gestured at us with the monster gun. "Tie 'em up and bring 'em along. We'll treat them to a little Sicilian hospitably first. I always had a soft spot in my heart for coppers," Capone said. "My older brother James was a cop. Bastard dropped the family name, Two Gun Hart they called him in Nebraska..."

Capone prattled on about his family as we were bound and hustled out the back and into a panel truck. Mobsters piled into the trucks and cars, and we sped off into the night. The trip to Red Hook wasn't long. As the truck settled on its hoverskirt, I could hear the sounds of tugs and cargo subs. We had to be near the north gate warehouse area.

Mobsters poked us with tommy guns, and we walked into the back of the warehouse. I caught Reg's eye. I gave her a little shake of the head. Nothing now. Wait for a better chance. She nodded.

We walked into an open but poorly lit area. I could see glass-walled tanks that seemed to hold bodies.

"Look," demanded Capone. "Behold the future."

I looked at him. "Listen," I said. "Maybe you're confused-"

"Confused nothing," Capone snapped. "I'm going to bring them all back," he said with a religious fervor. "All the great mobsters and villains. I'll raise them all from the dead, Pretty Boy Floyd, Ma Barker, Bonnie and Clyde, Machine Gun Kelly, all of them. I've found DNA in one place or another. We'll take over the whole ball of wax. You people are soft. We'll go through you like a hot knife through butter."

"Put them in the back room," Capone said. The hoods pushed us along to a small room below street level and locked us in. I looked around. A small eyelet window let us see a patch of sky, but it was nine feet up and too small for Reg to climb through even if she wasn't cuffed.

"Maybe we can use it," Reg said. "If we can break the glass and yell for help-"

"How?" Carolyn asked. "These plastic cuffs are tough."

"You two lean against the wall," Reg said. "I'm going to try and climb up your backs and break the window."

Carolyn and I moved to the wall. "Squat," commanded Reg.

"Yes, my queen," I said. Reg worked her way up onto our backs.

"Your bony knees," I gritted, "are causing me intense pain."

"Buck up, McManus," Carolyn huffed. "As soon as she's up on our shoulders we'll do a squat lift. Remember, lift from the thighs. Proper form is important."

Reg knelt on my shoulders, then using the wall to brace, worked her way up to standing. We lifted. It hurt slightly less than having the flamenco danced on your back with cleats. Reg eased up and stood with her back to the window. With a sudden convulsive jerk she slammed her head back into the glass. I winced for her. Glass splintered and fell on us, and I looked down quickly.

"Help," Reg yelled. "Is there anybody out there?" Reg repeated the call several times over a minute, then over five minutes. I watched the door, not that we could do anything if it opened. Either the guards didn't hear us, assuming there were guards, or they didn't care. The door stayed closed.

My shoulders began screaming. I glanced at Carolyn. She seemed to be bearing up better.

She noticed my look. "You know, if you would do those military presses and chest work I told you about-" she began.

"Please," I huffed, "not now."

Carolyn grumbled but subsided.

"Reg," I said, tears stinging my eyes, "can't hold you up much longer."

"Help," Reg cried. "Help, call the police."

We heard a vaguely familiar tapping sound. Then I recognized it—a woman in heels.

"Is that you Topless?" came a sultry Southern voice.

We craned our necks in incredulity. There above us we could see Freddie looking down.

"Quit looking up my skirt, McManus," Freddie said.

"What are you doing here?" I croaked.

"Looking for info to sell you, sweetums," Freddie replied. "Hey, is this a bondage thing? How Betty Page of y'all."

"Freddie, call for help," Reg rapped out. "There are a dozen hoods or more armed with projectile machine guns. We need SWAT teams. Now."

"Keep your top on, dear," he replied. "Freddie to the rescue." His face disappeared and we heard the sound of his running.

Pain returned. "Reg," I gasped.

"Yeah," she replied, hopping off and landing on her feet. I could see that the back of her hair was matted with blood from breaking the window.

"Who was that?" asked Carolyn. "Is she reliable?"

I was saved from having to answer either question as the door slammed open. Capone and two of his hoods stood there with the immense Thompsons. Capone looked at the transom and laughed. "What, did you think you were gonna grow wings and fly? Come on, you birds."

Outside we saw Agosta standing against a wall. He'd been freed of his bonds. Something in his face gave me pause. He didn't look defeated.

"Up against the wall," Capone growled. "We are about to reenact one of my favorite romantic moments, dedicated to St. Valentine." He laughed hugely as we lined up next to Agosta.

"Boss," called 'Anselmi' from further back in the warehouse. "We need you up front. They just delivered the containers with Bonnie and Clyde to the back dock."

"Don't go anywhere, Ness." Capone left, disappearing among the tanks of regenerating criminals, leaving us with the two goons. The goons backed away until they stood about twenty feet away, too far for a desperate rush.

"Brian," Carolyn said, "this isn't good. The St. Valentine's Day Massacre was when Capone wiped out his arch-enemy, Bugs Moran."

I looked over at Agosta. "You've got something up your sleeve. Give."

Agosta looked back at me. "Not too bad for a dumb cop. Yeah, our friend thinks 20th Century. I got a little transceiver under the skin. I broke the casing an hour ago. It sends out a tracking alert to my soldiers. They should be here soon."

"I hope your guys are prompt," Reg said. "Here comes Capone."

Capone returned, having dealt with the newest addition to his clone mob. "Sorry to keep you waiting," he said. "Now where was I... that's right, I was about to rub you out, Ness. Just like I did Moran."

"You didn't kill Moran," Carolyn snapped. "McGurn did it. You were hiding out on vacation somewhere."

Oh God, I thought.

"You dumb broad," Capone howled. "It's gonna be you first. Gimme a street-sweeper, Anselmi."

"Uh, a what, boss?" Anselmi asked.

"A tommy gun, you imbecile," Capone screamed, veins bulging in his forehead.

As Anselmi started forward to hand the massive gun to the enraged mobster, a flash of light hit him in the chest. With a surprised look, Anselmi toppled like a tree. Shouts and bangs sounded, and we could see running men all over the warehouse, up and down its various levels. A hail of particle beam fire splattered around us. Capone's gunmen returned fire with the ancient but lethal machine guns. Capone dashed forward and seized Anselmi's fallen gun as the other hoods fired at the running men. Bullets and PBs slammed into the clone tanks and fluid spurted in nauseating greens and pinks. Sparks flared. The particle beams touched off fires and smoke began to billow through the warehouse.

"So, Ness," Capone hissed, "your boys found you. Well, too bad for you." The machine gun swung toward me.

My mind raced. The clone seemed more deranged every second. Maybe I could use that. Something clicked, and I remembered what

Carolyn had said about the St. Valentine's Day massacre. "It's Bugs Moran," I shouted at Capone. "Police use stunners."

"Moran," said Capone turning pale. "Moran. He's come back from hell too."

Capone walked into the open. "Moran," he shouted, cutting loose at the gunmen at the end of the room. "Moran, come out and face me. This time I'll kill you with my own hands."

We used the distraction to run like hell. Agosta and I went right. Carolyn and Reg went left. Sal spotted me and cut loose, but he hadn't trained with the Thompson which bucked and climbed in his hands. Recoil, I remembered. I ducked between crates and kept running. I could hear Capone screaming, "Ness, Moran, I'll kill you both."

The fire blazed hotter. All the tanks were involved now. A nauseating smell of burning flesh filled the air. I stepped over a downed goon. He didn't have a weapon on him. Damn.

Smoke blinded me and I crashed into someone. We both went over. I found my face wedged between a set of firm and full breasts. "Reg," I said, or tried to, my voice muffled by the position. I rolled up to sitting.

"I got a knife off a dead guy," she said. "Can't cut my own bonds. Back to back."

We turned our backs to each other. "Hold it steady," I said and started rubbing the ropes on the dagger, slicing my skin as well. The goon kept a sharp knife, and I was free in a few seconds. I cut Reg's bonds. "Where's Carolyn?"

"She headed for the back door," Reg answered. "Where's Agosta?"

"Probably trying to hook up with his boys," I said. PB fire flashed and Thompsons stuttered. We heard indistinct screams through the smoke and crackle of the fire. "It's going to be hard to sort friend from foe."

Al "Clone" Capone

In the distance I heard the sound of sirens. "Freddie to the rescue," Reg murmured.

From somewhere out in the burning building Agosta shouted, "It's the police. Pull out- pull out."

"Run, you cowards," Capone screamed. I saw the blaze of the Thompson through the smoke.

Reg and I exchanged glances. "Let's get the bastard before he gets away." We made our way side by side toward where we had seen the muzzle flash. The smoke made us cough and stung our eyes. I stopped and pulled off my shirt, tearing it into strips and handing one to her. We tied the strips over our noses to cut down on the smoke.

Reg grinned briefly. "Now who's Topless?"

I grunted and peered into the blaze. Reg grabbed my shoulder and pointed. I saw two pair of feet through the smoke. The black and white shoes were Capone's. Then I recognized the track shoes facing them. Carolyn.

"Come on," I whispered.

We lost them for a second in the smoke. I nodded as Reg pointed to the top of a pile of crates. Up she went.

I peered around a barrel and saw Capone backing Carolyn against a parked hovercar. "You, frail," Capone growled. "Can you drive one of these?"

"No," Carolyn lied.

"Then I guess it's curtains for you," he said, raising his weapon.

With a wild yell, Reg leapt from atop the crates, sailing over Capone's head. He looked up in reflex. I slammed into Capone from behind. The tommy gun roared for only a second before flying out of his hands. I caught a blow to the face and went over backward. Capone scrambled to his feet just in time to catch a solid roundhouse to the mouth from Carolyn. "Take that, you historical revisionist," she shouted. Capone staggered. I kicked Capone's knee, and he fell. Carolyn and I landed on him.

Doors crashed open as armored police cruisers stove them in. SWAT troops charged in.

"Port Authority," Reg, Carolyn and I yelled over and over. SWAT guys surrounded us. Their comps identified us as cops, and we were hustled out of the burning building. SWAT cuffed Capone and dragged him. As we cleared the door, I saw Freddie standing by a hulking SWAT captain, leaning on his arm. Freddie smiled and waved.

Dead, stunned and cuffed goons lay everywhere. Agosta was face down on the pavement with two cops over him. He gave me a venomous glare. The SWAT team guys appeared behind us, dragging Capone.

"You people all right?" asked the SWAT captain.

"Good now," I answered. I smiled at Capone. "Let's move this party downtown Captain. We have a hell of a report to write."

Hours later we stood before a maximum-security cell. I was enjoying coffee and donuts. Carolyn had something made of vegetables that smelled bad. Capone glared at us. I smiled back pleasantly.

"So, Snarky—" I began

"Snorky," Carolyn said.

"—Snorky," I continued with a baleful glance at Carolyn, "back in the slammer again."

"You birds will never keep me here," Capone growled.

"I beg to differ," Regina said from behind us. A slim, almost skeletal man with a humorless face, dressed in a dark, poorly-fitting suit, accompanied her. "Allow me to introduce Internal Revenue Service Agent Quist. He has something to say to Mr. Capone."

Quist walked up to Capone's cell and looked at the criminal as if he were a bag of dog-shit left on his doorstep. "Are you Alphonse Capone?"

"Yeah," glared Capone.

"I understand you claim to be the real Alphonse Capone, raised from the dead?"

"Hell couldn't hold me," Capone laughed.

"Humph," returned Quist, producing a stack of papers from his brief case. "That being the case by your own admission, the UN-IRS, as heir to and successor of the United States Internal Revenue Service, wishes to inform you that you died the first time without satisfying all your debts to the sovereign government of the United States. The United Nations, having inherited the lien on you, has determined that with interest, you owe the UN four trillion dollars." Quist smiled thinly at Capone. "And no, we won't take a check."

Capone's mouth hung open. Defeat and despair covered his face.

"Poor Al," I said. Everyone turned to me. "He only remembered half of the inevitable. He escaped death, but he couldn't escape taxes."

CHAPTER FOUR

BLOODSUCKING GOURMETS FROM OUTER SPACE

THE FIRST BODY SHOWED UP IN THE EARLY MORNING HOURS, floating in the Gowanis canal in Brooklyn. Somebody did a bad job of tying it to a cinder block. The corpse broke free of the turgid, poisonous sludge at the bottom to fetch up against a freighter dock where the cargo subs from New Atlantis put in. Pretty standard for this part of town, until Forensics found two holes in the corpse's neck. Whoever she was, she'd been drained of blood. The vampire jokes started immediately. Forensic said it had to be a psycho or a cult or somebody more savvy making it look like a psycho. After all, vampires aren't real.

So it surprised everyone when the second and third bodies popped up, hookers, one male, one female, same sudden anemia. The murders came under NYPD jurisdiction, and they didn't seem too concerned about it.

Then the fourth body showed up, the sixteen year-old niece of the Mars colony governor-general. She'd landed on earth two days before. Her body had bite marks on the neck, arms, and thighs. Overnight the case went from a morbid curiosity to front-page news.

I came in early that morning, taking the tubeway in from Bay Ridge. My partner, the youthful and ambitious Regina Delmar, had called me the night before with news that Captain Fabacio wanted to see us first thing. Reg and I had been on paperwork for a few weeks, cooling down from our high-profile involvement in the

Snorge assassination plot. I hoped we'd get back to being regular detectives after the publicity died down.

Door guards waved me in to the Port Authority complex as I came up from the tubeway. They didn't even look at my ID. I was a celebrity these days. Great.

The elevator whisked me up to the ops center. I wondered how many more times I'd be taking this ride. I'd been a Port Authority cop for almost nineteen years and could retire in a year. For most of that time, I'd been a detective. My inability to keep my mouth shut kept me from promotion to the command ranks. Now I was Senior Detective and had the youngest Detective First in the force's history for a partner.

The doors whisked open and Regina Delmar stood on the other side. Reg still looked fresh from the Academy. Hard-bodied as an aerobic instructor, she had a tan, oval Spanish face and the temper to go with it. "Captain's waiting," she said with her usual economy of speech.

"Top of the morning to you too, my dear," I said in my best (also worst) Irish accent. County Sligo being long ago and far away.

She sighed. "McManus, try not to get us in trouble this time."

"Me?" I sputtered, shocked almost out of speech by the gross unfairness of it all. "*Me* get us into trouble? May I remind you of your part in the affair of the Lesbian Love Goddess? Shall we discuss how you acquired the street handle, 'Topless'?"

She sighed again. I followed her into Captain Fabacio's office to find Lieutenant Carnahan and Captain Fabacio already there. We sat after the usual pleasantries.

"What I have to tell you," Fabacio, a pleasant, motherly-looking woman who was neither, growled, "must remain absolutely confidential, or we could be facing a city-wide panic."

Reg and I exchanged looks.

"You've heard about the so-called Vampire Murders out in Red Hook and Lower Manhattan."

I nodded.

"At first we thought it was some kook playing Dracula. It isn't. It's far worse. It's a big galaxy out there, and there's no real order to it. Things go on that we on Earth never even hear about. This is one of those things."

"Captain?" I shrugged a question.

She looked me straight in the eye as if daring me to laugh. "There are vampires," she said.

"What?" Reg said.

"Not the ones of myth of course," Fabacio continued. "No evil undead here. These vampires are an old species from a red dwarf star three hundred light years from here. They are called the Draoi. Evidently they visited our world in the past, snacking on the locals and spawning the legends, but haven't come back to our world for several hundred years. The Draoi quarantined Earth after they realized how vulnerable humans are to shock and blood loss. Apparently we're the equivalent of beluga caviar. A small group of these vampires broke the quarantine, determined to get at- what I am told- is the tastiest blood anywhere."

"Oh my God," I said, "blood-sucking gourmets from outer space."

"Quiet, McManus," the Lieutenant said.

"Draoi authorities sent us a special police operative to retrieve these people, dead or alive. We don't have diplomatic ties or extradition to the Draoi. Hell, we never heard of them until last week. So this op will require special handling. You two, much to everyone's surprise, have proven you can handle the wild and unusual with the Snorge and Arcturian incidents. More, you can both keep secrets. You'll do both here," she gestured to the Lieutenant.

He stood and walked over to the window looking out toward Lady Liberty. With a wave he polarized the glass, cutting the sunlight. Then he walked to the rear door and opened it. "Come in," he said.

A woman followed him in and what a woman. Dressed from head to toe in a black leather and red fabric uniform with subdued buttons and insignia, she stood an easy six feet tall. Her skin was pale, flawless with an undercast of blue. Her eyes burned an emerald green, set off by blood-red hair that piled up like foam. Her body looked athletic but promised a full set of curves. She looked human only more so.

Of course, I thought slightly dazed. *They'd have to look human to pass among us, and vampires are all about seduction.*

"This," Captain Fabacio said with a look that mingled revulsion and fascination, "is Police Officer Jelena of the Draoi. They don't use last names outside of their own species, and we've given her a courtesy rank of Lieutenant, which seems to correspond with her own rank. She speaks our language."

"Is she a..." began Reg.

"Vampire?" finished Lieutenant Jelena.

She smiled, and I think everyone in the room backed up. She had a beautiful set of canines- for a Doberman.

"Yes," Jelena said with a slight almost middle-European accent. "It is the way of my people. But before you type me as some sort of demon, let me assure you that my kind does not live to kill. On the contrary, we are among the most gregarious of species. We live and mate with many others."

"And they live to tell about it?" I asked, swallowing. My mouth felt dry, and it got worse when those gem-bright eyes focused on me.

"Yes," she said, "and relish it. We are an old, and frankly decadent people, always seeking new sensations. We'd never found a species before that attracted us and yet is so fragile. This mechanism you call shock is unknown to us. So we put you aside, but the rumors and stories survived. Now my people have returned. The ones who have come are evil and do not care that their human lovers cannot endure the experience."

"Your job," Fabacio said, "is to work with the Lieutenant and to keep her under wraps while she is here. That means she stays with one of you at all times. Your stuff's been moved to a special office with its own entrance. We can't afford to have word get out about this and create yet another interstellar incident this year."

"Any questions?" she asked as if it were a dare.

One would be too many and a thousand too few. I stood.

"Then get to it," Fabacio said.

We walked over to our new offices, trailed by Jelena. I found everything there including, in its usual place, the holos of my wife and son. I closed the door after we walked into the windowless room.

"So," I said, "you're from a planet of blood-sucking fiends."

From where she had perched on a desk, Reg groaned. "Great moments in interstellar relations and 'You are there.' Ignore him Lieutenant. It's just his feeble sense of humor."

"I understand," Jelena replied. "The situation must be quite bizarre for you. Consider this though, you may think of me as a monster, but in truth your world is a hell for me. A few minutes under your fierce, yellow sun will kill me. If it wasn't for allergy shots, much of your plant life would make me ill, especially," she shuddered, "garlic."

Note to self, I thought. Don't take her to dinner at Riccio's.

"Being pierced by a large, wooden splinter could be fatal," Jelena complained, "it causes a reaction similar to anaphylactic shock."

"Makes you wonder why your people risk it all just to nibble on a human neck," Regina said.

"You do not begin to understand," Jelena replied in a suddenly husky voice. "We are a very sensual people, combining our need for sex and food into one act." The look she gave Regina sent my blood racing, and I wasn't directly in front of it. "You see," Jelena said with a languid smile, "you really do look good enough to eat."

Color flew into Reg's face, and I could see her breathing go ragged. I reached into the box I keep by my desk. Disturbed, Jelena turned to look at me.

"Donut?" I asked.

We spent the rest of the afternoon familiarizing Jelena with the case file, which didn't take long, then we went to the crime scene. Covered head to toe and with a tactical mask and sun goggles, Jelena dared the weak, early March sunlight to tour all three spots before collapsing in the back of the car with the a/c blasting on full.

After the little incident where Jelena looked Reg over like an hors d'oeuvres, Reg flatly refused to stay at home alone with her, so I got conned into taking her home with me. Figuring the Captain's top-secret orders didn't apply to my wife and not really caring if they did, I called Toni and let her know what was coming.

"You're bringing home what?" she said.

"An alien," I repeated. "She drinks blood but can enjoy cooked meat if it's rare. I'll bring home a pint of O-positive for her to drink. It's just for tonight. Captain didn't want to leave her in a hotel."

"Afraid she'd eat the staff?"

"Mebbe."

"Okay, prime rib and potatoes, cooked rare, served at seven. This I gotta see."

"Oh, honey, no garlic."

"Wonderful," Toni replied. "It'll be a regular Irish meal, no flavor at all. Just like when your Dad was alive."

We pulled out of the PA complex in an unmarked air car and flew up to the "official business altitude." I had the canopy fully polarized even though the sun was setting. You could still make out New York in all its sordid, muscular splendor. Streetlights and buildings lit up the darkling plain.

"Beautiful," breathed Jelena, staring at the city. The way she said it raised my blood pressure. "We have no cities so vibrant and huge as this. Our world is poor in metals. We are long-lived and reproduce slowly. Were it not for aliens who visited our world, it's unlikely we would have developed space flight."

She told me more about her people as we flew out. "With little plant life, we developed as carnivores," she said. "Blood became our way of life."

"Sort of is for everybody," I said, "one way or another."

We reached my home in Bay Ridge and dropped to street level. Toni and I owned a two-story with a garage in the basement and a small garden plot in back.

Toni greeted us at the door. My wife is Italian, short, pretty, fighting a few extra pounds. "Hey honey," she said, giving me a kiss. "This must be Lieutenant Jelena."

"Just Jelena," the red-haired vampire replied.

"Brian, darling," Toni asked, "do you ever meet any ugly women in your work?"

Yellow alert, I thought. There's a line of possessive, Sicilian blood in my wife's family.

"How kind of you," Jelena said. "And what attractive skin you have." She reached out and touched Toni's face. "So firm and moist."

"Good," Toni replied, drawing back a tad. "Let's hope the same can be said of the roast."

The women chatted for a while, about what I could not imagine, as I made up drinks. I fixed Jelena a Bloody Mary with real blood. After a while Jelena drifted in, sat on the couch, and we began to talk shop. I brought up a point that had bothered me in the coroner's report.

"How do they hold their victims with so little fight?" I mused. "There were no signs of struggle. Do they drug or stun them?"

"It's a response to our sensual nature," Jelena said.

I laughed. "No, really-"

She turned to face me. Suddenly it seemed we were very close and the room was warm. Colors became vibrant: the red of her hair, the green of her eyes. A heady perfume made my senses swim. I was dimly conscious of her lips on mine, tasting like ripe fruit. I could feel her nipples press against my shirt. Her lips moved off mine and down my neck.

"*Butana*! Whore!" someone screamed. I heard a loud whack.

I shook it off, my senses coming back to me in a rush. Jelena lay half-stunned on the floor. My wife Toni was climbing over the back of the sofa with the large crucifix her mother had given her clutched in one hand. Armed with Jesus, she advanced on the prostrate vampire.

Large wooden crucifix. Red Alert.

"No, Toni!" I yelled, grabbing for my wife and lifting her off the floor before she could get a second shot in.

"*Butana!*" Toni shrieked. "I let you into my house..." Toni switched to Italian for speed cursing. No annoying consonants to slow the process.

Jelena backed away from the crucifix, frightened, not of Jesus, but by the proximity of wood in the hands of an enraged Sicilian. "I was just trying to show him how the victims are taken," she said clutching her head. "We have great powers of seduction."

This of course was the wrong thing to say. It took fifteen minutes to restore decorum to interplanetary relations. I finally mollified Toni and got her back to the kitchen. She took the crucifix.

"Feeding doesn't have to be fatal," Jelena sulked. "I was only going to take a little nip to make you understand what my people can do."

"Actually," I said, "it had more to do with the presence of your lips on my neck, than your teeth. Human woman are territorial about their mates."

"How peculiar," Jelena winced as she placed an ice-bag on her bruised skull. Fortunately, Tony belted her with the flat rather than the edge, and she hadn't been cut. "How do they get enough sexual variety to keep it interesting?"

"Good question," Toni said, entering with a tray. "What do you say, honey?" she asked with a dangerous sweetness. "If you are going to keep showing up with naked partners and sex-starved vampires, how about I get to boff a mailman or a plumber?"

I sighed.

"Your partner was naked?" Jelena asked.

"Long story," I returned.

Dinner lasted forever. I envied the prime rib, which had at least died quickly. Jelena retired to her room, pleading fatigue and injuries. Toni and I went to bed after we wedged a chair under the door, and she hung garlic cloves over the window. In penance for the unexpected guest, I gave my wife a long back rub that turned into some unexpected fun. Afterward Toni turned to me. "I want you to wear a cross."

"Honey, she's not the undead. She's an alien. It was the wood in the cross that scared her."

"Do you love me?" she asked.

"Every minute of every day," I replied.

Bloodsucking Gourmets from Outer Space

"Then you'll wear the cross."

I smiled at my wife, enjoying how good she looked without clothes. "Sure, honey."

Morning came. I got up quietly, showered, then picked up the gold cross on its delicate chain. Jelena and I departed without waking my wife. I polarized the windows on the special cruiser I'd been issued and used the infrared to navigate. We got to the station to pick up Reg, entering from a restricted zone used to shuttle VIPs and other people we didn't want seen. To my surprise, I found Reg talking to Freddie, or Fredericka, as he preferred. I'd saved Freddie Bouvier from a group of outraged dockers one night. He peddled information along with his butt.

I hadn't seen him since he returned from Virginia, where I stashed him after he put us onto the Snorge assassins. He wore a white blouse, black leather pants and looked unfairly like a pretty girl.

"Hey, McManus," he said, tossing back long, black hair. "Still mad at me for dating your nephews?"

"Very funny," I said. I'd hidden Freddie at the American Museum of Frontier Culture in Staunton, Virginia where my brother served as curator. My nephews took him to a square-dance. They'd concealed the fact that they knew Freddie wasn't a real girl so they could have a little fun at my expense. I'd damn near had a stroke.

"Hey, is she the vampire cop?" Freddie asked, pointing with his chin at Jelena.

My jaw hung open. I looked at Reg.

She shrugged and looked back. "He knew when he showed up."

Jelena looked at me. "He?"

"Another long story," I said.

"How did you find out about the vampires?" I demanded.

Freddie smiled coyly. "I get information. It's why I'm so loved and useful. I can't reveal my sources, but in this case I have a lot of information."

"How'd you feel about taking a shot to the head with a police flashlight," I growled.

"I'd prefer a nice spanking."

I started to count to ten.

"Okay, okay," Freddie placated. "Don't get mad. I've got stuff you need to know."

I sighed and sat at the desk. "Usual rates?"

"Yes and no," Freddie said. "This is personal with me. I want in. I want to help."

I looked at Reg. "I think someone drugged my coffee."

"I'm serious, dammit," Freddie said. "I knew the first girl they pulled out of the Gowanis. Her name was Angela. We used to date a few years back when I first got to New York. We were very close for a while."

"You like girls?" I asked.

Freddie smiled. "I like everybody, McManus. I'm very democratic."

The room stayed quiet for a bit. "Sorry about your friend, Freddie," I said.

He looked at me. "Yeah."

"I mean it."

"I believed you the first time, copper."

"Freddie," I said, "we can't use you on a stakeout."

"Well then," said Freddie in a surprisingly grim tone, "I guess I'll have plenty of time on my hands to talk to reporters. That would be a shame, this being a covert op and all."

Bloodsucking Gourmets from Outer Space

"You want to be held as a material witness, Freddie?" Reg said.

"Thought of that," said Freddie, crossing his legs demurely. "If I don't make regular check-ins with my lawyer, he opens an envelope, calls the media, and files a writ of *habeas corpus*. As soon as I get out, I start singing in my husky tenor."

"You sing?" Reg asked.

"Yeah, I do some nightclub work. Lousy pay, worse hours. Life's hell for an artist."

"Excuse me," I snapped.

Everyone looked at me. I reviewed my options only to realize I'd been mouse-trapped.

"OK, dammit," I said finally. "We need bait anyway. But you'll sign a liability waiver so if you get killed in this op, no one can sue."

Freddie gave a bitter laugh. "McManus, my family would be delighted to learn I was killed while helping the police. I might even be reinstated posthumously."

I looked at Reg. She smiled enigmatically.

"Freddie, meet Lieutenant Jelena of the Draoi police force."

Jelena nodded. "I think she—"

"He," I interrupted, "he just likes women's clothes."

Freddie stuck his tongue out at me.

"—he will do very well as bait. He looks quite fresh," she said, canines in evidence again.

Freddie turned out to have a lot of information of dubious quality about goings on in Red Hook and the submarine dock area. Strange, pale people had been seen at night. We decided to stake out the scene of the most recent sighting Freddie knew of. Off we went, two Port Authority cops, a vampire, and a transgender informant. We pulled into an alley near a lot, around 2 a.m. I wanted to bring some garlic to supplement our hunting crossbows, but Jelena couldn't stand the stuff. She carried a wooden-bolt firing air pistol and a stunner attuned to her kind.

"Your stunners would be marginally effective against my species at best," she warned. "The crossbows will be more effective than your metal slug-throwers."

"How about holy water?" Reg asked.

"A myth your priests made up to sell holy water," Jelena scoffed.

I wired Freddie for sound and video, making him swallow a locator pill as well.

"Hey, how long does this thing stay with me?" he asked.

"Till you're disemboweled," I replied.

"Well, I guess I'd better get out on the street," he said.

"Last thing," I said. "No actual tricks. I don't care how you turn them down, but you aren't boffing anyone for pay on a police operation."

"Humph," Freddie said, "in addition to restraint of trade, what about blowing my cover?"

"Put it this way, your cover is the only thing you'll be blowing tonight."

"Oh," Freddie sneered, "great half-witticism, copper."

"Go be a vampire yum-yum," I replied.

Freddie opened the car door and walked out of the alley onto a street lined with three and four story brick buildings, some of them hundreds of years old. They housed the poor, some dockworkers, and the occasional artist looking for cheap space. Those that were occupied anyway. Some had small commercial businesses on their first floors. A few seedy bars operated closer to the sub docks, which never really shut down. Occasionally a commercial hover truck rumbled by. Freddie seemed to be the only hooker in the area. The vampire attacks must have made everyone cautious.

We settled down to do what so much of cop work is: waiting. Reg played with her crossbow. I watched Freddie's screen. Jelena sipped something from a sealed container through a straw.

Freddie turned down a few dockworkers and one guy who rolled up in a car, quoting apparently outrageous prices, or assuring them that what he had wasn't contagious. I shook my head. It felt voyeuristic. This was Freddie's life, if you could call it that. He was hardly any older than my son, at least in years. Freddie seemed to have been born with an old and very weary soul. I'd tried to get him off the street a dozen times. He laughed at each attempt. I wanted to give up on him, yet somehow never did. Now here he was, trying to avenge a lost friend, an enigma wrapped in riddle, wearing fishnets.

Nothing happened for hours. I caught myself starting to doze and slapped myself lightly, shifting position. I looked at the locator and frowned. "Freddie," I said hitting the mike that would whisper in his ear. "Don't wander so far from the car. You're almost three blocks away."

"Yes, mother," Freddie replied. He turned back, and I saw the mouth of an alley. "And stay back from-" I began.

Too late. Dark figures exploded out of the alley. Freddie turned to run and I could see more coming out of an open sewer hole. "Help!" Freddie screamed. "Oh, God help." They piled on him, no seduction here.

I slammed the car into drive, and we roared out of the alley, screeching into a left turn.

"They've got him," yelled Reg, watching the screen as I watched the road. "Maybe a dozen. He's fighting. Damn! The picture just went blank." Freddie's screams faded too.

We reached the spot in seconds, piling out of the car. Jelena jumped out first, her air gun and stunner drawn. All we could see was an empty street. I looked down and saw a manhole cover still partially open. Reg dove back into the car emerging with the locator and flashlights. "Underground," she snapped.

"Sewers," I said. "Why is it always sewers?"

Jelena flipped up the sewer cover without effort. "I'll go first," she said. "I see best in the dark." She dropped down into the hole in a jump that would fracture a human's ankle. *They're stronger than we are,* I remembered, *got to hit them harder.*

I climbed down. Reg handed me the locator and then cocked both her crossbow and mine.

"That way," I gestured, taking the lead from Jelena. We started down a side tunnel on the edges of a noisome trough. Reg made a retching sound, and my stomach lurched in sympathy. "Christ, what a stink," I managed.

"What stink?" Jelena asked. Her eyes glowed in the low light of the tunnel. The sight raised the hair on the back of my neck.

"Explains a lot," Reg said. "Taste and smell are linked in humans, must be different for Draoi."

"This way," I said, gesturing with the scanner. We headed through various chambers and levels sometimes crouching to get through. I tried to avoid the worst muck, but figured that I'd need a new set of shoes no matter what.

We came to a large, open area, dimly lit by a few naked, low-wattage bulbs on the walls. These were hooded, so I couldn't see how far away the roof was. "We're getting closer," I whispered. I started forward, then froze. Something felt wrong. Impatient, Jelena pushed past me.

"Wait," I whispered, trying to catch up with her. Reg followed me in.

A heavy fabric and rope net fell on us, fouling the crossbows. Through a tear in the fabric, I could see the glimmering eyes of vampires above us. They'd been hiding above the lights. More nets fell. I heard a familiar buzzing and got woozy. *Civilian stunner,* I thought, *not powerful, at least I won't have a headache when I—*

—*wake up!* Awareness flooded back. I looked around. Reg and I both hung from beams by ropes, our feet barely touching the floor. Two male vamps held Jelena's arms behind her back. A large, dark-haired man faced her, holding her bolt pistol. About a dozen men and women filled the space, which looked to be an old, abandoned subway station from before the electromagnetic tubeways. I could see Freddie, bound hand and foot, sitting with a goofy smile on his face. He looked stoned.

I looked at the male vamp. He looked back, his eyes glowing in the low light. "You're under arrest, asshole," I said.

He laughed, displaying the large canines. "So the older male is back with us. He doesn't look very tasty. Does he, Officer Jelena?"

Two young female vamps looked at me and laughed. "He looks good to us," they said. One had the same flame red hair as Jelena, the other was a cool blonde. They were gorgeous. They walked over to me and began playing with my clothes. At close range they looked and smelled even more wonderful. I wondered distantly if I wore the same goofy smile as Freddie.

"Snap out of it, Brian," I heard Reg yell. I was confused, snap out of what? I looked away from the girls with an effort.

Jelena stared back at the lead vamp. "Gregarth. Release us. You are only postponing the inevitable."

The one addressed as Gregarth smiled coldly. "I don't think so. If others follow, I will offer them the same thing I offer you. A long life in a feast of blood."

"What?" she said.

"Release her," Gregarth ordered, gesturing with the pistol. "Take the girl," he gestured at Freddie, "and amuse yourselves." He smiled at Reg. "I have plans for these others." Most of the vamps gathered around Freddie, picked him up, and disappeared up the stairs. Two remained with me.

"Gregarth," complained the cool blonde. "Let us stay and play."

He spared me an indifferent glance. "Very well." He walked over to Reg, who glared at him.

My fan club giggled appreciatively. They knelt and began pulling at my clothes.

"Just think of it," Gregarth said, turning back to Jelena. "You could remain with us. Dining on the most succulent blood the galaxy has ever produced. This planet is not so bad, so long as you stick to the cities and the night. But the food, the food," he said dreamily, drawing out the last word and stroking Regina's throat, "the food is wonderful." Reg turned her head in disgust.

I could see Jelena's breasts heaving, her teeth showed slightly, resting between parted lips. "You just use them," she said, "you give pleasure back only with death."

"So what?" Gregarth sneered. "If you find one you like, you don't have to eat him all at once. Give yourself the freedom to be selfish. It's not our fault they are so fragile."

The female vampires kneeling before me giggled as they finished undoing my pants. Then they began doing something to guarantee a good blood supply to the area they were interested in. With the part of my brain not totally dazed by pheromones, psychic suggestion, or whatever else they used to induce utter lust, I realized that after the little darlings fulfilled their objective, they were going to use their little pointies on my big pointy.

Jelena advanced on Reg, pressing against her. Reg struggled as Gregarth, grinning hugely, backed away, evidently content to watch. Jelena embraced Reg, her green eyes boring into Reg's dark-brown ones. Reg moaned and tried to arch herself away but only ended up pressed harder against Jelena, who pulled open Reg's jacket, running her hands over my partner's taut body. Unable to resist further, Reg whimpered, "No."

Jelena drew her close as Reg's eyes rolled up, and she leaned back in submission. The vampire's arms reached inside Reg's jacket, cupping her breasts. Her lips brushed Reg's pulsing throat. Jelena's hands moved, sliding down the back of Reg's pants.

"Yes," Gregarth cried, "yes."

Suddenly Jelena jumped back from Regina, who slumped in the ropes. Jelena turned to face Gregarth with a pistol in her hand.

Reg's back up gun, I thought muzzily, *how clever.*

Jelena fired three rounds into Gregarth's astonished face, right through the forehead, then spun toward me. He fell. Jelena's bolt-gun flew from Gregarth's hand landing somewhere in the dark with a splash. My vamps dropped what they were doing and hissed at Jelena. She shot both in the forehead. Dropping the empty gun, she leapt on Reg, wrapping her legs about my partner's waist.

She wants us all to herself, I thought, my brain starting to clear.

It wasn't the case. She boosted herself up on Reg's body and seized the ropes suspending Reg. In one swift move she bit through them. The women tumbled to the ground. A male vamp appeared at the head of the stairs, snarling at us.

Jelena hauled Reg to her feet. "Get McManus loose," she demanded.

"I can't bite through rope," Reg yelled, turning to engage the vampire coming down the stairs and stopping him with a side-thrust kick that slammed him into the wall.

Jelena cursed, ran over and leapt on me as she had Reg. My face disappeared into her impressive cleavage as she pulled up to bite the ropes. Knowing what would happen, I braced and didn't fall. I looked up into her cold, pale face, and she smiled, kissed me hard, and leapt off. *Damn,* I thought, *she bit my lip.*

The head-shot vampires stirred slowly, coming off the floor.

Of course, I thought numb with horror; those were just lead bullets. "Look out," I yelled.

Reg decked the male vamp again with a roundhouse kick, then dropped an ax kick on his neck with a sickening crack. He stayed down, alive and flopping, but out of the fight.

Gregarth, or what had been Gregarth, stumbled to his feet and stood there swaying, his forehead a mass of pulped flesh and bone. I tried to get my pants back up over the sort of erection you get when you're sixteen. Terror helped as more vamps flooded into the room.

Gregarth advanced on me. No intelligence remained in his eyes. The bullets had destroyed his higher functions. "Food," he drooled. "Fooooood."

"You've got to destroy his entire brain," Jelena yelled from the stairwell where she and Reg fought a clutch of femvamps.

Fighting revulsion and fear, I backed away from Gregarth. He advanced toward me, arms outstretched, an imbecilic smile on his ruined face. I looked around, spotting a fire ax the nest must have liberated while fixing up their new home. I seized it and turned to face the monster.

He was on top of me. I stepped back, screamed like a girl and swung for all I was worth. The ax sheared through flesh and bone and Gregarth's head dropped off, falling to the floor with a sickening wet sound.

Jelena and one femvamp were tied up in a knot. The second head-shot one lay unmoving, a stake in its chest. A third had Reg down. Reg was clearly losing. I ran over and slammed the ax into the thing's midsection. It shrieked like a human woman and I almost threw up. As it flopped away from Reg, I reversed the ax and brought the blade down. It's not a woman, it's not a woman, I kept repeating. Lord Jesus Christ, it's not a real woman.

Jelena grabbed the vamp she fought and slammed it into a wall. "No," screamed the femvamp as I advanced with the ax. "I surrender. I give up."

"Wait," Jelena demanded, as I stood irresolute. She produced cuffs and locked the prisoner. "You're under arrest." She looked at the male vamp flopping on the floor. "You too."

I stared in shock. *That's right,* I thought, looking around. *They're people. Not my kind, but people.*

Reg got off the floor and looked at me. "They didn't give us a choice," she said.

"No, but I don't have to like it." I'd been a PA cop for nearly twenty years, dropped lots of goons with stunners, clubs, and fists. I'd never killed anyone. God, I felt sick.

We heard a distant scream.

"Freddie," said Reg, her eyes wide. She spotted our crossbows lying by a wall and handed one to Jelena. I kept the comforting weight of the axe.

"Follow me," Jelena yelled. I hefted the ax and did. We raced up the stairs and into the next chamber.

We found Freddie tangled with a clutch of vampires. They seemed to be indifferent to his gender issues, people just playing with whatever appealed to them. The scream must have been of somebody's satisfaction. They were still playing and hadn't gotten around to teeth.

"Freeze–police," we yelled. The vamps looked up into the crossbows and ax. One made a sudden move. Reg shot him in the chest, and he flopped backward, the stunner falling from his dead hand. The others gradually abandoned Freddie. He snapped out of their spell, pulled his panties up, and slugged the nearest male vamp in the eye.

"No freebies," Freddie yelled. Then looking at me, he said. "Out-of-towners, they're all the same; cheap."

Reg and I left the cuffing and restraining to Jelena, wanting to keep our distance from the vamps. We marched them back to the sewer where we'd entered, making the prisoners drag the crippled vamps. I got to the cruiser and called the Captain's private number. An hour later a black van appeared. Men in what looked like spacesuits came out. We brought the vamps up from the sewers. They were hooded, bound further, and tossed in the van heading for the military base on Governor's Island. Lt. Carnahan closed the van door then turned to us. "Good job. Report to Governor's Island CP for debriefing."

I nodded as he hopped in the van.

"First," Freddie begged, "you've got to let me stop at home for a change of clothes and a shower, the sewer stink is killing me."

"OK. Reg and I can clean up at the station." Hours later we found ourselves at Governor's Island debriefing a UN diplomat and Captain Fabacio. A Navy doctor checked us over and pronounced us fit. They all disappeared as a full Admiral walked in. The Admiral kept it brief. "Good work," he said. "You two may have a future in Intelligence."

"It would surprise most people who know me," I replied. "Besides, I plan to retire before long."

"I don't see you as a man who could spend a lot of time sitting on his ass," the admiral replied.

"Watch me."

"Your vampire friend and her prisoners are leaving PDQ," the Admiral said.

"Where's Jelena now?" Reg asked.

"She was outside in the parking lot, talking with that young police woman you came in with."

"Freddie," I said, "is not—"

Reg kicked my ankle.

"—still on duty," I gritted, my ankle throbbing.

"If you want to say goodbye to Lieutenant Jelena," the Admiral concluded, "then you'd better do it now. I'll take you to the shuttle entranceway."

We followed him through the complex until we reached the shuttle gate. He bade us goodbye. We found Jelena standing by a window, looking out its polarized glass at the afternoon.

She turned to us with a small smile as we walked up. "Mission accomplished," she said.

"Yep," I returned. "Thanks to you. We were in serious trouble down there."

"And for a second you weren't sure I wasn't going to take Gregarth up on his offer."

We both laughed nervously but didn't answer.

"I don't imagine that we will see you again," Regina said. I could tell that, like me, she was somewhat relieved at the prospect.

"No," Jelena said, "our worlds will remain quarantined from each other. Our people will be told to avoid yours under penalty of law. Earth, with its killer sun is a version of hell to my people. It's only redemption is your delicious blood, which we cannot have. For those with discipline, the mating and feasting could be done safely, but few have such discipline.

"Goodbye, McManus, goodbye, Delmar," she turned and left without a backward look, disappearing into the ramp that would take her to the Naval shuttle at the far end. I wondered what the crew would make of her, or more, what she might make of them. We headed back to the parking deck.

"Odd," I said. "I thought Freddie would stick around to say goodbye. After all, she saved his mini-skirt clad ass too. He was here earlier."

"He might have said goodbye before," Reg said. "The Admiral said they were out in the parking lot."

"Maybe he's jealous about how much better she looks in leather."

Reg snorted. "Maybe. It looked as if Earth might be better for Jelena than she suspected. She certainly had better color than when we met her. Almost pink."

Suddenly Reg grabbed my arm. "Did you leave the cruiser door open?" she asked, pointing to our black aircar. It was parked in the shade of deck, but I could see she was right. The back door stood ajar. I could see a naked human leg hanging out. We looked at each other, drew our stunners, and ran for the car.

Freddie lay inside on his back, a fashionable, black dress up around his neck, underwear scattered about. I saw two bite marks on his pale, exposed throat.

"Is he?" Reg asked.

"No," Freddie said, opening one eye. "But damn, that woman is amazing." He looked down. "Whoops. Jeez, you'd think she'd pull a guy's dress back down."

I looked on speechless. Reg seemed fascinated by something.

"You know he's got a really big—" Reg began.

I looked at her. "Don't say it."

CHAPTER FIVE

GEEKS FROM THE STRATOSPHERE

THE HARSH BUZZ OF A TELECOMP SAWED ITS WAY INTO MY brain. I groaned. Toni and I had spent a late night celebrating our twentieth wedding anniversary. We partied on long past when people our age should have stopped.

"Honey," I muttered, "it's the hospital. Would you get it?"

My wife opened one eye under delightfully tousled brown hair. "Nice try, husband-mine," she growled, "but that's the police ring."

"Ah," I answered, "yet another disadvantage of decades of marriage. You're on to all of my tricks."

"You were happily enjoying some of the advantages of those decades of marriage last night. Tricks included," she replied before closing her eyes and rolling over.

I struggled out of the covers, walked over to the comp and hit the receive button after killing the video. "Detective McManus," I said.

"McManus," said a husky Southern tenor. "It's me. Put on the video."

"Oh no," I groaned. "Freddie, tell me that you're not calling me on my house at—" I looked at the computer screen, "three-thirty five in the morning. It's way after snitching hours."

"It's urgent," the voice insisted.

"Freddie, I'm standing here in my less than underwear, having thoroughly enjoyed my wedding anniversary—to this point."

"Congratulations," Freddie husked, "I just got engaged myself. That's why I called you."

My brain, already fuzzy, threatened to slide out of focus entirely. "You want some marital advice? First, you have to tell me which gender you got engaged to."

"Male—this time—but I don't need bedroom help."

I narrowed the focus of the screen to where it would show just my face and lit it. Freddie's face simultaneously appeared on the screen, black hair, tormented not teased, cat's-eye makeup, eyes that had seen too much in twenty years. As usual he provided a stunning example of not being able to judge a book by its cover.

Freddie gave a moue of disapproval. "You look like crap."

I glared at him. "I'm going to reach right through this computer screen and beat your silk-clad ass with a baseball bat."

"I get two hundred credits an hour for that," said Freddie, grinning wickedly. "And anyway I told you that I'm spoken for."

"I'm turning off the phone, Freddie."

"No wait. I'm in trouble and so's my fiancé."

"Okay," I said. "You've got me awake. Give."

"I'm singing at the *Radioactive Flamingo* right by the Koch Spaceport these days. I'm mostly off the hooking thing."

"Mostly," I said dryly.

Freddie blushed a little. "I wouldn't be much good as a source if I went entirely straight."

I looked at him.

"Don't say it," Freddie warned, lips pressed together.

"I don't swing at the easy ones," I replied. "Now what the hell did you want?"

"Oh, all right. I met a nice guy at the club. He really loves my singing."

"Humph," I said, eyes closing slightly.

"He was with a whole bunch of college kids about my age."

"Did you ever go to college?" I murmured. The sandman was winding up on me.

"Yeah. Like I had that chance," he said, bitterness twisting the pretty face.

"Ok," I prompted, "the college kids."

"Right. They call themselves the Geeks. Old word, has something to do with computers."

"Never heard it," I said. "So they're comptechs."

"Nothing so basic," Freddie replied. "They are the high-end visionaries. Metaprogrammers and wizards, holoworking the stuff that makes galactic trade work—the stuff that guards and defends the databases of planets.

"My fiancé, Nava, is one of them. He says they've formed a hacking group. They've done some minor illegal stuff but they've got a new leader named Sid who's taken over, and he has big plans. Nava's frightened and wants out, but Sid's got some ex-mob muscle, Swedes from the gang you broke up."

An unintelligible voice spoke to Freddie off screen. It held a panicked quality.

"They're coming," Freddie said. "I'll call back if I can—"

"Freddie, wait—" But the screen went dark.

"Computer," I demanded, "police emergency override code Piper Alpha Romeo three-three-four level one, launch a trace on call just received here."

The computer's toneless feminine voice advised, "No calls received at your location in the last six hours."

"Impossible," I muttered. "Recheck."

"Confirming no calls since 7:30 this evening."

I could only stare at the screen. Telnet wrong? I couldn't conceive it, but there it was. Slowly I walked back to the bed.

I arrived at Port Authority Headquarters at the New World Trade Center early, never having gotten back to sleep. With my last promotion I now rated an aircar slot below the Towers now. As I closed in on HQ I saw cars racing in and out of the parking deck with lights and sirens. The streets below were chock full of uniformed officers, NYPD cops and brass, who wouldn't normally be caught dead at NYPA headquarters. Something was up.

Feeling the need for fortification, I stopped at Katsulos donut and bagel stand for the necessities of life, only to find the lovely and talented Detective Regina Delmar standing there in a severe red pantsuit.

Before I could say hi, she spoke, "There's big trouble. Chief Fabacio wants us upstairs PDQ; the mayor is in her office."

I looked despairingly beyond her at the crullers, sinkers and bagels. My eyes must have welled with tears because she produced a bag from behind her.

"Coffee," she said, "light and sweet along with two powdered jelly donuts. You can eat them as we go, provided you're finished before we get there."

"Helen of Troy," I said, "could not have been more beautiful in my eyes than you are at this moment."

On the Case

"Oh," she said. "Oh, the sheer malarkey of it. I just know that you are simply unbearable without coffee and a donut. Still," she continued as we started toward the towers, "even if it's BS, it's nice for a girl to hear sweet nothings occasionally. Maybe I can get you to give Michael some tips."

"How is old Mike these days?" I said around a mouthful of donut. Master that I am, I contained the spurted jelly without the need of a napkin followed with a swig of perfectly mixed coffee.

"You know he hates being called Mike," she replied.

"Really?" I said, feigning shock. I remembered meeting Michael, a young, handsome and wealthy stock trader. I'd said, "Hey, Mike, nice to meet you." He visibly winced and said, "I prefer Michael, please." I'd despised him from that moment. He in no way deserved a woman who could anticipate the need for coffee and donuts for a distraught partner. I believed that I should probably shoot him but had not yet found the excuse.

"Yes, really. He took me out to the Galaxy Club last night."

"Where you got to hear all about him."

She grimaced. "Yeah, kinda."

I was instantly sorry for the comment. My dating days were an age ago. I tried real hard not to remember them. "Ah, he's probably just nervous. Guys babble around beautiful women."

Reg spared me a smile. "You're sweet, Brian, a dinosaur, but sweet."

I hid my embarrassment behind the second jelly donut. We reached the bank of Tower Two and shot up the eighty stories to Fabacio's office. I slurped and snarfed, apparently frightening the other occupants of the car. I managed to subdue the accompanying burp as the doors slid open.

Fabacio stood at bay outside her office with her broad backside to me. I ditched the coffee cup as Reg and I walked up. On the other side of her stood our mayor, Carlos Diviega, all five-foot six inches of him, with bristling mustache and flashing eyes. In the standard manner of NYC mayors from time immemorial, he rarely talked below a yell and waved his arms constantly.

"You've got to do something!" said the Mayor, semaphoring with his limbs.

Fabacio caught sight of us in a reflection and turned. "I understand, Mr. Mayor. My trouble team has just arrived. Let me brief them, and I will meet you in the press room shortly."

Trailing Spanish expletives, Hizzoner followed the aide Fabacio waved over.

Fabacio sighed and looked at us with the pleasant matronly face she used to mask her ambitious and ruthless personality. "Good. You're here. My office."

We followed her in without questions, which was how she liked it. She sat in the big comfy chair, and we got the metal ones.

"Nobody took this seriously until three hours ago, and the media hasn't yet been informed," Fabacio said, almost as if to herself. She leaned back in her chair, looking out and up from the window behind her.

I couldn't resist. "Is the sky falling?"

Reg sank lower into her chair.

"In a manner of speaking, yes, wise-ass," Fabacio returned. "Last night an old air-mining platform appeared in the air pattern over Koch Interstellar Spaceport. One second, nothing, next second all 1,500 meters of it is circling over them. Caused a lot of emergency reroutes."

"How is that possible?" murmured Regina. "What about air traffic control? Not to mention the NYC air defense grid?"

"Bypassed by these Geeks, as they call themselves," Fabacio said as if the incredible had no meaning anymore.

Geeks. All of a sudden the donuts turned to brick in my guts.

"They're a group of hackers and so-called visionaries," Fabacio continued. "They broke into the Interstellar Trade Commission database and put a rounding error on their savings accounts. Every trade made dropped a fraction of a cent in an account. They purchased an obsolete Indonesian air-mining platform, tons of holographic equipment, computers and supplies and moved onto the thing."

I whistled. "Hacked the ITC? That's supposed to be impossible."

Fabacio nodded, "Confidence in the ITC underlies much of the galactic economy. If this gets out, we could have a financial panic."

"These Geeks are circling Koch Spaceport in neutral trade airspace. They've declared their air-miner to be the sovereign state of Freedonia. They're offering plundered data from hundreds of supposedly secure systems to the highest bidder with deposits going to an irrevocable trust off-world. Freedonia's chief industry appears to be blackmail."

"I don't suppose they'll run out of supplies," Reg ventured.

"The air-miner weighs 6000 tons loaded," Fabacio replied. "They could live there for years. We don't even know how many Geeks there are. Their computer defenses whack anything we use to snoop on them."

"Considered shooting them down?" I joked.

"Yes," said Fabacio.

My jaw dropped. "In neutral tradespace?" I managed. Tradespace was inviolate, one of the basic tenets of the Galactic Federation.

"UNAF received authorization to destroy the air-miner, but no less than three alien governments threatened military reprisals if the UN enters neutral trade space. They've hinted that they are being blackmailed. The Snorge Republic on the other hand is threatening an attack if we don't destroy the air-miner. You know the Snorge and the secret they are willing to kill for. They can't afford to have the assassination fiasco you two broke up, made public. It would bring down their government and restart a civil war."

"There is only one political entity with the jurisdiction to enter neutral trade space over Koch Interstellar," she continued, "the Port Authority of NY & NJ."

"Why not send up SWAT?" I asked.

"We did, an hour ago. They hacked into our aircar systems and turned off the engines. Teams 3 and 5 fell right out of the sky."

Reg and I sat up. We had friends on those teams. They'd pulled us out of a burning warehouse once.

"Damn," I said. "Casualties?"

"The teams bailed out, but the aircars fell into Queens and hit an apartment complex project. We have twenty-two injured, one dead.

"That's why you're here," Fabacio said, leaning forward in her chair. "I'm putting you both in charge of the effort to seize Freedonia."

"What do you expect us to do?" I asked. "If SWAT can't reach the air-miner—"

"From assassins to interstellar vampires to resurrected clones," Fabacio interrupted, "you two manage to get out of more tight corners than a Norway rat. You'll find something. You have the complete resources of the NYPA. The UN and Interstellar Confed don't dare help for fear the Geeks will find out. You're on your own."

Reg and I made our way to the top of Tower Two and then across the skyway that joined the towers. The observation deck sat atop Tower One. Normally the deck would be open to the public, but today PA cops guarded the doors. Fabacio had it sealed off so we could use it as a command area. We were waved in. I wanted to see the bad guys with the naked eye—not over a camera screen. We walked out into the stiff breeze that always blew at this height. Reg's shoulder-length brown hair fluffed and whipped until she captured it back in a ponytail.

Tower One stood 2,000 feet and gave a good view to the northeast where Koch Spaceport lay in what had once been Long Island Sound before the galaxy burst in on us. We walked past the batteries of suits, politicos and brass. We'd deal with them later. To my surprise there were UN troops outside with portable computers and tables. Reg went over and checked on them. "UN Air-Defense Artillery," she said when she returned. "They've got Raptor SAMS ringing Koch."

"Brilliant," I said. "Dropping aircars on apartments wasn't a big enough fubar. Let's top it by dropping something the size of a destroyer on Queens."

"Well," said Reg, "it is Queens."

I looked at her.

"Kidding," she said. "Really."

I turned to the scopes that lined the parapets. While the wind slapped at me, I scanned north. "Got 'em," I said.

"Me too," said Reg. "One air-miner, ho."

The air-miner looked like a cross between a passenger jet and an aircraft carrier. Long and slender, painted a brilliant red and white, its flat-deck was topped by an enormous structure running a third of the hull and looking like a luggage handle.

"What do we know about it?" I asked.

"Air-miners are relics of the late 21st Century," replied Reg, "when aliens sold Earth the technology to clean up our polluted air. They rolled over the globe using electromagnetic fields to suck pollutants from the air—converting them to useful chemicals and metals or condensing them to be shot into the sun by EMG rail guns.

"After fifty years of operations and with cleaner technologies being developed, the market eventually collapsed. Only a few air-miners are needed these days. This is one of the early models. It had a brief career as a casino and a luxury hotel before ending up in an Indonesian conglomerate as a freighter," she concluded.

Now it circled at 15,000 meters over Koch Interstellar, its antigravity units supplemented by lift from the aerodynamic body. Lights twinkled along the side in a pattern. I upped the magnification. The lights formed the words, "Hail Freedonia!"

"How in God's name do we get onto that?" I wondered.

Eight hours later we were none the wiser, despite all the "help" from the mayor's office. While Reg ran interference, I sought a few quiet minutes in the back of the concession stand.

No such luck. Lt. Frisby, one of my least favorite cops, bore down on me.

"McManus," he growled. "Whaddya, hiding back here?"

"Unsuccessfully," I said.

"That nancy-boy snitch you pay is on Channel D," Frisby said. "He says he's got info about Freedonia. Hah, he can probably see it out his window." He tossed me a portable comp and walked off.

I flipped open its mini-screen. "You there, Freddie?"

"Jesus Effing Christ," said Freddie. "Keep your voice down." Freddie looked back at me, considerably the worse for wear. He sported a shiner and bruises. "Listen. I'm on Freedonia. Nava and I escaped from the Swedes, but they're hunting us. He wants to surrender to the police but he doesn't want to betray his friends. I've talked him into helping you and Delmar land up here."

"That's nuts," I sputtered.

"I know, I know," Freddie wailed, "but it's all I could do. If you come on board with power to make a deal, maybe we can get him to do more. Listen, I don't have time. Here's what you have to do..."

Two hours later Regina and I stood in the hatchway of a small UN vertical take-off and landing *Intruder* looking down at Freedonia. Even with its lights on, the air-miner was mostly just a dark shape occluding the lights of the Big Apple as it cruised on its circuit. Nava had intruded into Freedonia's defenses long and deep enough to allow the small VTOL to make one pass and drop two and precisely two people. Anything else and the VTOL would find itself tumbling to the ground.

A UN airman briskly finished the last adjustments on my artificial gravity belt as I stared into the blackness. The air-miner looked like a toy below us. The wind slapping at me felt as cold as the reaper's long bony claw.

I turned to Reg, like me decked out in a black sneaksuit, body armor and a helmet. "I am too old for this shit," I shouted over the drone of wind and engines.

Reg grinned.

Nut, I thought, *never happy except when there's trouble.*

"Yellow light," snapped the airman. "Stand in the door."

I shuffled over. "I am too old—"

"Green light, go!" shouted the airman.

Reacting to the order shouted in my ear, I stepped out into space. We'd switched off our coms to avoid being detected. That was good, as my screams probably couldn't be heard farther than Connecticut. The tether snapped and the low power AG unit switched on, holding me upright. As I slowed in the air, control returned to me, and I looked between my feet at the air-miner, steering toward the main deck.

The air-miner grew into a ghostly white shape and the deck developed features. Ten meters off the deck, the AG unit kicked harder and slowed me. I hit and rolled across the deck chased by gale-like winds.

I slammed into a stanchion rigged with safety lines and hung onto it like a politician hangs onto a kickback. After a few seconds Reg crashed into me. I grabbed her.

She clung to me, putting her helmet against mine so I could hear. "I am definitely too young and pretty to die," she shouted over the wind.

"Amen," I managed.

The deck, which had appeared so smooth from above, proved to be studded with pillbox shapes and piping of all sizes. In the distance we could see the flat area for aircars to land. I glanced around. The section didn't look like where we were supposed to have landed. From a pillbox shape about fifty meters away, a small red light began to blink SOS. I pointed and Reg nodded. She tied us together at our utility belts, and we painfully crawled over the pipes and decking toward the light.

It was an airlock. Beside the access door I could see Freddie's face through a small window, outlined by the red penlight he held. We opened the door and stumbled in. As it closed behind us, the room pressurized. Reg and I drew lasers the PA had issued us in place of our stunners as the hatch cycled. Freddie stood on the other side, wearing a black mini and silver blouse.

"They caught Nava," he said, eyes wide with terror. "Come with me." We dashed away from the airlock into an open machinery space, finding cover behind a huge processor.

"Great," I said. "Screwed before we start."

"Nava put some lockouts in the computer system," Freddie whispered, eyes darting around the huge machinery. The area was poorly lit and looked like a maze of catwalks and machinery.

It hummed with electronic and mechanical noise. "They won't lock on to the bio-signs of our bodies. But we can be spotted on camera, and they'll detect the opening of the airlock. We need to get away from this area."

The screens over our head lit suddenly. On it a smarmy, blond, teenage male looked down on us, flanked by two topless Indonesian girls in what looked native garb from a bad movie. In the background I saw more young men. They didn't look like Swedes so I guessed they were Geeks. Horns blared and a seductive female voice spoke. "Prepare to hear from King Sid the First, Lord of the Database and Master of Freedonia."

"Oh, please," said Regina. We followed Freddie as he pried open an a/c grill and we moved into the machinery spaces. We could see control panels, many of which featured King Sid's leering face.

"I know that you're here, Detectives McManus and Delmar," King Sid said in a nasal whine, that none the less held complete confidence. "Nava managed to cloak you with a holoblock, so my sensors don't see you or his so-called girlfriend. You know her, the one with the big dick. We all had a good laugh at Nava's expense before sealing him in the security hold. Still he couldn't stop me from finding the last message the cross-dresser sent you. It's just a matter of time until my court wizards and I penetrate Nava's wards. Then we will see you. Better surrender now."

"Tactical idiot," I muttered. "Give up some more information. Amateur. Snot-nosed brat."

We continued on through the machinery spaces, heading toward the air-miner's bridge.

"McManus," King Sid taunted, "I'm in the Port Authority payroll. Guess what I just did with your savings? Bought you 20,000 shares in a robo-bordello on Ceres. How will you explain that to Toni? Oops, there goes your pension too."

Hearing my wife's name on his greasy lips made my teeth grit.

"Let's take a look at those medical records," Sid laughed. "Gee, McManus, you're awfully damn boring. Never even managed to get the clap. Now your partner, she's a hotty. She even looks good in her file photo. Did you know she had an abortion at age fourteen? Hey Regina, who was the daddy?"

Ahead of me in the conduit Reg suddenly stopped, hunched over in the narrow ductway. Her back and shoulders spoke of pain. I put my hand on her shoulder. Even through the armor I thought I could feel the heat of her rage.

"Basic Psy-Ops stuff," I said, as if he had just announced the weather. "Done to throw us off our game and let him set the pace. Remember, he's talking, but we ain't listening."

Her head jerked once.

From in front of her Freddie spoke over his shoulder. "I've never met any perfect people myself."

"Thanks," she choked out.

Freddie nodded then changed the subject, "I think that we should turn right at this junction."

We exited into a room that looked like a dorm gone to seed. Pizza boxes littered the floor, computers of various sizes filled spaces not cluttered with dirty clothes. It smelled like combination locker room, brewery and drug den. A naked Indonesian girl lay sprawled and snoring in the middle of one bed.

"Found the rumpus room," I said. "I see they bought more than just the air-miner in Indonesia."

"Nava is being held in the secure cargo hold just forward of here," Freddie whispered. "I overheard King Sid ordering it."

We opened the door, leaving the snoring party girl to dream on in peace.

I used a small SWAT probe on a telescoping tube to look around the corner. It flashed an image onto my hand comp. Two guards, both big Swedes, stood in front of Nava's cell.

"Do the guards know you?" I whispered.

Freddie looked at the screen. "Not these two," he replied.

"Can you sashay past these guys and get them to look the other way?"

"I look like shit," Freddie protested. "I've got a black eye and bruises."

"Reg isn't dressed for it. You've got big fake boobs and nice legs," I said. "They won't be looking at your face."

Freddie hmph'd, then pulled a compact out of somewhere. A few seconds' work and the worst of the damage was covered. Freddie walked out into the corridor as if he owned it. Reg and I crouched by the wall, watching Freddie and the goons on the hand comp.

"Vell, vell," said one. "Vhat do we have here, Lars? She's not Indonesian."

"Hey boys," said Freddie, "looking for a party?"

The Vikings laughed and Freddie managed to get past them, wiggling in a practiced fashion that riveted their attention.

"Hey," said Lars. "I just remembered, the only non Indo-girl is — " moving fast for a big man, he backhanded Freddie, who bounced off the wall.

"Freeze, police," Reg and I yelled, jumping around the corner. We had our weapons leveled; the Swedes, being pros, didn't go for theirs. "Drop the weapons," I ordered. The Swede's guns fell to the decking.

Freddie calmly got off the floor, walked up to Lars and soccer-kicked the Swede's testicles into low orbit. Lars ate deck and then barfed on it.

"Open the door," Reg ordered after we frisked the Swedes. The other goon obliged.

"Come out, Nava," called Freddie.

A slim Indian boy in his teens came out, looking nervously at the goons and us, then glared at Freddie. "Oh, I am so mad at you," he said in accented standard. "You made a fool out of me."

"Yeah," said Freddie with apparent contrition. "I'm sorry. Couldn't help myself."

"Reunions later," I snapped. "OK, Viking," I continued, "take barf boy and get into the cell. Reg cuff and gag them."

A minute later we were hotfooting it down the passageways. "Our best chance," Nava said, "is to get to the auxiliary control room. I can hack into the system and lock out the other computer controls."

As I stepped toward the main corridor, Nava shouted, "Wait, the video-scanners—"

On a screen by the side of a comp panel, King Sid's face appeared. "Aha. Got you."

Live steam began venting from pipes behind us.

"This way," Freddie screamed. We raced forward. The air-miner had no internal security systems. It wasn't a warship, but emergency doors tried to crush us, panels shorted and spat electricity at us.

We jumped into one room off the main hallway. Another rumpus room, this time full of naked girls, who ran shrieking as we burst in. Most of them made it out of the room before King Sid struck. At the other end of the room, an exterior hatch began to slide open. Wind howled. A girl too close to the opening door screamed once as she was sucked out.

Reg launched herself at the far end. *She's going out too,* I thought. Instead she hit the wall and clawed at a hatch control. The door ground closed again.

"That girl...that girl," Nava stammered, "she's gone."

"Sid's not worried about his girlfriends," I spat.

Nava scrambled past me. "My computer," he crowed, snatching at a small, ornate portable. Before I could figure out if it was a good idea, his hands blurred over the controls. "Sid, you vicious maniac," he shouted. "Take that."

Sid's image derezzed on the computer screen.

"I left a back door," Nava said. "Good hackers always do. Mine is so deep none of his wizards can find it. Not even King Sid will. I can attack all his communication and control programs. Sid is good though; even my intruder software won't disrupt his control for long. Auxiliary control is a hundred yards ahead on this deck."

"Then we will have to make the most of the time," said Reg. "Let's go."

The air-miner lurched as Nava and King Sid's programs battled for control. We pushed out of the rumpus room, armed with lasers and Nava's computer, shoving our way past Asian girls.

"Vikings," yelled Reg as she snapped off a shot. A Swede tumbled to the deck and the others dodged into cover. We raced for the hatch to auxiliary control, Nava tapping frantically on his keyboard as we ran.

"I've overcome the locks," he yelled as the door rolled open.

We raced into the long disused auxiliary control room. I took up a position by the door and fired at the first Viking I saw in the corridor outside.

"I can break his control but I don't know how to fly it," Nava sputtered, looking at the banks of yellow computer boards and screens.

"I can," snapped Reg. "My father taught me to fly anything." She hopped into the center seat. "Get me control!"

The Swedes moved up the corridor. I pegged a laser shot at them, wishing I had my stunner. I didn't join the PA to kill people.

Hot metal splattered me as a return shot destroyed a nearby cabinet. My opponents were less filled with the milk of human kindness than I.

"Gimme a gun," shouted Freddie. "You can't hold 'em off alone."

"Can you shoot?" Reg called.

"Grew up on a bayou shooting possums," Freddie said.

Reg slid a laser across the floor to him. Freddie snatched it up.

"Hah," he yelled, firing. "Bitch-slap me, willya? Die, Viking scum." A cry indicated a hit.

"Nava, can Sid jam my police frequency?" I asked, ducking a return shot.

"Not now," he replied. "I've cut off all his exterior communications."

"McManus to Fabacio," I said hitting my throat mike and disregarding codes. Sid probably knew them anyway.

"Fabacio here. What's your sitrep?"

"We have partial control of the air-miner, but it's temporary at best. We need SWAT backup."

"No can do," said Fabacio. "There's an air battle breaking out above you. A Snorge Republic just sent fighters into Neutral Tradespace—heading for your position."

"Crap," I said.

A distorted image of King Sid appeared on the screens. "Nava, wait. We can make a deal. You've cut off my exterior communications. If I can't dump out people's secrets, we have no defense."

"What you're doing is wrong," Nava shouted back. "To hack is one thing—to destroy people's lives with blackmail is another."

"Imbecile," shrieked King Sid over the speakers. "That's all that's keeping the UN from blowing us out of the sky. Snorge Republic fighters are only minutes away from us. You've got to give me control."

"Never," Nava said.

The air-miner dropped from below our feet. Everybody screamed.

Reg looked at the boards. "I've got helm control. I'm heading us away from the spaceport toward the Connecticut shoreline."

"Good," I said, finding my feet and drawing a bead on the tumbled Swedes.

King Sid's face appeared again. "There's a Snorge fighter closing on us."

"Yep," confirmed Reg. "He's got two UNSDF *Corsairs* on him. Damn. He's firing."

The air-miner bucked and heaved sidewise. "Hit on the bridge area," Reg called. "I hope they didn't kill Sid. He's mine."

"We can't survive another hit," Nava whimpered, falling to the deck, clearly overwhelmed.

"Won't have to," Reg crowed. "*Corsairs* just splashed him."

"We're still dropping," I yelled.

"Impact in five seconds," Reg said. "I'm going to try and get her nose on the beach. "Brace, we're going to hit."

With an ear-shattering roar the air-miner slapped the ocean. Lights dimmed, panels blew out, and unsecured junk flew everywhere. With a final jolt, the air-miner stopped moving. I looked down the hall; the Swedes were running. Rats abandoning the sinking ship.

Reg scrambled up. "To the bridge," she said. "Sid's not going to get away."

"Wait, dammit," I yelled, then set off after her, trailed by Freddie and Nava. We ran into Indonesian pros and running Geeks. I clobbered the Geeks and cuffed them. Nobody opposed us. Reg ignored everyone and raced into the bridge.

When I cleared the door, I spotted Reg advancing on King Sid, circling the smoking control panel. Sid stood at least a head taller than Reg, but she was all lean muscle and trained. She push-blocked his straight right and slammed leopard punches to his midsection. His inept punches bounced off her blocks, and she booted him in the midsection.

"So, you've foiled my plans," he huffed. "I surrender."

Reg cracked him across the face and executed a nice spinning back kick to bounce him off the wall. "Nava, stay where you are," I called into the corridor.

I looked at Freddie. "He's resisting arrest," I said.

"Clearly," Freddie returned, watching Reg snapping punches into Sid.

"He attacked Officer Delmar with a pipe, while I was dealing with the Swedes," I continued. "You were cowering in a corner."

"I was so frightened," Freddie agreed, smiling as Sid missed a swing on Reg.

A minute reduced Sid to a sobbing, bleeding pile on the deck. Reg started to kick him. I moved in and wrapped an arm around her, lifting her off the deck and stepping back. Reg didn't fight me. She glared at Sid.

"You bastard," she managed. "Scum. Play with my life—"

"I'll make the arrest," I interrupted in a low voice. "You take Freddie and Nava. Keep an eye on the rest."

She nodded, breathing hard. I let her go. Freddie followed her out.

I looked at Sid. "I'll sue," he whispered between mashed lips.

"You want I should bring her back in, Sid?" I asked. I saw terror in the one eye he could open. "You won't sue and you won't talk to the press and you won't see a trial. You fucked with the ITC, you're going to wish Detective Delmar had finished you." I flipped him over on his side and cuffed him. He started crying. I had to steel myself against feeling sorry for him. Had to remember the injured SWAT guys, the people in the apartment when the SWAT car crashed into it, the Indonesian girl sucked out into the night air.

"You assholes always think you're different," I said. "Always think that just because you use a computer to loot people's lives that you're different from a robber. You probably think that killing that girl with a computer command is different than using a rifle. You're not different. And you're under arrest."

Reg returned. She'd rounded up the surviving Indonesian girls who clustered near Freddie. She had the two Swedish goons we'd locked up earlier and the tech geeks chained or cuffed. Behind her I could see the fires growing in intensity.

"Time to go," Reg said.

I looked at the lead Swede goon. "Pick that up," I said, pointing at Sid. The goon dragged Sid upright and carried him out into the corridor.

Reg stood facing me. Smoke drifted near the ceiling and machinery spat and crackled around us as the air-miner died. She looked at me for a minute.

"Nobody hears a word about anything from me," I said. "But anytime you want to talk…"

She looked away and then nodded, "Let's go."

We made our way to the deck of the burning miner. We'd crashed in by the shore and the upper deck stood well above the water. As we walked out onto it, I could see VTOLs and hovers closing on us from all directions.

The next day I sat with Freddie at a beach hotel table with a fine view of the still-smoking air-miner. Reg had accompanied Nava into Secret Service custody. She had friends there, and we wanted to make sure that Nava didn't get "disappeared." I spent most of the night reporting to various Confed and Earth government entities, Mayor Diviega and Chief Fabacio and trying to keep Freddie from being dragged off into custody. I even managed to get a call to Toni to let her know I was OK.

The blonde waitress finished serving breakfast. I had sausage, potatoes and eggs with a pot of coffee. Freddie nibbled on some toast. "Have to watch my girlish figure," he said. At some point after the air-miner crashed, Freddie had located and raided a beauty shop in the resort. His hair had returned to its former height and his cat's-eye makeup was impeccable.

"Something has gone horribly wrong with my life," I said, "when I find myself spending an ordinary breakfast at a seaside resort with you."

Freddie winked at me. "I always thought it would happen. More sugah in your coffee, Sugah?" he offered in his best Southern drawl, languidly waving a spoon.

I sighed. Retirement wasn't that far off. "Oh just pass the damn sugar bowl."

CHAPTER SIX

A BONE TO PICK

"JESUS CHRIST," DAVIS SAID. "I'VE BEEN A PORT AUTHORITY cop for fifteen years. I've never seen anything like this." He mopped his brow with a bandana, his dark skin gone ashen. Behind him on a launchpad about a kilometer away, a transport rumbled skyward on its impellers, adding to the drone of Brooklyn's Koch Municipal Spaceport.

"Take it easy, Davis," I said. "Just tell us where the body is."

Davis shuddered. "There ain't no body. Just clean picked bones lying in a pool." He pointed toward the marsh grass beyond the tarmac. I spotted the yellow crime scene tape.

"Ok. We'll go take a look."

I gestured to my partner, Regina Delmar, who'd remained quiet while I spoke to the unnerved patrolman. Reg was still relatively fresh from the Academy, new body, new mind, undamaged psyche and ambitious as hell. She had the looks of a model, olive skin, dark-brown hair and big brown eyes. She could also drop the carryall she was hauling and run a marathon. Only an actual appearance by the Grim Reaper could get me to run any distance. I was built for power, not speed, and about twenty years before her.

We walked into the weeds. Reg carried our bag of sensors and remotes, easily managing the uneven and spongy ground. Ah, youth. I crunched behind her, sinking deeper into the soil. It wasn't far to the tape and the shallow pool of rainwater from last night's storm.

We peered into the pool. A cool white skeleton looked back at us accusingly. The bones were as clean as if they'd been sent from a lab.

Reg put her bag down and set up the usual sensors. They'd sample water, air and soil. The robot, which looked like a mega-cockroach, stalked off to search for man-made items and fibers. Reg triggered a small disk camera. It flew over the middle of the pond to start imaging 360-degree holos.

"Dial up a satellite look-down," I said. "Let's get a full photo run down to one millimeter length."

"Got it," she keyed the request into the portable comp, then joined me in my morose study of the skeleton. "Male," she observed. "Big guy, about your size."

"Less handsome," I returned.

"Damn. You know you'd gone nearly a whole hour without a wisecrack."

"He hasn't been here long," I said, ignoring the jibe and kneeling by the skeleton's left arm, which projected from the pool. "These bones aren't discolored. And here, look at this."

"What?"

"Cut marks on the bone. Saw something like this on a National Geographic special on cavemen. Somebody took the meat off these bones."

"Yuck," she responded. "So someone carefully skinned and gutted a human somewhere else and dumped the bones here to be found by a patrolman looking to relieve a full bladder."

"Yep," I replied, "and dumped him right here in the spaceport grounds. I wonder if this is related to the anti-alien riots last week?"

Reg's portacomp beeped. She consulted the screen. "Air normal, water normal, the grass has been crushed but no tracks. There are

126   *On the Case*

a number of very odd hairs that the roach picked up. They look canine but they aren't coming up in the DNA database."

"Any DNA on the bones?"

"Negative. That's going to take the crime lab guys."

I looked around for a last time. "Call them in," I said. "Time to collect Mr. Bone-a-part here."

Reg sighed and reached for her belt comp.

An hour later we were back in the PA station at Koch. Reg and I normally worked out of the New World Trade Center, but we'd been loaned to the actual spaceport detail after the Rigellian flu put half of New York on its back.

I was savoring a donut and coffee when Reg walked up with her usual bad timing.

"Brian, you have crumbs on your suit," she observed. "What will your wife say?"

"That I was saving them for later."

"Crime lab checked in," Reg continued. "The bones belong to one Walter Brice Primorse of 1312 86th Street, Apartment 301 in Bay Ridge. I've arranged for the landlord to let us in."

"Wife, children?"

"Ex-wife," Reg said. "One child, a boy of fourteen, there's a court order barring the deceased from contacting them. Bad domestic, evidently."

"Okay, we'll see them later. Let's check out the apartment."

Reg drove the aircar as we zipped over the Gowanis. With cop clearance we could land on the roof. The building computer opened the roof door and summoned the manager. A squat and unlovely creature, he met us at the door of 301.

"So," the landlord grunted. "He's dead, huh?"

"Extremely," I answered. "Gonna miss him?"

"Nah," said the landlord. "Guy was a freak. He hated people. Loved animals and their rights. Saw no difference between McDonalds and Auschwitz."

"He must have missed the barbed wire," I muttered.

"Know the weirdest thing about him?" the landlord asked.

"What?" Reg said.

"He didn't own any animals. Not even a fish." He opened the door and padded away chuckling to himself.

We walked into the spartanly furnished one-bedroom apartment. The walls were festooned with animal rights posters and photos of what looked like demonstrations. Several of them bore the markings of the *Society for the Preservation of Prey Animals.* The SPPA logo appeared to be a very militant looking rabbit. In many of the images stood a man about thirty-years-old, balding, with cold, washed-out blue eyes. I picked up a large framed photo of Primorse with his arms linked with other demonstrators. He had the face of a man who always knew WHAT THE RIGHT THING WAS for everyone, all the time. No wonder he was divorced.

An hour's perusal confirmed it. Primorse was an animal rights fanatic. A rabid vegan who'd tangled with the law at farms and restaurants.

"We're through here," I said.

"Time to see the former Mrs.?" Reg asked.

"I hate this part," I said.

"She's already been told," Reg shrugged. "Wasn't too upset when I spoke to her. Wife's always a suspect when the husband ends up dead."

"She didn't do this."

"Just because your wife likes you, for reasons that elude me, is no reason to be sentimental about other people's marriages. Primorse's ex had a restraining order on him."

"Doesn't feel right," I said.

"We'll see."

We flew for an hour into what had been New Jersey a century ago before the aliens landed and opened up the universe. The Port of New York ate northern New Jersey over the next hundred years. As we flew over the remnants of New Jersey's ancient swamps, the car comp beeped and flashed information on the console screen.

"Well," Reg said, "so much for my theory. The family has an alibi. Her boy, Adrian, was on stage for a piano recital last night. Forensics places Primorse's time of death during the warm up. We even have local media tape of the recital. They're both on it."

"It would be unkind of me to say I told you so," I said generously.

"Very unkind, possibly causing me to sob with shame and kick you in the groin," she said with a flash of her Spanish eyes.

"Out of respect for your tender young feelings we shall let it pass," I replied with a dismissive wave.

We dropped into a tidy yard of a nice suburb. Sonya Rickett, the former Mrs. Primorse, stood in the yard waiting for us. She was a pleasant-looking black woman of about thirty. She walked up as we got out of the aircar. "Hello."

"Ms. Rickett," I said. "I'm Detective Brian McManus. This is Detective Regina Delmar."

"Call me Sonya," she said. "I've got some iced tea on the back porch. We can sit there." We sat on the porch and exchanged some awkward pleasantries.

"Well, I guess you want to hear about Walter?" Sonya said.

"I'm afraid so," I said. "We've read the domestic file."

"Damn fool," she said bitterly. "Can you imagine beating up your own child for having a meatball sandwich with some friends?"

I thought about my boy, Tim, and the many reasons to beat teenagers. That wasn't one of them. "No."

"That was the last straw. Walter wasn't always a narrow-minded fanatic. Or maybe he was and I didn't see it. So many things start with hope and end badly."

"Too true," Reg whispered, almost as if to herself. I looked at her curiously. She glanced away.

"Something went wrong with him," Sonya said. "I couldn't help him and I wasn't going to let him ruin Adrian's life."

"Yeah." We talked over the matter for a while longer. I asked all the necessary questions, learning nothing new or useful.

"You don't need to talk to Adrian?" Sonya asked. "He's pretty upset."

"Not now," I said, rising. "I don't see a need. It's got to be tough losing your Dad regardless of how he was."

Sonya's eyes welled. She looked away and nodded.

"We'll leave you in peace," Reg said. We showed ourselves out.

"That was a good woman," I said as we got back into the car. "He wouldn't have ended up as bones if he'd made it work with her."

Reg gave me a rare smile. "You're a romantic, Brian. The real world is a cold, cruel place."

"That's why I eat donuts," I said.

We returned to the office and started studying the data. I sat at my desk and yawned. It was getting near the end of a long day.

Reg, looking as fresh as ever, was digging into Primorse's financial records. She had the better head for math.

"Primorse hid money in a variety of shell companies, and in one of those he'd spent a huge sum of money to visit, Inkporlin IV, locally known as Gratia," Reg said.

"Yeah?" I keyed the Confed Encyclopedia and brought up information on Gratia. What I saw made everything click.

"Reg, check the immigration and visa records for aliens called Gratians, arriving anytime in the last month."

Reg's fingers flicked over the screen. "Not a common species for Earth, one hundred twenty seven have passed through Koch Spaceport since May 15."

"Any still onworld?"

"Yes," she said. "I'm showing a party of twelve staying at the Spaceport Hilton."

"Okay. Let's roll. Get the car. I've got a call to make to Forensics. I'll explain as we go."

"Backup?"

"Not yet."

Reg dashed out. I called Forensics and pulled up the results of our field tests. Fortunately the Forensics chief was still in. Even with computers, my request would take a while, she said. She'd call back.

We slid into a parking spot and flashed our tin at the Hilton carparkers as they came over to tell us to move. We entered the towering hotel and walked to the marble slab of the front desk. It featured live help to handle the peculiar troubles of alien and space travelers. I cut ahead of a party of trollish Snorge. Reg showed them a badge before they could kick up a fuss.

"Police business," I said to the middle-aged clerk. He hardly reacted, doubtless having seen much weirdness in the hotelier trade.

"What do you need?" he said.

"Are there any Gratians checked into the hotel?"

"Not anymore," the clerk said with a bored shrug. "A big party just checked out. They're over there waiting for the airbus." He pointed to the other exit.

I looked at Reg and nodded. We hotfooted it through the lobby. The Gratians were still there waiting for the airport shuttle. A late-night TV wag had christened the Gratians "Poodle Men from Outer Space" and the resemblance was striking. The dozen of them looked like the sort of dogs that people used to dress up and take photos of. It would be funny except for the fact that they, poodle-cut hair and all, had made it to the stars ahead of us. I pulled out my shield. "Excuse me. Detective McManus, Port Authority of New York Police."

One of the Gratians, wearing a dark suit and sunglasses, came forward. I half expected him to bark, but he spoke fluent Standard. "Yes, officer. May I help you? I'm Vesh Dekaann. I'm afraid none of my companions speaks Terran very well."

Bullshit, I thought. "I am going to have to ask you to return to the hotel with us and answer a few questions."

"I am afraid we have a ship to catch and lack time."

I looked at the Gratian. "I'm afraid that I must insist. You are in neutral tradespace and within our jurisdiction. Under Confed Treaty 109, Section 34, you're required to cooperate with us."

"Of course," Dekaann replied. He turned and spoke to his friends in what sounded like a series of hoots. They exchanged what seemed to me to be anxious looks.

Reg bought up the rear as we returned to the hotel and commandeered a small conference room from the no longer bored clerk. I set up scanners and an interrogation recorder. My phone beeped, and I stepped away from everyone. It was Forensics with the answer I expected. "Thanks," I rang off.

"Officer," Dekaann said. "We do have a ship to—"

"Why did you kill the human, Walter Primorse?" I asked.

"I have no idea what you are talking about."

"Unfortunately and in common with many furred creatures, you shed. I just received a call from our Forensics department. The murder site contained the hair of six different Gratians. Your party are the only ones of your species on Earth in the last seven days. DNA testing will tell us which of you were there and the rest will go in as accessories. So let me restate the question. Why did you do it?"

The Gratian looked at me and growled, his fangs suddenly in evidence. Reg drew her stunner in a liquid move. I just stared back.

"My people" Dekaann said, "are carnivores."

"Yeah, I noticed the teeth."

"Primorse came to our world on a tour, or so he told our immigration authorities. Truth was that Primorse believed us to be an abomination. His actual plan was to release a virus into the staple animal of our diet. The virus is harmless to the animal, but if consumed by a Gratian, causes severe illness, sometimes death. He broke into several of our major food processing centers and spread the virus. He then used our package delivery service to infect many other locations. We did not know it until after he escaped our world. A time-delayed broadcast warned us that we had been judged guilty by the Society for the Preservation of Prey Animals.

"We suffered billions of credits of damage and had to import offworld foods or face real hunger on our world for the first time in centuries. My mate's family fortune was destroyed, her father killed himself—"

"Why didn't you file charges and demand extradition?" Reg interrupted, still holding her stunner but pointing it at the floor.

"Such procedures can take decades," the Gratian huffed, his gray whiskers bristling. "They are uncertain at best. To you, this is a crime. To us it is an attack on our species, on our entire way of life, on the balance between predator and prey. It is a mortal insult."

"So you hunted him down and ate him," Reg said.

"Yes. We lured him to the airport on the promise of meeting with like-minded ecoterrorists. He was dispatched...humanely... you would say. Then, in accord with the rituals for sacred prey, for those that have killed or injured a hunter, he was properly dressed and prepared."

"Prepared?" I asked.

"I like to think of it as stewing him in the juices of his own self-righteousness," Dekaann said, "with herbs of course."

"He was evidently quite full of those," I murmured.

"Unfortunately, we lacked the means to dispose of the bones and made a poor job of it."

"Yes. You realize that you and your companions are under arrest."

"Of course," Dekaann said. "There will be no trouble. We are a very civilized people."

"Good," I said. "We'll make sure your cages have nice fresh paper in them."

We quickly frisked them and secured their arms with crooktape then marched the Gratians out of the conference room. In the hallway outside, a buffet was being set up for the insurance seminar in the ballroom across the hall. The Gratians stopped as the

On the Case

preparers set up a large warming pan. They seemed to be breathing deeply.

"Problem?" Reg prompted.

Dekaann looked at us. "It was just the smell, delicious, very reminiscent of Mr. Primorse. Indeed I imagine it tastes very similar."

Against my better judgment, I looked at the server. "What do you have there?"

The young Puerto Rican girl smiled at me and opened the pan with a flourish.

"Of course," I said. "Tastes like chicken."

Reg sighed.

CHAPTER SEVEN

MARS NEEDS MEN!

"**M**ARS NEEDS MEN!" THUNDERED KESTRA DOMINIE, Governor of Mars to the assembled hordes of hopefuls in Madison Square Garden.

My partner, Regina Delmar, raised an eyebrow. "Well, Brian, you going to go?"

"An attractive offer to be sure," I said, eyeing the governor's blonde hair and impressive décolletage as both filled the screens overhead. "Though it didn't work out so well for the last bunch."

Reg leaned against the glass, scanning the crowds of hopeful men in the stands below. "Hardly their fault that militant lesbians wiped out most of the male population of Mars with a bio-plague."

"Leaving a hard-working ten percent to take up the slack," I replied.

"Sounds like a typical male fantasy." Reg had recently broken up with her Wall Street broker boyfriend and my gender's stock was low with her.

"Thinking of joining the Martian Sapphists?" I asked.

She shot me a cool glance. "Could be. But I like you, McManus. For a big Irish mug, you're OK. I'll give you a head start."

I laughed. Reg was nearly young enough to be my daughter. She ran multiple marathons a year; I always watched them on Tri-Vee. Whapping thugs on the chin kept a Port Authority Cop in good shape, but I wasn't built for jogging.

We'd drawn security detail for Her Excellency, Kestra Dominie because Reg and I had an established reputation for dealing with the weirder aspects of interstellar relations: Arcturian kitty-smugglers, alien vampire cops, and Snorge assassins. We'd been so successful that the powers-that-be overlooked my habit of mouthing off to Captain Fabacio. I now held an enlisted rank invented just for me, Command Detective First. The powers would do anything, rather than promote my wise-ass out of the enlisted ranks.

"Any buzz?" Reg asked, brushing a lock of brown hair out of her oval Spanish face.

I checked my command comp. "Nothing since the Japanese ambassador got locked in the can."

"Good," she said. "Let's hope it stays that way."

Of course, it didn't....

"You're kidding," I said to Captain Fabacio.

Fabacio's bulldog face glared at me out of the aircar's screen. "Hardly, McManus. Governor Dominie's daughter, Avalie, slipped out of the UN after seducing her chaperone. The Governor advised us that her daughter has issues with men. As in: can't keep her hands off them."

"We're not babysitters."

"Shut up, McManus. Avalie's overdeveloped sex drive seems to have burst into full-blown nymphomania since the bio-plague. Now, she's loose in the New York underground sex scene. Unfortunately, she's familiar with the area, having graduated from NYU two years ago."

"Isn't this a job for a psychologist?" Reg asked.

"It will be, after you quietly and quickly get her back. If this gets out, the scandal could bring down the Martian government. Dominie was elected on a 'family values' platform after the plague.

In Mars' precarious condition, complete chaos and a UN takeover might be the result. Get the little minx back and keep it quiet. Fabacio out."

Three hours later, we'd discreetly prowled through the better-known sex clubs and lowlife spots. We checked the hospitals and the morgue as well. Big nothing. The trail was getting cold and we couldn't enlist extra manpower without fear of our bimbo hunt becoming front screen news.

"You know who we should call," Reg said finally.

I sighed. "The little trollop was busted last week for possession of a controlled substance. I am not getting his butt out of the lockup this time. I told him if he couldn't drop the drugs and hooking, I was through with him."

"No one knows the New York sex scene like Freddie."

"Problem is," I grumbled, "he is the New York sex scene."

Reg smiled. "Oh, McManus, quit playing so tough. I know you nudged the warden to drop him in with the non-violent offenders as a trustee. Face it, you care what happens to him."

I sat back, shaking my head. "I just got him to where he could serve his time without a group proctology session in the shower."

"Brian," Reg said. "We need him. If anyone has the connections to find Avalie quickly, it's Freddie."

"I hate it when women use logic and intelligence on me."

"There, there," she soothed. "Now make the call."

The warden arranged for Freddie to be released into our custody. We flew to Riker's Island to find Freddie waiting for us on the airpad, dressed in prison orange. There'd been a bit of confusion about Freddie when he was arrested. Freddie Bouvier looked like a pretty girl, thanks to artifice and surgery. But he hadn't gone the whole way. They finally threw him in the men's cell-block after they found him relieving a lot of tension over on the women's side of Riker's. From the height of the black hair and cat's-eye makeup, he'd already found a contraband cosmetics supplier.

"Come to collect the Cajun Queen?" the guard asked.

"Princess," Freddie corrected in his languid Southern accent. "I'm too young to be a queen."

The guard shook his head and handed me Freddie's paperwork.

Freddie looked at us. "I am just dying in this color."

"I think it suits you," I snapped.

"So, you'll help us," Reg said, before I could launch into my bit about truth, justice and the American way.

"I'll do anything," he said. "If I can go home, have a hot shower, and pick up some decent clothes."

"You own any decent clothes?" I asked.

Freddie gave me a mournful look. "Still mad at me, McManus? I said I was sorry. I just fell off the wagon."

I shrugged. "It's your life, what's left of it anyway. Come on. We've got a Martian nymphomaniac to catch."

Midnight found us with a freshly scrubbed and outfitted Freddie, flouncing happily in a black mini and a red silk top. We ate a mercifully quiet meal at an Irish pub, then headed into the West Village on foot. Many of the old three-to-five story brick homes remained, hunkered under pedestrian walkways leading to larger, modern apartments. The old meatpacking district sat near what had once been the West Side highway. In the late twentieth century, it turned from honest mob-run butchery and money laundering, to sex, drugs, and rock and roll. The party had raged one hundred and fifty years, so far.

I gestured at a neon sign that blared, *The Pink Pussycat.* "What about there?"

Freddie rolled his eyes. "Do I tell you how to blackjack a suspect? Please. Our nympho is straight, young, and trendy. She wouldn't be there."

"Yeah," Reg said. "Everybody knows that. Let an expert work, willya?"

I looked at her as we walked on. "I've obviously been a bad influence on you."

She nodded. "The worst."

"This is it," Freddie pointed.

The sign over the door read, *Plato's Last Stand*. The old storefront was covered up and a large bouncer in an ill-fitting suit stood outside. We could hear the thump of Arcturian synthesizer music, the latest craze.

"All right," Reg said. "Let's go."

We walked up to the bouncer, who judged us worthy and waved us in. "Have a good time," he said, clearly not caring if we expired in front of him.

We strode into the vestibule to confront a scene that would have killed an interior designer. Red velour drapes hung over a thickly carpeted floor. Despite the dim lighting, I could see the dance floor where lights strobed to the throbbing music. Small bars dotted the hallways to either side. Girls danced on anti-gravity pads floating on several different levels. Roaming prismatic crystals swam through the air like schooling fish, randomly stopping to light up dancers and patrons alike. The place boasted a good-looking crowd, men and women from their twenties on up, clad in silk pajamas, robes, or, in some cases, far less.

In the cloakroom, a buxom blonde looked us over. "First-timers?" she asked.

"Yes," I admitted.

"Lucky you, it's Pajama Night,"

"Oh, good," Freddie said.

"OK. Out of the clothes. House rules, you know," she said. "Everybody into your PJs or less."

Freddie casually stripped. Behind him, Reg gulped and then followed suit. Reg wore a black brassiere and panties with novel cutouts and little leather bands joining them. It highlighted every fabulous detail of her tan, tight body.

I decided that I had already studied as much of her as was good for a happily married man and looked away only to find Freddie, who, disturbingly enough, looked almost as much like a girl as Reg. I wasn't sure quite how he managed to look like he didn't have a penis, then decided I'd thought too much about it. I started counting ceiling tiles.

"Think you'll find Avalie up there?" Freddie whispered, while throwing his silk blouse to the blonde. "Your turn, Sweetums."

Surprisingly, Reg also smiled. "Come on, Sweetums."

I was grateful for the low light and undressed hurriedly, trying to keep my stomach tucked in as I scrambled into blue silk boxers and matching robe the blonde handed me.

"You look good," Blondie grinned, "chest hair and muscles. But you'll pass out unless you breathe. Save some energy. I'll be out on the floor later." She winked, put our street clothes in a locker and handed me a ticket.

Reg pinched me to get my attention back.

Girded for perversion, we headed onto the floor, bumping couples who laughed and reached for us. Freddie led, having more experience at fending off hands. Reg stood on my right, clutching the bag that held our badges and police stunners. We ventured into the pits, unobtrusively searching the alcoves for any sign of the Governor's daughter.

As we passed a couple in a writhing tangle, Freddie whispered, "You know, we should spend a little time having some fun ourselves."

"Quiet, Freddie," I said. "I have a son your age."

"Don't you ever misbehave?" Freddie pouted.

"Father O'Hannon advises against it."

Reg raised an arm. "McManus," she whispered. "There, in the back."

I turned and looked. A young blonde woman, tall and willowy in a cobalt danceskin, was chatting up two guys.

Avalie.

Behind her I could see a couple of her gal-pals looking the boys over, as if planning to order them for dessert. They were too far away to hear, but I read the scene well enough to interpret Avalie inviting the boys downstairs.

As soon as they were out of sight, we followed. The stairs descended to a small room. As we slid through the doorway, we saw the party boys face down on the floor.

"What gives?" I began.

The door clicked shut behind us and the air began to smell funny, then the world went black.

We woke in a concrete-floored basement, tied up. Thumping music told me we were still in Plato's. Whatever gas they'd used acted quickly and left no headache. I scanned the room. Reg and Freddie were both sitting up, backs against crates of champagne.

"This happens to us with distressing regularity," Reg said.

I looked at her. "Do you own any underwear that isn't black?"

"What?"

"Every time I see your underwear, it's black."

"It doesn't happen *that* often," she protested.

"I've seen you in underwear, or less, on at least three occasions," I said. "I worked with Frank for fifteen years and never once saw him in his underwear."

"I prefer hot pink," Freddie said, "but the customers think red's sexier."

"If I get lucky," Reg muttered, "somebody will shoot us soon."

The door to the room swung open.

"Be careful what you wish for," a sultry voice said.

Avalie swept in, followed by two attractive women in dance clothes. Behind them, more women wheeled away gurneys loaded with KO-ed party boys. Avalie and her duo watched us. They held cheap, civilian stunners.

"What's this?" I asked. "The graduating class of NYU '69?"

One girl turned to Avalie. "How'd he know?"

Avalie ignored her. "Your badges say Port Authority Police. I assume Mother sent you to bring me home."

"Yep. Of course, that was before you assaulted PA officers, and did whatever you were doing to those guys," I said, gesturing with my chin toward where the gurneys had disappeared.

"They'll serve the needs of Mars."

"What?" Reg said.

"My mother's a fool," Avalie spat, "to come begging to Earth for new men, taking the sex-starved rejects of Earth. Mars is the future. We deserve the best. So I'm taking the best. Selecting men for my own use and for those women with wealth and power enough to take what they want."

"Wow," Reg said in an admiring tone. "You're one twisted vixen. Didn't anybody tell you men are people, too?"

Avalie looked at her taller, chestier companion. "Linnea," she said, "we don't have a market for either of the females. The male is a bit old but sturdy."

"My wife makes the same observation," I said. "Still, I'm not going anywhere with you except to in-processing at PA jail."

"There are drugs that will make you more pliable," Avalie said. "We'll have to dump the women in the river along with the other rejects."

"Hey," Freddie said, sitting upright. "Don't judge the book until you peek under my covers ... I own a penis, too."

Avalie and Linnea laughed. "So what?" said Avalie. "You're useless to a woman anyway."

"Hey baby," Freddie husked, "you want to put your mouth where my money comes from?"

Avalie laughed again, but her face went a little flush and her breathing seemed to get ragged. "OK girlie-boy. Why not? Natalie, help him up."

The red-haired girl pulled Freddie up. Avalie stood nearly a head taller and made Freddie look almost stocky by comparison. "Keep an eye on them, girls," she ordered, then left with Freddie in tow.

If I could film this, I thought, I could retire early. I decided not to worry about Freddie. He was, after all, a professional. Occasionally, in the hallway, a gurney with an unconscious male went by. I wondered how many men Avalie had harvested from Plato's.

Linnea regarded us with an enigmatic expression. The other gal-pal, Natalie, lounged in the doorway looking bored. "I don't see why she should have all the fun," Natalie complained, brushing back her long, brown hair. "Ever since we graduated, she's been ordering us around."

Linnea looked at her. "If you close the door, I'll keep an eye out and you can have some fun with Big Daddy here."

"You told her my nickname?" I asked Reg, who rolled her eyes.

"You might not like it, Daddy," Natalie taunted as she walked toward me. "I like to hurt my toys."

A stunner buzzed. Natalie's smile froze on her face and she toppled over. Linnea strode past the fallen Natalie, cut our bonds, then stepped back, covering us with her stunner.

"Not everyone wants to see Mars overrun by big, hairy men," she said.

"You're a Sapphist?" Reg asked, rubbing her wrists.

"No. Sapphists believe all men are servants of Satan. I believe only my ex-husband was. I'm with the Magalen party. We disapproved of the Sapphist plague, but, now that men on Mars are mostly extinct, we don't want them reintroduced. A small, strictly contained breeding population will do. We'll oppose Governor Dominie at the polls, but Avalie's man-jacking required immediate measures. I'll help you now on one condition: that you let me go afterward. No mention of me in any report."

"Deal," I said.

Linnea kicked Natalie's stunner to me.

I scooped it up and nodded to Reg. "Let's go."

We burst into the hallway, indiscriminately raying down the NYU class of '69 with our stunners. The short hall fed into a storage room containing cold-sleep chambers full of slumbering studs; the results of Avalie's slave-shopping spree. Two muscled goons, doubtless from *Plato's* staff, leapt up as we ran in. I rayed them both. We raced past them down a long hall, into a garage.

I spotted Avalie out of the corner of my eye and backpedaled just as she fired a military-grade laser. The laser seared the plasterboard, which immediately started smoking.

"Where the hell did she get a laser?" Reg yelled.

"Load the cylinders in the truck!" Avalie shouted screamed from somewhere around the corner. I leaned out and waved my stunner. The pathetic thing buzzed in Avalie's direction. Laser shots flared back. The wall behind me caught fire.

"Back, Brian, back," Reg yelled. "It's going to flashover."

I whipped around and followed her as the smoke and flames beat hotter and hotter. Reg and I grabbed the stunned NYU grads and the goons, dragging them to safety or slapping them awake. Alarms began to shriek. We ran up the stairs and into complete chaos. Dozens of nearly naked people pushed past us as smoke billowed up into the club. Avalie must have used her laser to start several fires. There was no time to grab our clothes. We ran out onto Bank Street with everybody else.

"We've got to rescue Freddie and the boy-toys!" Reg said.

A naked girl standing next to her asked, "Oh hey, is that like the band?"

"Shaddup," Reg snapped.

We shoved through the shivering mass of people, and headed for the corner. Police and fire units closed in from everywhere; I remembered Fabacio's orders to keep the case hush-hush and groaned.

"They've got to be around back in a truck," Reg said.

"There's no way through," I said, looking at the street. "We'll have to run around the block."

We sprinted, Reg in her leather-strapped bikini, me in silky boxers and too-thin robe. We got about fifty meters before two of New York's finest wedged a cruiser in our path. Both cops jumped out, leveling stunners.

"Drop your weapons!" yelled the big cop.

Mars needs Men!

"Port Authority police!" Reg yelled back.

"Yeah?" said the driver. "Let's see some tin."

Of course, our badges were somewhere back in *Plato's* inferno.

"Drop 'em, or we drop you," added the other cop.

We dropped our civilian stunners. The cops bent us over the cruiser hood and frisked us. They frisked Reg twice.

"Quit feeling me up, you morons. There's a woman with an M-grade laser and a truck load of unconscious men around back. She started the fire."

"Too many dopesticks," the big cop said, shaking his head.

"Honest, guys," I added. "We're undercover detectives. PA detec–"

"PA pukes got no jurisdiction in the East Village."

An old sore point between the two forces. "We got jurisdiction anywhere in the Port of NY when it comes to alien trade relations," I said.

"What's this?" a familiar voice sounded behind me.

"Hey, Sarge," said the big cop. "These perps were running from the scene with stunners–"

"Bishop?" I said. "Is that you?"

"McManus! Let him off the hood, boys."

I stood up. Asame Bishop, the Police Benevolent Rep from my chapter, looked at me, jaw hanging open. Then he looked at Reg.

"Not what you think," I said.

"Better not be," he replied. "I dance with your wife at the PBA benefit, man."

"We're undercover," Reg snapped. "Can't tell you what or why. A woman with a military laser may be on the other side of the block with a load of unconscious men."

Bishop stared at me, "On the level?"

I nodded.

He gestured at the two cops. "Check it out. Warn everyone there may be perps with M-lasers." They jumped into the cruiser. "Got any description?" Asame asked me as he took off his jacket and handed it to a grateful Reg. Behind him, fireman raced into the burning building.

"Can't," I said. "This operation is undercover. By now they're probably long gone anyway. Damn."

"McManus, what do we do?" Reg asked

I had an inspiration. "Did you grab anybody else?"

Asame raised an eyebrow. "Yeah, we grabbed all the naked people. It's fun."

"Let's see them."

We walked back. "I don't suppose you have any spare pants?" I said.

He looked at me. "Doesn't come up much on NYPD duty."

"Yeah."

The face I wanted to see was in the group cordoned off behind a barricade, Linnea.

"Release her to me," I said.

Asame looked at me, chewing his mustache for a minute. "OK, McManus. This better be on the level or there's going to be a grievance."

"Hey," I said. "I'd never do anything to a union brother."

"OK, OK," Asame said. "Take her."

"Thanks, Asame. I'll catch you at the Spring Fundraiser. See if you can find it in your heart not to mention this little incident to my wife."

"Reg, get the car. Call Carolyn Halford, we need some backup. Tell her to get our spare clothes out of our lockers, draw two stunners, and meet us as soon as I figure out which spaceport Avalie's fled to. If she's using a ground truck, we may have time."

I grabbed Linnea by the arm. She'd found a jacket somewhere, but her shapely bottom peeked out from under the black leather.

"We have one chance to contain this before it's a disaster and you're going to help," I said.

She shrugged. "A public relations disaster for the governor may suit us, now that Avalie's man-jacking project is stopped."

"Might it?" I asked. "You think the collapse of the last functioning government institution on Mars is a good thing? It took Mars seventy years to work its way out from under a UN protectorate to independence. You want to be occupied by the UN again? They've been calling for it since the plague. Governor Dominie is the chief reason they've held off."

She bit her lip. "We had a deal. You said you'd let me go."

"Avalie fled with some guys ... and Freddie," I added. "That's not politics. Those are real lives and you're an accessory. What will she do with them if she can't get them away? She didn't seem too worried about people burning to death in *Plato's*."

"I don't know everything," Linnea said. "She has a ship chartered somewhere at Kennedy. I don't know names, but I saw some of the crew."

Reg sped up to us in an unmarked aircar. "Hop in."

We roared into the emergency transit lane and headed for Kennedy. I spotted Carolyn Halford's sturdy, gray-haired form standing by the PA landing pad. A reserve officer and gym instructor,

Carolyn wore her usual disreputable tracksuit. Her jaw dropped when we coasted to a stop in front of her.

"Old friend," I begged. "Don't ask."

She handed me the clothes. "Not bad, Brian," she said, looking me over with a critical eye. "But you better start watching the love handles."

"Please," I groaned. "No fitness lectures today."

She smiled. "Don't need to, the young ladies are in great shape."

Reg hastily donned her spare clothes and grabbed a stunner. There were no extra clothes for Linnea, so Carolyn gave her a bath towel, mercifully unused, from her gym bag. Linnea improvised a wrap-skirt as I explained the situation to Carolyn.

"We can't call any more attention to ourselves," I said. "If this gets out it could mean political disaster for Mars and the Port Authority."

"No problem," Carolyn yelled, as a liner took off behind her. "I've got a good right arm to lend to the cause." She flexed a bicep capable of lifting 75 pounds and grinned. "But without help how are we going to search all of Kennedy?"

"It's probably a small, intersystem freighter or private yacht," Reg said.

I shook my head. "A yacht would be too visible, there aren't that many and they berth in the luxury section."

"Your aircar is too big for some of the passageways. I'll requisition a hovercart from the baggage station," Carolyn said. "We can head for the tramp freighter area." She returned in a minute with the far smaller, silver and blue utility hovercart. We piled into the open four-seater and zipped toward the tramp section. Vessels of many colors and shapes poked out of the ground and gantries around us, like fairytale castles. The dull rumble that Kennedy generated was always in our ears as millions of pounds of metal slugged it out with gravity overhead.

"Anything look familiar, Linnea?" I demanded.

She shook her head. "It was night. I wasn't paying attention to the ships."

Reg interrogated the hovercart's traffic computer. "There are thirteen small freighters and one cruise ship bound for Mars in this section. I eliminated the ones that won't leave this week. That gives six good prospects including the liner. Nearest freighter is the Medexo Combine's *Fantastic*. She's in berth 27A."

"OK, go." I said.

The *Fantastic* proved anything but, just an old first-generation FTL vessel downgraded to insystem traffic. Neither crew nor vessel looked familiar to Linnea. We sped off to the *Annubite*, then the *Campania*. We worked our way through all the prospects. Nothing.

I pulled the hovercart over. "This is bad," Reg said. "I don't know how much longer we can keep this under wraps. If Avalie clears atmosphere, God knows what will happen to those men, particularly Freddie. McManus, we've got to call Fabacio and have her close Koch and Kennedy, maybe Newark as well."

"All right," I said. "We're out of time, and choices. Head for the main tower."

As we pulled away from the *Campania*, Linnea grabbed my arm. "Wait, that ship...the symbol on its side."

"The winged foot?" I said, looking at the colorful symbol.

"Yes, I saw it that night. There were two ships there. This was one, but I don't know which one she was working with."

"Wingfoot is the *Hermes*," Reg sang out, studying the portacomp Carolyn had brought. "The vessel next to her is the *Ho-sien* and she arrived only yesterday. Ah!"

"What?" I said.

"*Hermes* isn't on a Martian route, but her plot chart says she puts in at the Trekkia drift station. They transship a lot of material from Jupiter to Mars on that route."

"You sure?"

"Brian, remember my mother's family are merchants."

"Let's pay a visit to *Hermes*," I said. As we got out, I cuffed Linnea to the hovercart. "Sorry, can't risk you taking a powder on me now."

She sniffed, and sat back in the fabric seat. "Men are always worried about premature releases."

We ran up to the metal companionway and flashed Carolyn's badge at the Port Comp. It called the ship to demand entry. A middle-aged man sporting a belly greeted us at *Hermes'* hatchway, though greeted was an overstatement.

"What gives? We've got liftoff in three hours; our papers are in."

"You misspelled, 'Mother, may I,'" I snapped. "Who are you?"

"Second Mate, Joshua Gisley," he muttered, still blocking the hatch.

"I want to see the captain, the manifest, and passenger list," I said. "Put your countdown on hold. This is a Port Authority spot inspection."

"Ah, shit," he said. "We stop the countdown and we lose our launch window. Could be days before we get another. Don't you have something to do beside harass honest businessmen?"

"You're locked down as of now," I said. "Want to add interfering with an officer to that?"

His dark brown eyes flickered about. "Look, friend. Perhaps we could come to terms, maybe get you and your lady friends a free dinner at Luchows 3000–"

"That's it, buddy," Carolyn snapped, "out of the way."

Gisley backed up. "OK. My mistake."

We followed him in. As we passed the inner hatch, Gisley suddenly hit a wall plate. An alarm hooted. Three crewmen jumped out from behind the open hatch and grabbed us. I booted Gisley in the groin as he rushed me. He dropped to the deck, retching. A spacer threw a barroom swing at Reg. She stepped into it with a right block, then snapped a back-fist into his temple. A huge crewman lassoed both arms around me and heaved me off the deck. I fishtailed and drove both knees into his crotch. When he dropped me, I hooked a combo to his face. He jolted me with a surprisingly fast left jab. I grabbed his extended arm, yanked him past me, and drove him headfirst into the wall.

I pulled my stunner. Reg held her own with the other crewman, but he was soaking up her punches. Carolyn wrestled with the remaining thug. I booted the spacer fighting Reg away from her, then dropped him with the stunner. The stunner discharge in the small space made my teeth vibrate, but I swung the stunner and shot the big guy, too.

The crewman struggling with Carolyn raised his hands. I turned toward Gisley, to demand answers, when I heard Linnea shout my name.

"Cuff them," I told Carolyn, who'd finally drawn her stunner. "Reg, you're with me."

We ran out onto the gantry. Linnea gestured at a large, gray cargo hauler with a line of trailers. I spotted Avalie behind the wheel. Reg and I dashed down to the hovercart, hopped in, and shot off in pursuit.

We dodged among and around clusters of ships and up and down little passages for cargo and airport workers. I sideswiped a passing cargo carrier, spilling luggage all over the tarmac. Reg saved

Linnea from toppling out. "Uncuff me!" Linnea wailed. "He's going to get us killed." Reg leaned over, struggling with the cuffs.

Ahead of us, Avalie swerved and the tail-car on her trailer tore free. Its contents rolled out onto the airport road. Boy-toy cylinders broke free, one opened and a naked guy got a case of road rash on his tush. We slowed to dodge him and the falling cylinders – this gave Avalie a lead. She vanished into the airport terminal. We zigzagged around screaming airport workers.

"There," Reg pointed.

Avalie's cargo hauler crashed into a wall of baggage-dispensers. She scrambled to her feet, hoisting her laser in both hands. Its beam flashed out. I cut the wheel and the beam danced and scored a hit along the side of our hovercart. We tumbled out of the hovercart, ducking for cover. Workers fled pell-mell in all directions. Linnea joined them. I chanced a stunner shot back at Avalie but the range was too great to do more than make her woozy.

A cylinder at Avalie's feet opened and Freddie tumbled out. Avalie grabbed Freddie and put the laser to his head. He yipped in terror. She threw him on the luggage conveyor and then jumped on top of him like he was a sled.

Reg and I hoofed ahead as she rolled out of sight with Freddie into the bowels of the conveyor.

"Take a different conveyor!" I yelled to Reg. "Maybe you can get ahead of them."

I slid onto the conveyor behind some silver metal luggage. Then the track sucked me into the airport underworld. I looked around at multiple conveyors angling in dozens of directions and heights. For a few seconds I could still see Reg, her stunner held high, riding a nearby belt. Then she vanished behind a wall of machinery.

Kennedy's automated underground wasn't intended for people. The conveyor seemed awfully narrow as it looped over canyons of great depth, lit only by the flashing telltales. I lay in the middle of the beltway, looking for any sign of Avalie and Freddie. Dark towers of ascending luggage loomed in the dimly lit distance. I felt like I'd been drawn into one of the lesser known rings of Dante's Inferno.

Ahead, a sorting machine shunted luggage into two channels. I could only hope my silver luggage was bound for the same place as Avalie. I ended up piled onto a low-railed, open elevator platform, ascending at an alarming rate. When it stopped, I was looking at Avalie and her laser. She still sat on Freddie in the adjacent elevator. "Lose the stunner!" she snarled.

I pitched the stunner, thinking about how many forms I would have to fill out for losing two weapons in one day. I looked back at Avalie and saw something go mad in her eyes. Freddie saw it too, and grabbed for her weapon. Avalie whacked him over the head with the barrel.

I used the distraction to grab the silver luggage. Avalie fired just as I lifted it. The laser refracted off the silver case into a thousand smaller beams. Avalie flinched as one nicked her. Before she could fire again, something hit her from behind. Reg.

I dropped the luggage and sprang forward, but Reg already had Avalie face-down in an arm bar.

Freddie struggled upright. "You OK?" we asked each other simultaneously.

A minute later, the elevator brought us onto the main concourse. We tossed a jacket over Avalie's head. Freddie held a blood-soaked handkerchief to his own. Travelers stared at the smoking, silver luggage and us.

"Hey," said one middle-aged woman. "That's my case."

I looked at them. "Malfunction in the conveyor." We trotted forward. "Gotta get these workers to the hospital." I gestured at Avalie's muffled form. "Out of the way, her face is all cut up." Shocked people scurried aside. "All claims for damages go to the baggage counter," I shouted over my shoulder.

An hour later, naked guys and lost stunners had been collected and order returned to Kennedy. I called Fabacio from the Kennedy substation.

Fabacio glared out of the screen. "This was quiet?"

I sighed.

"The Feds and the UN will be along to collect Avalie," Fabacio continued. "She's leaving Earth shortly."

"What?" Reg exclaimed. "No charges after all she's done?"

"We can't afford it, Delmar. Keep her under control until the Feds arrive. Fabacio out."

"I can't believe it," Reg said. "Kidnapping, assault, attempted murder–"

"Ravishing me without paying for it," Freddie added.

We looked at him.

"Alas," he said, "you were too late to save me from a fate worse than death."

"Kindergarten was too late to save you," I replied.

Avalie laughed wildly. "Well, you've got me. And so what? You heard the fat lady sing. Mother is already making plans to bury the whole matter. I'll never serve a day."

"She's right," Reg observed.

"I can't deny it," I said.

"You know," Reg said. "I'm going to do something your mother should have done when you were ten." Reg grabbed Avalie's arm and in a second had her in a kagi hold, standing on her toes.

"You can't do this to me," Avalie wailed, as Reg sat on a bench and forced Avalie across her lap. Reg wrapped a leg over Avalie in a modified scissors hold and pulled Avalie's slacks down. Avalie bucked and Reg squeezed. The Martian nympho gasped and subsided.

Reg's hand came down on Avalie's pale white cheeks. She screamed.

"Now," said Reg, "repeat after me."

Crack.

"I will not kidnap men..."

Crack.

"...assault police..."

Crack.

"...or otherwise misbehave like an arrogant, twisted brat."

Avalie was still sobbing when the Feds came and collected her.

After they left, Reg sprawled out in the chair and draped an arm around a surprised Freddie.

Freddie smiled and laid his bandaged head on Reg's shoulder. He winked at me. "Why so glum, McManus?"

"How am I going to explain to my wife that I lost yet another set of clothes while on assignment with Reg!"

"Don't worry," Freddie said. "I'll be your character witness."

CHAPTER EIGHT

SEACHANGE

I SAT DOWN AT MY DESK, WITH A SIGH, JELLY DONUT IN ONE hand and a coffee, light and sweet, in the other. I looked around the Port Authority of NY cophouse that had been my home for the last 22 years. As usual it was filled with the helpless and the hapless being shuffled around in the endless dance of law enforcement. Some of the skells haunting the spaceport and subdocks were second generation criminals to me. Future generations of miscreants rode in their pants just waiting to be born. When I had joined the force after my military service, I'd had dreams of making a difference. Maybe I had, but it wasn't visible today.

I tried to shake off the gloomy thoughts that had haunted me lately; they'd taken hold right after two significant events in my life. My young partner, Regina Delmar, had been promoted, the youngest Lieutenant in the NYPA. Her meteoritic rise had happened despite being my partner. The PA brass and the politicos always had a sour taste in their mouths when it came to me. Largely it was my own fault. I brought home the bacon on the big cases but with my Irish temper and big mouth I had shared too many of my opinions, too publically.

The idea of breaking in a new partner, who would unquestionably be nowhere near as good or as easy on the eyes as Reg, filled me with ennui. I was beginning to consider life after being a cop. The unions, thank God, had hung onto to "twenty-years and out" despite the fact that people now lived to 150 in good health. So another career awaited me after the obligatory couple weeks of beer-drinking, card games and sleeping in late, which would be as much as my wife would put up with before kicking my butt out the door. But what to do? I had entertained the idea of becoming a private investigator, but the life of a shamus was hardly as glamorous as seen on Tri-Vee. I didn't want to divorce work, so that meant working for insurance companies, and in comparison the cophouse suddenly didn't look so bad. I diverted and consoled myself with the coffee and donut and checked the morning report. Mercifully I had not been assigned a new partner and remained in that sort of limbo between formal assignments.

Lieutenant Frisby walked by, which suited me fine. Squat and dyspeptic he was one of the few cops I actually disliked. Suddenly, he stopped, made a show of remembering something and put a finger to his forehead. "Oh, McManus."

Crap, I thought, *I knew it was too good to be true.* "What?" I said. I was too close to retirement for "sir" for the likes of him, even if he did outrank me.

"You know a Freddie Bouvier, don't you?"

I felt a slight chill. "Used to. He was an informer for me and Reg up till last year. I dropped him as a source."

"That's right," he said with ill-disguised relish. "Little transgender hooker, got back into the life. He was kind of your pet project. Wasn't he?"

I nodded sipping my coffee and taking a bite of jelly donut. "Yep. Why? Is he dead?"

"Nah," Frisby said, visibly disappointed by my lack of reaction. "Not last I heard. Some perp stuck him with a vibra-knife last night. He made it to the hospital anyway."

I shrugged and turned back to my computer screen, determined not to give him any satisfaction. Freddie had indeed been my project, I even owed the little...whatever he was, my life. For a while there, Freddie had ceased being a street informer and had graduated to people. On some of Reg and my worst cases, Freddie had been an essential part of my success. I didn't care about his confused sexuality, or voyages between the genders, but I wasn't going to allow a prostitute and drug addict in my orbit. The last relapse had broken the camel's back.

I put it out of my mind and started scanning through the morning reports. The usual trade of a senior detective: drug shipments intercepted at Kennedy, illegal aliens rounded up at Koch Spaceport: some from Peru, two from Mars and one drunken Arcturian. Then there was a small starship that had been held for false identity, there was some thought that it might have been the hijacked courier *SS Bambury*, on which an heiress had disappeared along with the ship seven years ago. That one looked the most interesting and up my and Reg...well now my solo alley.

A shadow fell over me. For a moment I felt an instant of blind rage. If Frisby was back, I swear I was going to deck the son-of-a-bitch. But the shadow had a far more delightful shape and an oval Spanish face with a perfect complexion: Regina Delmar.

"Reg," I said with the first smile of the day. "Good to see you."

Her smile lit up the area. "You too, Brian. I see you're still into health food."

I gave the donut a guilty but longing look. "I had to do so something to console myself after being abandoned."

"I was at your house for dinner Friday!"

"That was Friday, today I had to shoo Lt. Frisby away from my desk all by myself."

"There there," she soothed. "Come with me."

I grabbed up my jacket. "Where we going?"

"Now that I'm a Lieutenant," she said, "I don't have to tell you."

I followed Reg, who drew admiring looks for her tall, athletic form and stylish clothes. We rode the elevator down to the basement where an unmarked aircar awaited us. I was betting on the missing heiress case, something that required more than a detective. We zipped out of the underground lot and into the police lanes through the skytowers of NYC.

After a minute, I turned to Reg, "Hey this isn't the way to Koch?"

"No," replied Reg. "The heiress has been missing for seven years; the trail won't be any colder tomorrow. We're going to NYU hospital because you want to see Freddie and you won't go because it would mean you don't see him as a skell, bound for a body bag and a toe-tag. So I am taking you, and you can blame it on me."

"I've been down this road too many times," I said.

"Maybe it will lead to somewhere different after this."

"When did you become a girl scout?" I grumbled.

She smiled. "You were a bad influence."

I sulked and sat lower in my seat. It took ten minutes to fly and park at the hospital. She hit the locks on the door. I started to get out, then noticed that she wasn't moving. I looked at her and raised my eyebrows.

"You have stuff to talk about with Freddie," she said. "You'll pull your punches if I'm there. Go get it done. I'll head up to Koch check in on the freighter and be back for you in two hours."

"Ain't gonna take that long."

"Maybe it should."

I made my way through the immense medical fortress, wondering how anybody could find a patient in such a warren. Human, alien and the odd robot, all clad in white and green, scurried through its passages. I found a medbot at an information station, and it gave me Freddie's ward. He was in a section kept for patients with only basic medical, still, thank God for socialized medicine. An elevator and a hike took me the rest of the way. I used the time to work myself up with righteous indignation. I'd done everything to get Freddie clean and out of the life, but that self-destructive streak of his asserted itself each time.

I walked into a ward that held even more of the antiseptic smell typical of hospitals. The beds here were curtained off, but there was a buzz of hushed conversations in various languages. A dark-skinned nurse looked up as I peered into each bay. I held up my tin in response to the look. "Bouvier?"

"She's in the last one near the window."

"She?"

She gave me a look. "He wants to be called she, he gets called she."

I nodded. "Good for you."

"If this is official," she said, "keep it short."

"It ain't."

"Then take your time, honey. Baby is hurt bad and needs a friend."

I started to open my mouth, decided nothing useful or intelligent would come out and shut it. I walked up and slid past the curtain.

Freddie lay pale and bruised in the diagnostic bed. I pulled the curtain behind me so that we had our little bit of isolation in the midst of the other suffering. The sun struck across Freddie's face, and his pale complexion was waxy, deathlike, for all that Freddie still looked more like a girl than many girls do. No cards or flowers lay on the bed stand, Ghosts of Christmas yet to come?

Freddie stirred and opened his eyes as I walked up to the bed. I felt my righteous indignation ebbing and began to wish I'd brought something, flowers, a teddy bear, something with me. Something to break the morgue-like atmosphere.

"Hello," he whispered, his husky whisky voice much reduced.

"Hey," I returned. "You gonna live?"

"Seems so," he replied listlessly.

I pulled a chair up by the bedside. "Still love the night life?"

His eyes focused on mine and suddenly he looked very young and in pain, rather like my son when his first marriage broke apart. "I want out," he said, tears starting down the pretty face. "I don't want this anymore."

I steeled myself against sympathy. "How's this different than the other times I got you on your feet only to find you drugging or hooking a month later?"

He slowly shook his head from side to side. "I mean it this time. It's gone too far. You always said you would see me like this sometime—"

"I said worse. I thought they would call me to identify a body. This is better."

"The knife," he said, "it felt so cold going in, and it vibrated, half my insides came out. I remembered how he smiled. McManus, please, please help me."

"I've walked this path with too many people, and most of them don't make it. You never seemed like that good prospect before. I'd have to know you meant it."

"I swear to God."

I could see he was too hurt and tired to even wipe his nose, so I got him some tissues from the bedside cabinet and handed them to him. Freddie caught at my hand instead of the tissues.

"McManus, please don't give up on me. You're the only chance I have. I can't do it on my own."

I took a deep breath and slipped free of his fever-warm grasp. "If we do this, it's on my terms. You backslide on me once and we are through. No drugs, no hooking, you stay on the right side of the law."

"I can't change what I am," he said, gesturing to his face and hair.

"If you mean being transgender, I don't care. I don't understand it but I'm a grownup and I'll deal. It's not like we'll be dating. But you sabotage yourself with every other breath and you try desperately hard not to live up to anyone's expectations of you."

"I'll try."

"Nope. You'll do it. No mental reservations or excuses, none of the 'I tried and it's too hard' crap. Commit or don't. Live or don't. One last chance."

Freddie held my eye. "I want to live. I won't if I keep up as I was. That knife was always out there waiting for me, but now I've seen it, felt it in my flesh. Honestly I don't know if I can make it, but I will do it with all I have left. To tell you more would be to lie to you, and whatever you believe, I tried to keep the lying to you to a minimum."

I considered his pale and bloodless face, the strained look of a desperate child.

"Ok," I said, before I could think further about it. I tried to ignore the wash of relief that stole through me. "Ok, we'll do it. As I said."

"Someday," Freddie whispered, "you can tell me why a traditional-minded Irish catholic cop cares what happens to me."

"Someday, I will, right after I figure it out myself."

"So what follows?" he asked.

"For now, nothing. You concentrate on getting better. Reg or Toni will check on you daily. There's no drug besides Firefox that they can't take care of the withdrawal from these days, but you will be seeing someone whose name I'll give you. It's the mental game that will be the challenge. Then we will start looking for a real job for you. Where are you living these days? We'll get some clothes for you."

"I'm still sharing a flat with Keesa Zela. My sonic key is in the drawer."

"Keesa? Oh, yeah the Russian girl. Ok. I'll get you some clothes from your place." I fished the key out of the drawer and tapped it to my porta comp to transfer the data. Freddie gave me the address code.

"McManus?

"Yeah?"

"Let Keesa pick the clothes."

"Hey I know the rules, no white shoes after Labor Day."

Freddie groaned and closed his eyes.

"I'll talk to the NYPD about your case too..." I realized Freddie was fast asleep. I sat quietly beside him for a minute wondering what the future held.

The curtain rustled, a young resident looked in and scanned the diagnostics, then looked Freddie over without waking him. I motioned to him when he was finished. We stepped away.

"How is he?" I asked.

"And you are?"

I showed my tin.

"The physical injuries were very bad. A year ago, before we received Vegan nanobot technology and skin-welding, we couldn't have saved him. As it is in a few weeks he won't have any physical scars, hell, even the ones from his breast enhancement surgery will disappear. But his chart indicates a long history of self-abuse issues, not uncommon with transgender people, especially those like him that don't commit entirely to one gender. Even in this day and age there's discrimination."

"He came out of a conservative religious family in Louisiana," I replied. "Some good and some not so good. He's never been back."

"I am going to refer him to social services for what good it will do."

I waved a hand. "Leave that to me. My wife, Toni Bellaqua, is a trauma nurse and she's done some of this work, knows the right people. She'll be dropping in."

"What's your involvement with him?" the doctor asked.

"He's helped out on a lot of cases. For mini-skirted tart, he can do all right in a pinch. It's the rest of the time he spends fucking up. I owe him one last one. This will be it."

"I hope it works," the doctor said. "I've seen this sort of story end badly before."

"You can't save people," I replied, "until they want to save themselves. I honestly think he wants to now."

I called Reg from the hallway and asked her if she needed me on the Bambury case. I wanted some time to look into who'd knifed Freddie.

"No," she said. "This is a bust; it's just an old freighter of the same type that's been sold too many times. I'll finish up here. But Brian, Freddie is an NYPD case."

"Yeah, but I have friends there. Besides Freddie did work for us, it may give me grounds to at least see what's doing."

"Ok. Watch your step."

I hailed a cab and went down to the 6th Precinct on West 10th Street where my old pal Asame Bishop worked and where Freddie's case was being handled. The new diagonal air tunnel from the Upper East Side to lower West was crowded again, but the trip wasn't too bad. I found myself in front of another old building with the generic look of officialdom and had to spend a minute convincing the child manning the front desk that I was a real police officer from an honest-to-God different police force in

NYC. I hoped her mother would come by and pick her up at the end of watch. She didn't seem to appreciate my mature attitude.

I found Bishop on the second floor, he was cursing sonorously at a coffee machine. He had a little less hair than last time I saw him and was a bit thicker around the middle. His pleasant, dark-brown face split in a grin when he saw me. "What McManus? Come to see how real cops fight crime?"

"Yeah I hear you NYPD are leading the charge into the Eighteenth Century, next thing you know they'll start issuing you revolvers."

"Droll. You must have passed the Port Authority Wise Ass Test."

"I wrote the Port Authority Wise Ass Test."

Asame shook my hand. "What's brings you here? I haven't seen you since Plato's Last Stand caught fire and I stopped the uniforms from re-frisking your mostly naked partner. Has Topless learned to keep her clothes on?"

"That's Lieutenant Topless to you, and if you want to keep what's left of your hair, I would forget about that incident."

"Forget about her wearing an outfit of leather straps? Ask for something more possible."

"Sure, tell me about Freddie Bouvier's stabbing."

He grimaced. "Thought that might be what brought you out of the Towers. What interest does the NYPA have in an attempted homicide?"

"Used to work for me."

"Thin, Brian."

"Let's see how much weight it will carry."

He looked around. "Come on back to my office." We walked past the familiar desks, cops and criminals into a small glass-walled cubicle. It didn't have a door but was reasonably private.

"I'll show you the case file in a minute, but there's more going on."

"What gives?" I asked settling into a metal and green fabric chair.

Asame turned a worried face to me. "There's been a dozen killings of police informants in the last seventy-two hours. Most have followed this same pattern, use of a vibra-knife in a disembowelment. Nobody has been as lucky as your boy Freddie. They're all wearing toe-tags." He tapped a clear-board and a list of names and faces appeared.

I scanned the list. "All of these people worked with the NYPD. Freddie only worked with Reg and me in the Port Authority. What connection could he have had with them? I don't see any other pros. Most of these guys are in organized crime."

"Yeah, but if you think about police informants, Hell, Freddie was the damn poster child for informants. Too many people knew he was practically on the team with you and Delmar in between your various fallings out."

"True," I muttered, "it had started to interfere with his value as a source except that people then started bringing him information when they wanted revenge of someone or to screw someone else's operation."

"Pity he couldn't say straight," Bishop said.

I raised an eyebrow at him.

He sighed in exasperation. "You know what I meant. Clean, outta the life."

"I think though he's finally seen the light."

"More like he's seen his intestines in his own lap."

"The light comes in many forms, that was a harsh one."

"So what now?" Bishop asked.

"I want in. Nobody does shit like that to someone I know and walks free."

Bishop stared at me. "McManus, I think joint-ops are a good idea, but you know how touchy the NYPD is about jurisdiction with the NYPA, there's no indication of any spaceport connection here, not even a hint of an alien involvement."

"Vibra-knives are illegal on Earth, not manufactured in Sol System," I said.

Bishop pursed his lips and gave me a measuring look. "You really willing to hang it out so far for this kid? I heard you were through with him."

I shrugged. "I've always had a soft spot in my head for the little trollop. Plus my wife, my brother's family, even my son knows him. How do I explain letting him get cut-up go unanswered?"

"You know you are giving Frisby a shot at canning your ass if he finds out."

"Asame, old buddy. I've had my twenty years and to tell you the truth, if staying with the force means much more of guys like Frisby, well without Delmar, I just don't see it as worth it."

Bishop barked a laugh. "You? Retire? And do what?"

"Sit on my ass and drink beer in a cop bar and bore the youngsters with tales of derring-do?"

"Come on," Bishop said. "Let's go catch this bad guy. My partner, Karolina, has been down on South Canal shaking up some people. Maybe she's found something."

Karolina Nolikova was a tall woman with a cap of bright blonde hair, a Slavic face and cold blue eyes that belied her easy smile. She'd gone to see one of her contacts who was busy leaving town for an indefinite period. The informant wouldn't have talked to her at all except that Karolina threatened to hold her on some trivial charge. That got her information in exchange for a uniform to escort her to the Port Authority and see she got an airbus for Lima, Ohio. We found Karolina lounging against her cruiser, a sausage and pepper sandwich in one hand and soft drink in another.

"Hey McManus," she piped, her voice was high for such a tall woman. "What are doing slumming around here? Are aliens after our women again?"

"If they were, you'd be in trouble. A tall cool blonde is never out of style."

"Amen," she replied as she looked beyond me at Bishop.

He shrugged. "I told you he'd show up. You owe me five credits."

"Put it on my tab, it will reduce what you owe me out of four figures."

"What do you know?" I asked, putting my back against the cruiser. I felt a pang as I remembered how often Reg and I had stood like this.

She glanced at Bishop who nodded. "Word on the street is that there's a new guy running the South of Canal Street gang, Bal Rurik, also known as Rurik the Gag. He did ten years upstate because of an informant. Now that the SOB is in charge of the Socanals he's been making an example of any known informers. Too many Socanals been cutting deals when they get pinched, so he thought it would be a good way to discipline the gang and eliminate some snitches."

"Two birds with one stone," Bishop said, "and present company excepted, most cops aren't that concerned about their informants so he probably figures it's relatively low risk. Assuming he thinks that much. He's a real bastard. I suspect he just looks for an excuse to do this sort of shit. The only good thing is that guys like him usually get wacked fairly quickly. The streets have a tendency to self-correct."

I thought of Freddie lying pale and bloodless in a hospital bed. "Not soon enough."

"We have only one thing going for us," Karolina said. "He's missed only one target, the highest profile informant in NY. A target he wouldn't normally have a good shot at because of his connections. However Freddie went and screwed up those connections and hung his own lily-white ass..." she looked at me speculatively. Bishop grinned.

"I have no idea what color his ass is," I grated, "but I assume that if it's as pale as the rest of him, then your description is apt."

She grinned. "I was just curious if you knew."

"Is she always like this?" I asked.

"Frequently worse," Bishop assured me.

"Great."

"As I was saying, Freddie lost his protection and then went in harm's way and got harmed. But, he is still alive. Rurik may want to make sure of a clean sweep, especially as Freddie is a witness and could identify him."

I shook my head. "Freddie told the local cops he didn't see who cut him."

"Rurik may not be sure of that," Bishop grumbled. "Hell I'm not sure of that. Bouvier... Freddie could be lying. You know a lot of witnesses remember more after the assault trauma fades and no one ran a holo of Rurik past him."

"Why haven't you?" I asked.

"Because I'm pretty sure it was Rurik and if I am going to use Freddie, I want it on a lineup with no prospect of a smart defense attorney saying I prejudiced the witness."

"Makes sense. So you think he'll try for him at the hospital?"

Bishop shook his head. "Nah, too much security."

"I don't know," I said. "It's a big place. Kinda anonymous. I could see somebody getting in, but he is on a ward. There'd be a dozen witnesses. Odds are good you're right."

"Odds are."

"Show me this punk," I said.

Karolina finished her sandwich and flipped open her hand comp. It unfolded in her hand like a flower. An image of a hoodlum glowed into sullen life on its surface. Rurik was a human, like so many people these days he was a mix of all different types of human and no one group had the disgrace of claiming him. His chief characteristic was a dark, brooding glare and a curled lip from a scar that he evidently took some pride in as he hadn't bothered to have it corrected. He was about five foot ten and stocky. I studied him until I was sure that I could spot him no matter what he was wearing. I read his rap sheet and wondered again about the world that provided such an infinite supply of such scum.

"Seems to me that our best play would be to have the hospital start telling folks that he is getting out tomorrow," Bishop said. "Then we have someone dress as Freddie and head for his apartment and hope Rurik tries something."

"Freddie and I are about the same height," Karolina said. "I'd need a fright wig and to shelve my fashion sense for a day but I could pass for him."

"He has bigger boobs than you do," I added helpfully.

She glared at me. "I'll stuff."

"A lot," I said.

Bishop's grin broadened.

"Call me when you have the details set," I said.

"Where you going?" Karolina asked.

"Hospital," I said. "There's comfy chair by Freddie's bed, well comfy enough anyway, just in case we are wrong about Rurik trying the hospital."

Bishop nodded. "We'll pick you up in the morning. I'll call the hospital and get them to change his chart, then we'll have him moved to another ward under an assumed name. Best we can do with the op this far off the boards. I just hope your buddy Frisby doesn't call our Captain looking for you."

I grimaced. "I left some bullshit about doing cleanup outside work on a statement and needing a couple of personal hours, on his phone. I got enough comp time saved up I could have retired two years ago."

"God bless the union," Bishop said.

"Amen, Brother," I said.

I got to the hospital by 6 p.m. Toni dropped by to check on Freddie and me and snuck in some lasagna and Barolo. The three of us had a quiet little dinner together behind the drawn curtains, with Freddie on his best behavior, as he always was in front of my wife. I filled Freddie in on the part of the plan with him being moved.

At the end of the meal, we hid the evidence and Toni got ready to leave. She kissed Freddie on the forehead and then walked around to embrace me. I was almost a foot taller than her so I had to bend down to kiss her good night.

"You're up to something," she whispered. "Should I get Regina?"

"No," I whispered back. "I have Bishop. I don't want Reg involved in this one. Wouldn't be good for her career."

"Good, tell Bishop he still owes me a dance at the next PBA ball."

"Will do. Love you. Good night."

The nurse came with a pill for Freddie, and we were spared any deep conversation by the sedative, Barolo and a full tummy of lasagna.

The next morning came with bad hospital coffee and a backache from sitting in a chair all night. Freddie was still asleep when they came to move him in the morning. I stopped at the security desk to make sure the Captain knew enough of what was going on so that the rentacops would keep an extra eye out.

I was out back of the hospital when an unmarked with Bishop and Karolina pulled up. I did a double take as I slid into the front seat and looked at her stretched out on the back in an LBD, heels and a wig of black hair.

"Pretty good imitation," Bishop said.

"You forgot to give me his cup size," Karolina said with a wicked grin. "How did I do?"

"I think you went for G's."

She looked down. "What?"

"Gee those are too big."

"Oh very funny," she snorted. "Bet you haven't used that since high school."

"Those were the best nine years of my life," I said.

"Okay," Bishop said, "Karolina, go on into the hospital. They'll take you out the front in a wheelchair. It took hours, but I finally got the goddamn AccessaRide to send a car to take Freddie home. We'll tail you."

"Hospital staff said there were about a half-dozen calls last night asking about Freddie," I added. "Only one didn't use a visual line. I think our boy is on the hunt."

"Then let's give him something to hunt," she said.

"You got body armor on under that thing?" I asked.

She sighed and looked at Bishop. "Does he think I'm brain-dead? Of course, finest ultra-thin body sheath underneath."

Bishop laughed. "What? Old Mother Hen here? Nah, he's just old-fashioned and a worrier."

She considered. "Well that's kinda nice. Yeah I got BA on and my back up stunner on my inner thigh."

"Which is stunning enough on its own," I said.

"Nice of you to notice." She winked and slipped out of the car.

We circled the block and pulled up opposite of where a white and green AccessaRide car sat waiting for Faux-Freddie.

"You know," I said. "That armor will stop a vibra-blade for about three seconds, tops."

"Yeah. We don't take chances on this one. Psycho has already killed twelve people."

Karolina came out in a robotic wheelchair which took her up to the car. The AccessaRide driver did not get out to help her. Karolina did a good job of looking sore and hurt as she made her way to the car.

"When this is over," Bishop said gritting his teeth, "remind me to give that punk's ID to Traffic."

I nodded as the car pulled away and we slid in behind it. It took the better part of an hour to get to the part of Queens where Freddie could afford an apartment. We'd sent his roommate away for a day. I checked my comp screen using the bugs that Bishop had placed there. There was no sign of anyone in the apartment or the hall outside, and the building lobby showed nothing on the concierge scanner.

"Best place to grab her is that vestibule by the entranceway," I said.

"In daylight?" Bishop said.

"This is Queens, not that many people on the street as in Manhattan, it will be 9:30 soon, most of the commuters are gone. If he's quick—"

"Yeah."

I tapped the comp I wore under my jacket, only Bishop, Karolina and I were on this circuit. "Karolina," I said as low voice as I could. "Stop the guy at a market or somewhere to kill a few minutes, Bishop will speed ahead and drop me off so I can get in position."

I heard her talk to the driver who immediately started to argue with her. Bishop passed them. "I am so going to get that ball-buster."

We got to the block of Freddie's street, and I slipped out of the car. Bishop turned to fall back on the AccessaRide. Karolina had persuaded the SOB driving it to stop at the corner shop for bread and milk by offering him a ten-spot. I could hear Bishop cursing him under his breath.

The street was an old one with four and five story buildings fronted by too small and struggling trees. Cars and aircars lined the far side of the street, as the alternate parking rules were in effect. Only a few people could be seen, well-spaced out. They were mostly elderly.

I had a shopping bag with me because bad guys look for large men like myself with empty hands, but assume anybody carrying a bag lives nearby and isn't a cop. So I walked slowly down the street, studying my hand comp as if I was reading a grocery list or text. I knew Freddie's block well. The building next to his had a stoop, and from the entrance atop it I could see his entranceway. I used my cop ID to get the building computer to let me in and not go nuts over my standing in the hallway. I put the bag down and checked my stunner. Then I checked the street. I couldn't see anything. Still Rurik could be in one of those cars. In that much the onerous traffic laws of my hometown were helping us. There were no parked cars on this side of the street, he'd have to come across. But it also meant Bishop would be further away.

The AccessaRide pulled up, and I watched as Karolina paid and tipped the SOB, who again did not get out to help her as she slowly gathered a bag of groceries and her bag from the hospital. He sped off as soon as she was out. I saw Bishop pass by. He'd have to go to at least the next block to make a u-turn without making it obvious he was tailing Karolina. That left me and Karolina alone for a long minute.

Not alone. Across the street a car door opened. Rurik must have been lying down in it as I'd been watching the cars. I'd been afraid he'd detailed this hit to one of his flunkies, but evidently he preferred the personal touch. He got out of the car, wearing a long coat for all that it wasn't cold or rainy. His hands were empty as he looked left and right watching for a break in traffic. I drew my stunner and slipped the door slightly open.

Karolina stopped on the street putting the bag down and holding her middle in a convincing display. She was still ten feet from the outside vestibule, but he was coming fast and I didn't think he was going to wait, he'd push her in. I thought about her body armor. I knew we should wait until he tried to do something but 2-3 seconds was too slim a margin and what if he stabbed for her face or throat?

As he started to rush forward, I stepped out stunner leveled. "Freeze! Police."

Karolina spun around. Rurik had just pulled his vibra-knife, and the weapon, with its characteristic golden shimmer, glowed evilly in his hand. He was only two steps from her, and she was reaching under her skirt for her weapon which in another time and place might have been fun to watch. I saw Bishop's car accelerating back down the other side of the street. Just then some asshole pulled out of a parking spot ahead of him without looking. The unmarked crashed into the side of it with the wet crunching sound of collapsing metal and plastic.

The distraction gave Rurik a second to fling his vibra-knife at me and dive at Karolina. I ducked as the weapon flashed past me to imbed in the wall behind me and slowly start sinking down as its energized monofilament sawed through the brick. I looked up. Rurik had hit Karolina with a tackle, sending her and her weapon flying in different directions. He ran into the vestibule and crashed through the interior door. My stunshot missed him, but came close enough to Karolina to make her woozy. She sat on the pavement with a confused look as I ran down the stairs of the stoop and into the vestibule after Rurik. The broken door was still swinging; I could see him heading down the stairs, heading for the fire door in the back basement. I leapt over the banister and dropped on him, sending him crashing onto the landing. I fetched up against a wall and my stunner fell from my hand. Rurik and I both scrambled up. He ignored the fallen stunner, it was cop-keyed and wouldn't fire for anyone not on the force.

Rurik screamed a curse at me in a language I didn't know and waded in. But I wasn't a 130 lb woman he could knock over. I hit him with two hard shots, and when he tried to clinch, I moved into it and shot for the ribs, then back to the face. I'd boxed guys way younger than me for years. Rurik was street-tough but not trained. He almost got a knee in, but I managed to turn my leg, then snapped out another pair of hard straight ones. I stopped a roundhouse punch on my arm, it stung badly, but I got two more straight shots to his face and blood started pouring out of his nose. Suddenly there were footsteps. Bishop and Karolina appeared over the barrels of their stunners. "Freeze! Police."

Rurik looked up at them. "Fuck." He raised his hands.

"Put the stunners away," I said.

They stared at me.

"If you can get past me, Cutter," I said. "You get to walk away."

"Fuck that," he said.

"McManus," Bishop added. "Don't be a fool."

"I ain't playing," Rurik sneered.

I shrugged. "Then you can just take this." I stepped forward and slammed a series of punches in. I could hear Bishop and Karolina arguing, but it stopped quickly as she made sure no one came out to interrupt. Rurik took the first few shots then grappled with me. He was wiry, tough and managed to bang me into the marble wall hard enough to daze me. His fist caught me in the lip. I clinched, gave him an upper cut then a right cross. He got one more in on me before I landed a combination that left him staggering, eyes fluttering.

"Don't cut on people I know," I snarled and let him have all I had in my right arm. He bounced face-first off the wall and slid down, leaving a pleasing streak of red behind.

Bishop and Karolina stood above me on the staircase as I huffed and tried to breathe through the pain in my ribs and my mouth. I tasted blood but all the teeth were there.

"Aren't you a little old for this kind of behavior?" Karolina said. She held her stunner in one hand and mine in the other.

I nodded. "Definitely."

Asame just shook his head. "Well he was resisting arrest and attempting to flee. Mostly."

"Assaulted me too," Karolina added, smiling as she handed me back my weapon.

"So this is what you've been up to," an unwelcome voice cut in.

We looked up to see Frisby walking down the stairs, a triumphant smile on his face as he surveyed everything.

"Yes, Lieutenant Frisby," Bishop began smoothly. "Detective McManus was just helping us with—"

"Can it, Bishop. Everybody knows you're his asshole buddy."

"Wow," Karolina said. "He's everything you promised he'd be. For your information Lieutenant, this is the guy who cut up thirteen people in our city, caught with an illegal vibra-knife in hand."

He stared at her Freddie wardrobe. "I'll leave you two to your own superiors. This is your turf and if this is how they think the job should be done, God help New York."

Frisby looked down at the prone form of Rurik and smiled. "As for you, oh boy, McManus. You sure put your foot in it this time."

"It was my fist actually."

"Running an unauthorized joint-op with the NYPD, excessive force—"

"He resisted arrest," Karolina said.

"Stow it, sister," Frisby barked. "That line ain't worth a rat's ass."

I smiled at Asame. "Have you ever wondered why a rat's ass is such a popular unit of currency with some people?"

Asame's eyes widened at my tone. "Hey Brian…"

"And all for your little girlfriend in the hospital," Frisby continued.

"He's better people than you are," I said.

Frisby stalked up to me. "The next thing you say to me better end in, 'Sir.'"

"Sure," I replied and hit him on the jaw with a straight right that came up from my hip. His head snapped back, and he went down like a felled tree.

"Sir," I added.

"Wow," Karolina said, admiringly, "that was quite a shot."

"Sure was," Bishop replied. "I hope it was worth it."

"It was."

Bishop gave me a thoughtful look. "You know a shot like that could lay a guy out for an hour or so. Might be that when he came too, his brother officers would think he was confused. Make sure that he went to the hospital and took a battery of tests."

"Especially," Karolina said with ill-concealed glee, "since he was injured going hand to hand with a suspect who escaped our custody and would have got away but for the fact that the heroic Lt Frisby stopped him."

Bishops eyebrows threatened to crawl off his forehead. "That what you saw, Karolina?"

She grinned. "Sure. Isn't that what you saw?"

"Ah jeez," he replied. "McManus. You remember what you said about retiring?"

I touched my split lip. "Yeah."

"Before Lt. Buttmunch wakes up might be a good time to do so. Bet you can get your papers in before he can get out of the ER; with a possible decoration hanging over his head, he might decide not to make an issue of it."

"You know Asame, old friend. I think you may be right. Yep, today's the day." I reached out and shook hands with him then with Karolina. "I leave these mean streets in your capable hands. And thanks, I won't forget what I owe you." Without a backward glance at Rurik, or Lt. Buttmunch, I headed for the street and the subway to the NYPA, for the last time.

CHAPTER NINE

RERUN

I TOGGLED THE SWITCH ON THE ELECTROPHOTO IN THE DOOR. It obligingly lit and displayed the brand new logo of the, McManus Detective agency. The golden logo of an eye and magnifying glass looked pretty good, if I did say so myself.

"Very nice," Toni said.

"Yep," I said looking over my wife and liking the view. Her short, glossy dark-brown hair was perfectly cut and she'd put some extra effort into makeup tonight. The few extra pounds looked good under the crimson sweater and black skirt she wore. We'd just come from a celebratory dinner at Guytano's, fine wine and a new business. What a night.

"It will give you something to do besides playing cards at the Rusty Badge with Frank and Reg, or hanging around the house driving me crazy."

"Here I thought you were looking forward to my retirement."

She grimaced. "You Port Authority cops have such a racket. Twenty years and out, that hasn't changed since the 20th century, when people lived half as long as we do now."

"God bless the union," I said fervently. "It does give me chance to start a second career as a hard-boiled detective with you as my Gal Friday."

"Hah," Toni said. "You think that after a ten hours shift in the ER, I'm going to do filing for you?"

"Guess I'll just have to hire somebody. Maybe one of the strippers at the Pink Flamingo by Koch spaceport—"

"Oh no, you don't," Toni wagged a finger. "I've already hired a Gal Friday for you."

"Really?" I said, raising my eyebrows. My wife had a possessive Sicilian streak. I could only imagine the appearance of any woman she would hire to work all sorts of odd hours with me. "Is she gorgeous? A detective's Gal Friday has to be beautiful and have a checkered past."

Toni gave wicked grin. "Quite beautiful and as for a checkered past, it could hardly be more so."

"I'm intrigued.

Toni strutted over to the outside door, leaned out into the street and waved. I heard the tapping of high heels and for a moment a silhouette filled the doorway, backlit by a streetlight. It was a delightful form: busty, long-legged with a pile of black hair. The vision stepped into the light of the vestibule.

"Oh, no" I groaned.

"Hi McManus," came the husky Southern tenor. "Happy to see me again?"

The face was smooth and pretty, with cat's eye makeup under black hair that had been tormented, not teased, and it belonged to Freddie Bouvier. Despite being an amazing simulation of femininity, Freddie was as male as I.

"See," Toni said. "Beautiful."

Freddie pirouetted.

"And there can be no question of the checkered past," Toni added sweetly, closing the door behind her.

"None whatever," I replied. Freddie had worked for my partner, now Captain Regina Delmar, and me, as an informant between bouts of drugging and prostitution. I had finally gotten him out of the nightlife last year after a psycho stabbed him. Toni had kept tabs on Freddie through the hospital and he'd finally honored his promise to me to stay off drugs and avoid his old hangouts. I hadn't seen much of him while he was in rehab.

"And finally," Toni continued. "I can trust you alone in an office with this Gal Friday."

"Don't be so sure," Freddie winked

"Be sure," I nodded at my wife.

A serious expression stole over Freddie's face. "You don't mind, do you McManus?"

I looked past Freddie at Toni. She gave me a quick nod. Freddie wasn't just here for a joke, I'd find out what was up later.

"OK," I growled. "Can we tone down the hookerwear though?"

Freddie nodded. "I can do demure."

"We start in the morning," I sighed.

"Freddie is going to stay here tonight," Toni said. "I fixed up a bed in the storeroom."

"Then he won't have any excuse to be late," I said. I looked at him. "Coffee light, and a—"

"Donut," Freddie rolled his eyes. "Yes, I know, powdered sugar."

"So, now that we are through here," Toni said, picking up her coat. "How about we head out to the ballroom and dance off some of that fine dinner?"

"They're your feet," I warned.

As I walked by him, Freddie whispered, "Thank you."

I nodded. "See you in the morning."

We stepped out into the brisk night air of Brooklyn. Toni took my arm as we walked. Streetlights cast pools of yellow in the darkness. Overhead a few aircars flitted by, the street level was empty of traffic.

"So shamus," Toni said in a throaty whisper. "Did you bring the dingus?"

"Oh, yeah, baby." I replied.

I returned to the agency the next morning to find Freddie dressed in the promised demure pants suit and freshly made coffee and powdered donuts on my desk. Toni had told me that Freddie was broke and that it was hard for an ex-hooker to get a regular job. I grumbled about becoming a social worker but gave in easily. Either I held his nose out of the water or he went under—simple choices.

I looked at small box wrapped on my desk then at Freddie.

"A present," he said with a languid smile.

I opened it up. A date crystal winked at me from inside, then a holo of a gorgeous blonde appeared. "Welcome to the Lair of the Lesbian Love Goddess—"

I snapped the lid close and gave Freddie a glare.

He batted his eyes in mock innocence. "Isn't that one of your favorite films? I thought the sentimental value would make it a fine housewarming present."

"I wouldn't mention it to Captain Delmar, when she comes around."

"So formal," Freddie sniffed and after all we've been through? She'll always be Topless to me."

"I can see," I said putting the box in my desk, "that it is going to be one of those days."

"If we're lucky," Freddie said as he sashayed to the outer office.

Cases came in the door quickly, mostly insurance stuff. Surveillance on worker's comp cases or the occasional check on a wayward spouse. The weeks sped by and the agency began to pull in dollars. I should have been happier about it, but it wasn't police work and I missed Regina. Course she was busy being the newest and youngest Port Authority Captain. I still saw her on poker nights but we were starting to drift and I was old enough to recognize and reconcile to the truth.

Freddie worked out as secretary. He made a good cup of coffee, handled filing, billing and office work. After the first month, he got an apartment nearby. Life started to settle into a routine until...

Freddie sauntered into my office wearing riding boots, skintight breeches, a red riding blazer and carrying a crop. "Morning, McManus, detected anything yet?"

"Either you're joining the horsy set," I said, eyeing my transgender secretary over the newsholo on my desk, "or you have a gig as a dominatrix for this weekend."

"Intriguing idea," Freddie smiled wickedly. "Dominatrix used to pay well. Of course y'all did make me give up playing for pay."

"The IRS insisted," I said.

"I have a case for us," Freddie said, perching on my desk.

I took my feet off the desk and flicked off the holo. "You have my attention."

"My uncle, Henri Comeaux, called. He's about the only relation I have that stays in touch. He's an assistant trainer for the Hancock family, who own Calumet Farms. The Hancocks want an investigator to check out something fishy at the track. Uncle Henri wouldn't say more, just that they're looking for discretion."

"Discretion is the watchword of the McManus detective agency," I said.

"Ooooohh," Freddie said. "I thought donuts was our watchword. How do you keep so fit eating those things?"

"My heart is pure," I replied, standing and reaching for my jacket. "My wife watches what I eat, cause God knows I don't, and then there's about ten hours a week in the gym on a heavy bag."

Freddie rolled his eyes. "I'll get the aircar."

"Lose the crop," I said.

We flew out to Belmont. I mourned for my days with the Port Authority police, when we could have hopped into the express lanes reserved for official business. But I had served my twenty, retired and gone private. So now we were stacked up over New York with everybody else. I put the aircar on automatic and looked out over the city, which ran out to the horizon in all directions. Koch Spaceport sat in what had once been Long Island Sound, and I could see the steady supply of ships and aircraft dancing attendance on Earth's main source of trade.

Belmont Racetrack lay nearer to Kennedy. We dropped down through the air-control layers, got off at exit 26D and drove into the grounds on our wheels. The track stretched out as it had for hundreds of years, four hundred and thirty acres of woods and graceful buildings devoted to the sport of kings.

We parked and walked over to the huge barn, drawing a few wary looks. We made quite the pair. At 6'1" and 200 lbs, I was usually spotted for the flatfoot I was. Freddie stood 5'9" but with the hair and boots he was nearly as tall as I. A variety of earthy smells confronted us, and we did the two-step over some truly formidable piles of poop. To my surprise there was something like an office in the back of the barn.

"Uncle Henri," Freddie waved, looking uncertain for the first time in my experience with him.

"*Tee-do*," the short dark man grinned. He ran over, picked Freddie up in a bear hug and shook him.

"*Tee-do?*" I asked.

Henri noticed me and put Freddie down. I was amazed to see Freddie blushing.

"It's a Cajun nickname," Freddie said.

"Means Little Sweet One," Henri boomed in an accent liberally seasoned with Cajun and pulled Freddie down to kiss him on the forehead.

"Hey, big man," Uncle Henri grinned at me and stuck out a hand.

I gave it a solid shake. Henri seemed to overflow with energy, the sort of guy who was always on the verge of busting into song or dance. I decided that I liked Uncle Henri.

"You must be McManus. I hear my *jeun fils* here is working for you now."

"Yep," I said, wondering if Uncle Henri knew of Freddie's prior life as a streetwalker.

"That be an improvement in his life." He gave Freddie a mock glare. "Maybe next he settle down and have a mortgage and a passel of children."

"Uncle Henri," Freddie wagged a finger.

"Stranger things happen, Tee-do. Never say never."

I changed the subject. "I understand you were the one who brought us in."

"Yeah," Henri said. "Mr. Hancock come to me since I told him about Freddie. Course he knew your name from when you stopped those aliens trying to kill the UN president."

I nodded.

"Mr. Hancock want this looked into quiet-like. So I figure we call you and I get to see my nephew here." He reached out and mussed Freddie's elaborately teased hair.

I expected a shriek of protest from Freddie, but he merely grinned, looking for a moment like the boy he must have once been.

"Come on," Henri said. We headed for the exclusive section of the clubhouse, where the big money players lounged. Uncle Henri and Freddie did most of the talking, at a rate that taxed even a New Yorker's ears. Freddie's nominal Southern accent had returned to the bayou and became incomprehensible.

Henri quieted down as we came up on an elderly white-haired gentleman seated by the window at a linen covered table. He wore an elegant seersucker suit, which matched the veins in his hands. "Ah, Henri. Are these the folks?"

"Yes, Mr. Hancock, Brian McManus and my relation, Freddie Bouvier."

"Pardon my not rising to meet you, young lady," Hancock said to Freddie in a genteel Kentucky accent. "My old knees aren't up to it."

Freddie gave one of his most winning smiles. "Please don't worry about it."

"Please sit," Hancock gestured. "Thank you, Henri."

Henri nodded. "See you later, Freddie."

Hancock took in Freddie's outfit. "I see you ride."

"Oh, I've been known to use a crop on a naughty stud from time to time," Freddie winked.

I rested my head in my left hand and sighed internally.

"Know much about horses, Mr. McManus?" Hancock asked. His old but clear blue eyes studied me.

"One end bites, the other poops?"

Hancock laughed. "Well, that's a start."

He gestured toward the track. "This is a sacred place to horsefolk. It's a battleground where each year the best horses vie with each other. See that statue there?"

I looked out to see a bronze of a horse. It sat on a marble block. Curiously it seemed to be running on a bed of white carnations.

"That's Secretariat. Two hundred and eighty three years ago he set the track record here, and it has never been broken. That may change this year."

"I don't follow racing," I said. "But even I've heard about Play-it-again."

"Yes," Hancock said, his mouth drawn into a tight line. "Play-it-again came out of nowhere. He had a fair to middling record in out of the way tracks in South America. His backers paid the premium to enter him in the Kentucky Derby, and he became the longest shot winner in history. Two weeks later he destroys the Preakness field. Now he stands ready to run in the Belmont, favorite for the first Triple Crown in fifty years. There's a prize of twenty million credits if he does."

"Not sure I can help you on handicapping," I said.

"Thanks, but I do well enough there when the game isn't rigged."

"And you think there's something rigged with Play-it-again?" I asked.

"Yes. Damned if I know how. But horses don't come out of nowhere, not like this."

I looked at Hancock. "There's something more."

Hancock gave me a long searching stare. "Something happened at Calumet last year. We kept it quiet because we don't like scandal.

The great warrior," he pointed to Secretariat's statue, "was buried on our grounds."

"Was?"

"Last year someone snuck in and excavated the entire grave." A deep anger lined his timeworn face and the genteel accent did not disguise the hurt. "We put it down to a sick prank at the time."

He shifted. "I'm an old man, Mr. McManus, one hundred-forty on my next birthday. But my wits are with me, and I know horses like few people do these days. Play-it-again looks enough like Secretariat to be him. Same height and weight, the markings are slightly off, but I have it on good authority that they use a dye on him."

"A clone?" I asked, remembering my last encounter with a vicious resurrection from the past, the clone of Al Capone. "Wouldn't the tests show it?"

"They should. There are genetic engineering marks from cloning, especially from dead tissue, which should have been picked up during his vet work. Of course, with Secretariat's grave empty, there's no way to do a one-on-one match to prove it.

"I want you to look into this. Racing has been my whole life, and I've loved Secretariat as if he'd been mine. If Play-it-again is the real deal, then he should have his run, but I won't see Secretariat's record fall to trickery."

"Do you know who owns Play-it-again?" I asked.

"Yes, my lawyers dug around for me. It's buried in transactions, but he's owned by Vendala Scheer. Know her?"

"By reputation," I said, "former showgirl. She made a raft of money in the casino business on greyhound racing. Now she owns the Gemini Casino in Atlantic City. Rumor has it she's had some big scores recently. She's not mob herself, but like most casino owners, she's connected."

"Yes. I wonder if some of those recent scores involved backing the biggest long shot in Derby history?" Hancock handed me a package. "This has all the data I could assemble that might help you. Will you take the case?"

"I'll see what I can do."

Hancock smiled. "Anything else I can tell you before I leave you to it?"

"One last question, was there anything unusual about the burial?"

"Unlike most racehorses," Hancock said, "Secretariat was buried whole."

"What happens with the others?" Freddie asked.

"Normally, they cut off the head, remove the heart and the testicles."

"God," Freddie gave a delicate shudder. "Who does that job?"

"Recently divorced women," I replied.

Hancock raised an eyebrow. "Good luck."

We set out the next day. Play-it-again wasn't housed at Belmont. Vendala Scheer had him parked at The Finish Line Farm in Oakhurst, New Jersey. With Henri's Calumet credentials, we could gain entrance and look around on the pretext of boarding a Calumet-bred there. We flew over and grounded at a tree-lined and wood-fenced complex. Horses ran in the fields and a variety of green-and-white trimmed barns and farm buildings dotted the landscape.

Henri met a tall, dour fellow named Quentin, and we got the tour, though Quentin seemed mostly interested in eyeballing Freddie. It gave me an excuse to slip away, leaving Freddie with

Henri and head for the section where Play-it-again was kept. I reached an area where I could see his stall. Curiously, the ones near him were unoccupied, by horses anyway. A couple of husky men and one tall, lean woman lounged around. All wore nice suits and sunglasses and looked very fit, high-class muscle.

I watched as a short, slim man petted the horse on the nose and spoke to it at length. I recognized him from the material Hancock gave me as the jockey, Al Frieze. He'd been a comer about a decade ago, then got involved in a doping scandal. Nothing was proved, but he ended up in South America on a C circuit. Then came Play-it-again.

The jockey left, and for lack of anything better to do, I followed him. He got in a sporty, red aircar and disappeared. I wandered back to watch Play-it-again. The muscle noticed me and started getting edgy, so I did a fade.

As I hiked back to the lot, I ran into Freddie. "Anything?" I asked.

He shrugged. "Uncle Henri is still with Quentin. All we learned from him is that the other animals don't like Play-it-again. Even the barn cats stay out of his stall. Scheer keeps guards on the horse, even brought in her own barn help. Only the jockey and his own grooms enter that stall. Quentin seemed a bit put out by all the fuss."

As we walked back to our aircar, Frieze came back, grounding nearby. He got out of his aircar with insulated bags under his arms.

"Hey Al," I said. "What do you know?"

The jockey gave a guilty start and his head jerked around. "Who are you? What do you want?" he snapped.

I smiled. "Nothing, Al, just recognized you from the papers. What's in the bag?"

"Some burgers. Do ya mind if a guy eats? Jesus. What are you harassing me for?"

I looked at the sack and savored the smell. "Take it easy. I just wanted to know where you got them. They smell good."

Al seemed to relax though he still watched me with narrow eyes. "Just go out the main gate and turn left about half a mile down. Place is called Beauty's. Tell em I sent ya."

"Sure. Good luck on Saturday."

Al gave Freddie a once over, then grinned and sauntered off.

I turned to Freddie. "Follow him and see what's going on."

Freddie raised an eyebrow. "What gives, Shamus?"

"Freddie, jockeys spend more time worrying about their weight than you do. He ain't eating burgers and fries this close to the race. It's not much to go on, but we're nowhere on this case and the race is in forty-eight hours."

"Right," Freddie smiled and pointed at me with his index finger held like a pistol. "Count on me."

Freddie followed Al as I wandered about looking for clues. None presented themselves. I checked in with Freddie by portacomp. Al had gone into the guarded barn where Freddie couldn't follow. It was becoming obvious that we weren't going to learn more and it was getting on toward sunset. I got our surveillance equipment out of the car and ditched it behind some large rocks, hoping no one would spot it in the meanwhile.

Henri had run out of things to ask about and beeped me on my portacomp, and I beeped Freddie. We met back at the car. "Henri," I said as we slid in, "drive out on the ground wheels. Freddie and I are going to bailout. Go to Beauty's diner and wait for us there."

Henri nodded. As soon as we drove out of sight of the barn, Freddie and I slipped out of the car and raced into the pinewoods. Freddie, I was pleased to see, had left his high heels in the car and traded them for sequined running shoes.

We used the fading sun and afterglow to make our way to the rocks where I'd cached our spy gear and then back to a small grass-and-brush covered hillock that gave us a fair view of Play-it-again's stall. With nightfall the barns had shut down. The animals were settling in. Two guards remained: a man and the tall woman. They seemed more interested in each other than in watching the wood-line. City people that they were, they stayed in the pool of white light from an overhead lamp, killing their night vision.

"I hope there aren't any dogs," I whispered.

"Quentin said he had to move them to the far end. Terriers kept yapping at Play-it-again," Freddie whispered.

"Good," I nodded, ignoring the buzzing of insects. We set up the scanners and sensors. I flicked on my telephoto and set it for thermograph and low light. The sensor combined the view through the Dutch doors with a thermal image through the wall.

The horse sat on his ass, facing Al the jockey across a bale of straw.

"I don't know much about horses," I whispered to an astonished Freddie, "but I know they don't sit that way."

In what looked a lot like a human hand, the horse held a half-eaten burger. In the other, he held a couple of cards.

"This animal is supposed to be talented, but this is a new level," Freddie said.

I pointed my boom mike at the pair.

"Raise ten," Play-it-again said.

"Call," Al said. "Read 'em and weep."

"Weep yourself, human, full house."

"Damn. Well, that cleans me out."

The horse emitted a titanic belch. "Good burgers, Al. If I hadda eat another fucking flake of alfalfa, I'd have shit a rocking chair."

"Just don't get too loaded down. We gotta big race Saturday. Besides didn't you get enough protein out of Secretariat's skeleton?"

"Don't be disgusting, Al. I absorbed the bones for the DNA so I could clone him. I didn't taste them. Besides, everybody's worried about your weight, not mine. I got Secretariat's body, remember that. His heart was nearly three times as big as a normal thoroughbred. That's how he outran everything."

"Yeah, we get outta this, the first thing I'm going to do is eat a five-course meal with extra bread. No more making weight for me. What about you? What are your plans?"

"Nothing personal, Al, but as soon as I'm free from Vendala Scheer, I'm blowing the cruddy dust of your planet off my membrane and getting back into the galaxy. You should come with me. We'd make a good team."

"Long as you don't mind a fat traveling companion."

They laughed, and I'd heard enough. We packed up and moved out.

Henri couldn't believe it when we caught up to him at Beauty's and showed him the images. "I don't understand," Henri said, staring at the computer screen. He flipped the screen down as the waitress brought some pie and coffee. After she left, Henri continued. "This animal has been tested and examined a dozen times in the last few weeks. How could this be?"

"I don't know," I said. "Obviously, it's some form of shape-shifting alien. When it wants to, it mimics a horse perfectly and not just any horse—Secretariat. It seems to have cloned him down to the atomic level and without any of the hallmarks a laboratory would leave behind or it would have showed in the standard tests."

"We have this scan," Freddie said.

"Proves nothing," I said, "too easy to fake. And we know the horse can pass the medical tests. No, we have to find some way to expose the creature where there can be no question."

"How?" Henri asked, throwing up his arms.

"Dunno," I said. "But if there are any answers to be had, I know where they'll be."

"Feel like placing a bet, Freddie?" I looked at him.

Freddie lifted a forkful of pie. "Oh goody, let me guess, the Gemini Casino?"

"Finish your pie," I said and drained my coffee.

The Port of NY had long ago eaten northern New Jersey and developed a tremendous case of gas for its trouble. After a huge subterranean eruption engulfed Las Vegas, in what most hailed as proof of an activist God, Atlantic City went on to become ten times as gaudy and wild as Vegas had ever been. Fake pyramids, volcanoes, and a Chinese pagoda complete with a Great Wall, fought for attention with a neon-lit casino shaped like the planet Saturn. We landed in the parking area and walked over to the towering imitation *Gemini Seven* cruisers that flanked an immense glass and glitzy building. A hoverbus pulled up and disgorged a horde of retirees who were sucked into the casino, packs of coins clenched in their hands.

We wandered into the casino proper, a vast and noisy room full of blinking lights, then headed over to where the racing bets were taken. We talked racing to anyone who would listen and looked around, getting a sense of the place's layout. I'd obtained a building diagram from city records but a lot of it was marked, *confidential, building security.*

"Hey," a gruff voice sounded behind me.

Freddie and I turned. Three stocky men in nicely tailored suits were giving us hard looks.

"This is private property," the biggest one said, the lights glinting off his silver reflective sunglasses. "Move on."

I stared at Sunglasses. "You must be the customer relations specialist. I can tell by your charming manner."

"Okay, smartmouth. Move along."

"We might feel like doing a little gambling."

"We don't want your trade."

"Something wrong with our money?" I crossed my arms. It would make it easier to throw a block. Sunglasses' buddies flanked out on us.

Sunglasses moved up. "You don't want us to get rough."

"No, cause then I'd have to watch my assistant here," I gestured at Freddie, "kick your collective asses."

Freddie buffed his nails on his blouse.

Sunglasses shrugged. "You asked for it." He reached for me, and I feinted a left jab. He fell for it and wasted his block. My right fist connected with his nose, and his sunglasses went flying. The left-hand bozo decided to ignore Freddie and stepped toward me. Freddie kicked him behind the knee. He howled and went down clutching his leg. I squared off with the right hand bozo.

"That's enough, gentleman." The voice was authoritative and female. I didn't take my eyes off Bozo Two, but sidled around so I could watch him and see her.

She was worth the look. A big cool blonde, with a heroic figure doing battle with the silk of her very expensive suit. She had wicked legs only barely covered by her skirt. I guessed her to be about thirty. Three more husky men stood behind her.

"Ms. Scheer," Sunglasses said, clutching his nose. "We'll get rid of these—"

"Shut up, you idiot," she said wearily. She gestured to Bozo Two. "Get them off the floor." She gestured toward Sunglasses and Bad Knee. The other huskies moved over to help their comrades. She turned toward us.

"My apologies," Ms. Scheer said. "You've been mistaken for someone else."

"Like who?" I asked.

She ignored me. "I'm Vendala Scheer, the owner of the Gemini. Allow me to make the mistake up to you. Roger," she said, "give these folks a thousand credits each and take them to a table. Comp their drinks and meals."

I looked Vendala over and enjoyed the view. "That's very generous of you for a case of mistaken identity."

She raised a delicate arched eyebrow. I couldn't read anything in her arctic-blue eyes, but there was a dangerous and playful quirk to her bright red lips.

"Take your 2K, sport. Enjoy the buffet and the free drinks. Luck *may* be with you."

"I think it might have already been," I murmured.

She cast me a sharp look across her chiseled nose. "This place was built by people who misjudged their luck." She walked away, her ample hips swaying in a way that was enough to make a good dog break his chain.

For lack of any better plan, we followed the huskies. The cashier gave us our chips. The huskies dropped us by the blackjack tables and faded away as a girl dressed up in a sexy spacesuit with strategically placed cutouts waved a tray of cheap champagne under our noses. Freddie grabbed two. I ordered a rum and coke as we wandered over and perused the buffet.

Freddie kept his champagne glass at his lips. "Clearly something is up. First, the goon squad, now the red carpet. What gives?"

"I don't know. But I'll bet if we could reach Vendala's office, we might learn something."

"Hard with them watching our every move," Freddie said.

I stared at the backstage door. A couple of leggy showgirls stood about, giggling and talking. Some wandered off with customers. Another showgirl came out the door. She had a mass of black hair, just like...just like...suddenly I had an idea, a terrible grinchy idea, an awful idea. I turned to Freddie.

"What's with the hideous smile?" he groused.

"I just figured out how we can get in there."

"How?"

"See that showgirl?"

"Yeah," Freddie said. "Hot babe. When I'm in my hetero phase, I could really go for her."

"Right now, I just want you to go for her clothes. Offer her a few hundred to get lost for an afternoon."

"Oh, for Christ's sake, McManus," Freddie rolled his eyes. "I can't wear that get up."

"Sure, now you decide to get modest on me."

"Modest my silk-clad ass. It's not that. Showgirls are almost a separate species. She's got eight inches more leg and neck than I have and no waist at all. Not to mention where would I hide all of my package in that little bottom?"

"You managed it when your butt got thrown into the women's prison three years ago. They didn't figure it out until they found you banging a couple of matrons."

"McManus, I can't pass for a showgirl."

"Well, I guess you've been letting yourself go a bit, slack through the middle, not to mention a bit broader across the tail."

"Ha," Freddie said. "I've got a tight middle and an ass like a rock."

"All talk, Freddie. Yes, your prime is behind you."

"Ok, Flatfoot," Freddie waved his finger. "You're on. I'll get the bimbo's costume. If this works, you owe me two months' salary."

"And if it doesn't, I'll arrange a high class New Orleans funeral for you."

"What a sweetheart! Good thing I changed back into real heels," Freddie grimaced and set off to stalk showgirls.

I cashed in my chips and went back to the car. There I changed my shirt and jacket and switched into heel-less shoes that dropped my height an inch. A few minutes work with a quick dye darkened my brown hair to black, and I put on a baseball cap and brown contact lenses. Human guards remember only gross details, and automatics remember too much detail. I was now shorter and differently colored. Thin disguise, but the best that could be managed in a short time. I slipped back into the casino.

About twenty-five minutes later, what looked like a striking showgirl flounced over to the corner I'd tucked into. "Jesus, Freddie. Where have you been?"

Freddie stuck his tongue out at me. "I had to talk the girl out of her outfit. Told her I had a John who wanted to do a showgirl." Freddie shimmied, causing the erotic chain mail corset he had on to tinkle.

"Was she wearing that?" I asked, searching my memory.

"I got it at the gift store and charged it to your private account."

"How did you get access to my—"

"Do you want to get into Scheer's office or not?" Freddie sniffed.

"All right!"

Freddie wiggled off. Ten minutes later my portacomp bleeped. I opened the receiver.

"McManus," Freddie whispered. "There's a backstage door in the basement level. It says K-19 on the outside. Knock when you reach it, and I'll let you in."

I slipped away toward the basement. It took a few minutes to find K-19 and knock. Freddie opened it. "This way."

I followed Freddie, trying to see round the headdress and the ostrich feathers that stuck out of his tail.

"Just about there," Freddie threw over the plumage.

Just as we reached the red and gold checked doors with Vendala Scheer's name on it, footsteps sounded. Freddie turned and threw his arms around me and buried his face in my neck.

"Oh, darling," Freddie said, his voice higher than usual. "Really, I must get back to work."

Deprived of wit by surprise and of sight by the headdress, I couldn't say anything. I could barely see through a gap in the feathers.

"Jeez. Keep it out of the corridor," an exasperated voice that sounded like Sunglasses said.

"Oh, sure," Freddie said, sliding around to my left side to keep my face out of sight. Hopefully, they were looking at Freddie's butt anyway.

"Boss sure was mad at you," another voice said. I peered through the feathers to see Bad-Knee. "I told you we should have ignored them."

"Shit," Sunglasses snarled, "I know that guy, Brian McManus, used to be a Port Authority detective. He's trouble with a big T. There's only one reason for him to be here now: Play-it-again. He may be the big guy that Angela said was hanging around the barn. We should have stuffed him in the compactor."

Voices and footsteps faded away before I could hear more.

Freddie leaned back and smiled up at me, arms around my neck.

I sighed. "We will add this to the long list of things we don't mention to my wife."

Freddie winked and we slipped over to Vendala Scheer's door. I used a robo-spider picklock that I had relieved Louie the Lizard of during my last police bust. The spider unfolded and made quick work of the lock. We were in.

The office was like Scheer herself, big, bold and a bit brassy. A portrait of her in a showgirl costume dominated one wall. I wished I had more time to study it.

"There," Freddie said, "her office computer. It's isolated from the net. We'll need to place a sensor on it."

I walked over to the brass and wood console and dropped an intruder on it. The jewel-like machine emanated dozens of tiny microfilaments and began to infiltrate the stand-alone comp. We searched the room as best we could while the intruder searched the computer. A small green light glowed when the data-miner found what we wanted. I snatched it up as soon as it extricated itself from the machine.

"We'll read it later," I whispered. We slipped out the door and back into the corridor, Freddie leading.

"Hey you!" A hand reached around the door we'd just slid through and grabbed Freddie by the tail feathers. I slammed the door with my elbow and whoever it was bounced off the wall. Freddie was running, and I was hot-footing it behind him. A man stepped out of the side hall. Freddie lowered his head and dove into his middle, driving the air out of him. I clocked him in the temple, and down he went.

A shot cracked behind me, a slug-thrower. Plaster exploded off the wall by my shoulder. I grabbed Freddie and thrust him out the door, pulling my stunner and raying back in the direction of the shot. I don't know if I hit him or just made the shooter woozy, but Freddie and I made it out the door and into the parking deck.

Freddie managed to stay in the lead despite the heels and feathers. He bleeped open the car and dove in. I ran around the other side, jumped in and gunned the engine just as another shot spidered the bulletproof glass in the rear window. The aircar shot forward, and I made an illegal exit off the second story. We fled New Jersey for the safety of our Brooklyn office.

I parked on the street before the agency. We put up with some whistles and hoots from the *gavones* hanging out at the corner pizzeria, as Freddie strode in full showgirl regalia into our storefront. The sliding door shut off the catcalls.

"Dammit," Freddie said, as he flopped on the couch.

"Now what?"

"I left my clothes back at the casino."

"Don't you have anything here?" I asked. Freddie had slept in the back office for the first few months after I hired him.

"Not since I moved out to my apartment."

"Never mind. Let's see what our little data-mining bug found." I plugged the bug into our system. Data and pictures scrolled across the screen. Unfortunately, while it showed Al Frieze was doing very well on the payroll, there was nothing useful.

"What about that file?" Freddie pointed.

"Which one?"

"It says, 'Disciplining the special staff.'"

"Trust you to find that one," I opened the file. "Eureka."

"The alien is similar in drives to most sapients, desiring to live and prosper. His species developed in a predator-rich environment, and shape-changing is a primary defense. It perfectly duplicates

the physical characteristics of any animal it absorbs, producing an undetectable clone.

He's been a real moneymaker as a racing greyhound. We're bulking him up to see what he can do as a larger animal.

Projectile weapons are useless on him. Energy weapons can destroy the whole creature, but should persuasion be needed, an electromagnetic pulse in a special range will cause him to lose control of his form, something which causes him an analogue of pain and humiliation. A short burst set at...”

"Freddie, get hold of Mr. Hancock. We are going to need some special equipment and access trackside.”

"Roger, Chief."

I sighed. "Did you save the receipt to return that iron corset?"

Freddie pouted. "But I really like it."

"Freddie."

"You don't want to call any more attention to our little casino visit do you?"

"Oh, all right. Get home. Get some decent clothes, assuming you own any, and we're off to the races."

Late Saturday afternoon we stood at the Belmont rail. In the air over us, holo images unfurled. We could see Play-it-again and his jockey loading in the gate. Another panel gave us a view of Vendala Scheer, dressed in a hot pink suit and matching hat, in her private booth, surrounded by friends. Sunglasses stood in the background. He must have had regenerative therapy, as his nose was back to normal.

I looked over my shoulder at the closed van with our emitter, then at Freddie, who smiled and opened his purse to show the transmitter button. I nodded.

"They're loading in the gate," the announcer said. "As usual, the horses next to Play-it-again are acting up. Look at Snorting Rum, rearing in the gate. Yes, folks, the other horses are definitely spooked by Play-it-again.

"And they're off," the announcer shouted, as thousands of fans cheered and waved. Above us we could see a close-up as the field of seven burst from their gates.

"Play-it-again broke well and is running easy, stalking the leader, Old Sweet Honey. Snorting Rum is right on Play-it-again's tail. Wild Weasel is fourth."

"Easy fractions at 26 seconds," the announcer continued. "As usual, Play-it-again is giving his rider a push-button trip. That's a smart horse, folks."

"Ready," I said. Freddie nodded.

"Coming into the back stretch, Play-it-again is overtaking the leader. As Old Sweet Honey fades, Snorting Rum has hooked up with Play-it-again. And the two are pulling away from the pack."

"They're approaching the top of the stretch, and there goes Play-it-again. He's hit another gear and is pulling away. Opening the gap with every stride. I've never seen anything like it."

The roar of the crowd swelled. I could see the announcer on a holo, hopping up and down.

"Ten lengths, eleven. He's eating the field alive."

The holo switched to a triumphant Vendala Scheer, shouting Play-it-again's name.

"He's flying, sixteen lengths, seventeen—"

"Now," I said. Freddie's finger snapped down on the button. From the van behind us, inaudible, invisible, and to all but one creature, imperceptible, a carefully frequenced electromagnetic wave rippled out.

Play-it-again stumbled, his outlines wavering. The jockey hung on to his neck for dear life. Now screams and confusion peppered the roar of the crowd. Play-it-again looked like a child's drawing of a horse. His neck and legs seemed blobby and viscous. Eyestalks protruded out of his head.

"What the hell!" the announcer shouted. Vendala Scheer's mouth hung open in shock.

Play-it-again rallied. He visibly shook as he tried to reestablish his form. Suddenly he stabilized, but not as Play-it-again.

"He's turned into a greyhound," Freddie observed.

"He spent a lot of years as one. It must have been second nature," I said, observing a 1200-pound dog in the center of the track, jockey desperately clutching at him, pick up speed. He still had lengths to go back to the nearest horse.

"A really big greyhound," Freddie continued.

The huge hound and its rider bolted across the finish line, still in the lead to a now thunderous silence. They didn't stop at the line, but cut right, leapt the fence and raced into a passage leading out of the track. Red-coated outriders pursued them like avenging cavalry.

All freaking hell broke loose. Boos and shrieks of outrage began. I could see Vendala Scheer and her security team, pelted by anything that could be thrown, retreating out of their box.

"Hold all tickets. Hold all tickets!" the announcer shouted over the din.

Freddie smiled up at me and waved a ticket. "Uncle Henri recommended Snorting Rum at fifty to one. I imagine that the steward's sign is going to be up for a bit."

"Oh, for like a week or so," I said, with a grin.

CHAPTER TEN

DROWNING IN THE PAST

"**I** CAN'T EFFING BELIEVE IT!" I SHOUTED, LOOKING AT THE aircar's mangled fender, the Louisiana bayou and insects the size of bats hovering beyond the aircar's fading lights. "I mean who would believe we'd run into a flight of Canadian Geese at that altitude and this season?"

"Anybody, who listened to me when I screamed, 'Hey look out for all those Canadian Geese just ahead of us!'" Freddie Bouvier's languid Southern accent was syrupy with mock sweetness as he sat on the aircar's trunk lid. The black miniskirt and hose he wore under a black leather vest matched the aircar's decor perfectly, but not the primeval surroundings. One leg was stretched out, ankle in a fresh air-bandage. His pale arms were crossed, and he glared at me through cat-eye makeup.

"Hey, you were the one who just had to visit your old stomping grounds in the land that time forgot for Halloween. Who knew there would be demonically-possessed geese in the way?"

Freddie sniffed in derision. "We finished the investigation on that runaway case a week early, and I haven't seen my family, the part that acknowledges my transgendered existence anyway, in three years. AND, the only thing those geese were possessed by was an insufficient sense of self-preservation. Finally, to you New Yorkers, anything south and west of New Jersey is Terra Incognita."

"What's that," I said, "some sort of Cajun food?"

The car's emergency system had brought us down on a bit of road on what passed for a hillside in the swamp. But we'd hit some trees and landed partly in a drainage ditch. Nothing had driven or flown by in the hour since we crashed.

I tried my comp again; it lit but wouldn't hook up to anything. "How is this even possible?" I groused. "There's no place on Earth where we don't have satellite coverage. No response to the car beacon either. What about your comp?"

"It went out the window in my purse when we hit the trees."

As the car's battery failed, the lights dimmed to extinction. I waited for my eyes to adjust but it seemed to me that there was a ruddy overtone to everything. I looked up at the moon. "What the hell? The moon is red."

Freddie looked up. "What? Wait, what's tonight? Oh, no. A red moon means a lunar eclipse and on Halloween night too. Oh Lord, my grandma always said the powers of darkness are exalted in the dark of the moon and all good Christians should stay indoors." Freddie's eyes grew round.

"Well then you should be fine," I said.

"We are in the wrong place at the wrong time," Freddie intoned.

I looked into the valley, where I could see the lights of a small town by the glimmer of a river. Odd, I hadn't noticed it before. The car lights must have ruined my night vision.

"Well let's see what we can do about getting out of it," I said folding my comp and putting it back in my jacket. "You wait here. I'll hike in and get help."

"You are outta your mind if you think I'm staying here by myself. God knows what's out here."

"What happened to, 'don't diss my home place'?"

He glared darkly at me. "I left for a reason."

"Well you won't get far on that gimpy ankle even with an air-bandage and the best quasi-legal painkillers you stuffed in our med kit."

"I wasn't planning to. I mean a big fellow like you, former boxing champ, all-around athlete, could surely carry a skinny little thing like me on that broad, strong back. You wouldn't be so unchivalrous as to leave an injured lady behind? Just think of what your wife would say if she heard about such behavior from her knight in shining armor."

"Oh all right," I said, walking over. "Hop on Pop." With Freddie settled on my back and my arms under his legs, we headed down the road. I did find it mildly distracting how much he felt like a real girl when I was carrying him, especially the impressive rack he was resting against my back. Oh well, at least he smelled good and wasn't very heavy. I kept hoping for some sight or sound of a vehicle, but our luck did not change and we trudged on.

"The road," I said, peering off to the right, "doesn't seem to be heading toward that village."

"Is that a cut off just ahead?" Freddie asked.

I looked. If there had been a sign, it had long since disappeared, but clearly a surfaced road bent off into the valley below. "Doesn't look like it gets used much. The surface is all cracked, and there's weeds and grass growing up on it."

"Well we're not in Brooklyn anymore," Freddie said. "Lot of bayou folk prefer hover cars to wheeled and they don't care about the surface. At least it's going in the right direction. Giddyup."

"You squeeze me with those thighs again, and I will feed you to the first crocodile I see."

"Well then we'll be vacationing in Egypt, Sweetie, that's where they keep the crocodiles. All we got hereabouts is gators."

We walked down the old cracked road with me taking the occasional rest break and Freddie sometimes limping with an arm over my shoulder. It was faster with him on my back, and, with the light of the moon growing dimmer and redder, I opted for speed.

Finally we came up on an old wooden sign that read in faded letters, "Sarapeta, population 113, It's a quiet town."

"Great," I said. "Here we are after midnight in East Cupcake. Bet nothing's open."

We stepped off the cracked road surface onto better paving and walked into a collection of buildings that passed for a town. I guessed two roads met there as I saw an intersection and a few lights ahead. As we walked on I noticed the old style lights and the quaint shapes to the houses, the land that time forgot, indeed. We came to a two story building with a porch and a sign that said, "Murrow's Dry Goods." Not far away stood the tallest structure in sight, a water tower that climbed forty feet into the sky.

I gratefully put Freddie down. "No more of Toni's lasagna for you, Missy."

"Hah. Despite your wife's best efforts with cannoli and pasta, my gorgeous butt is the same size it was last year."

I stood, turning in a circle. "Wait a minute. Did we walk into a theme park or a museum?"

"Yeah," Freddie said. "Everything looks old-style. Look at those wheeled cars and the street lights. I don't see any automatics or server bots either."

"Well it sure ain't Time's Square." I walked up onto the porch passing a half-dozen well-worn rocking chairs and a bulletin board with honest to God paper on it, to peer into the store. The shelves inside were lined with metal cans and other oddities I didn't recognize.

Freddie leaned on me as we walked down the porch looking in windows and waiting for the house security system to do something... anything.

"Odd there are no dogs," Freddie whispered, looking into the darkness.

"Yeah, good news is less bugs too, and it's cooler." I felt Freddie shiver and remembered he was, as usual, only minimally decent.

"This isn't usual even for October," he added.

I looked for a comp pad by the door, couldn't find it, then recognized a bell and pressed that. There was no sound. After a minute I banged on the door in frustration. It rattled but there was no other response.

"Poor Mrs. Redcliffe," a voice sounded behind me. "I wonder if they'll find her—"

I spun on my heel, but there was no one behind me on the porch.

"Did you hear that?" I demanded of Freddie.

"Yeah. God, it was almost in my ear."

"No," I said, "it was right behind me." We stared at each other and then into the darkness of the street beyond. It was dead silent now. I didn't even hear crickets.

"Come on," I said. "Let's try that house next to, I guess it's a gas station, over there."

We walked over to the house. A solitary light bulb of an antique style glowed in a fixture. I knocked on the door, which to my surprise, opened under my hand. Inside, I could see lights on in the next room.

"Hello," I said. "Anybody home? We need some help. Our car crashed on the hillside..."

Freddie brushed past me to sit on a chair just inside the doorway with relief. "Hi y'all, so sorry to barge in."

I walked in slowly, hoping not to face a shotgun or a dog – calling every few feet. I turned toward the kitchen. There was a meal set on the table, the food was hot. Glasses of tea beaded with perspiration sat next to the food.

"Hello." I walked through the one story house with its four small rooms of antique furniture. There was no one. I returned to the kitchen where Freddie was washing his hands and face in the sink.

"Maybe they ran out the back when they saw your homely Irish mug coming in through the front," he added with his sweetest smile.

"As I recall you were in the lead. Maybe it was your makeup."

"OOOOOooohhh," Freddie said, limping to the chair. "Are you hungry?"

"No, not really. Odd, usually I'm starving if I have been up this long."

"Me neither, but God knows when we'll get a chance to eat."

"You wanna play Goldilocks?"

"I'll leave the check to you; tip handsomely when someone shows up." Freddie spooned up some stew, chewed and then stopped. He grabbed another spoon. "Taste this."

"What? Now you're a food critic?"

"Taste it."

I took the spoon. The stew looked good though there was little...no scent. I chewed it. "No flavor. None at all. Just like my Irish mother used to cook."

"It's not funny," Freddie said, picking up the tea. "The same. I have the sensation of drinking something but there's no flavor at all, not even as much as water."

The lights went out. Freddie screamed and dropped the glass. I pulled my stunner. There were silhouettes through the curtained front windows. "Ned's not going to let this go, and that monster of a son of his is backing him up," a man's voice said.

The other silhouette nodded. "Government's paying good money. They promised to rebuild the town above the new lake. We have to do it."

"Ned won't go. He's trying to ruin it for all of us."

"Got to do something..."

I ran out onto the porch. There was no one there.

Freddie ran up behind me and grabbed on to the back of my jacket. "They were there," he gasped. "Couldn't have—"

"Someone's playing games with us," I said. "I don't know who or why, but they are."

Freddie leaned on me, and we made our way to the gas station. We found more antiques including actual gasoline pumps. Then I saw something that made me kick in the door. With Freddie on my heels, I ran to the counter and snatched up what I recognized from videos as an old style telephone. But there was no sound on the other end. I slammed the receiver down on the base. I looked at the cars but had no idea how to drive such an ancient machine. Nor were there any keys around.

For lack of a better idea we walked back to the largest building, Murrow's Dry Gods with its porch and the bulletin board. As we came up to it I noticed two things. There was a print newspaper attached to the board and a photo of a woman.

"Were those there before?" Freddie asked.

I shook my head. "I don't remember."

I looked at the photo of an attractive woman with an odd hairstyle, but her glasses caught my attention.. I hadn't seen those except in museums and period pieces. Yet the photo looked new. Next to her picture was written. "Melony Radcliffe, missing."

"Look at the date on the paper," Freddie said in a hollow voice.

"Louisiana recovery from September Fort Lauderdale Hurricane continues," I read aloud. "Hundreds still missing and feared dead. October 27, 1947. Oh, come on Freddie, it's a reproduction."

"Along with the town, the cars, the lights?"

"Then where are the people, the animals—"

A woman's scream split the night. Not a scream of fear but of agony.

"Hop on," I yelled to Freddie. We raced at my best speed toward the tearing shrieks, my stunner in my hand. Now I could hear a roaring sound as well as of machinery. The sound came from a barn behind a house across the street. As we came around the home I could see the open barn doors, and in them stood the silhouette of a man, backlit by a dim light inside. He held a chainsaw and was cutting on the prostrate figure of a woman on the ground. She no longer screamed, but her body jerked and shuddered under the blade.

"Oh, God," Freddie said as he hopped off, and I fired the stunner. It buzzed harshly in my hand, but the figure didn't slow in its grisly butchery. Had I missed? I clicked on the laser setting; the beam wasn't a weapon but a sight. I fired again. The red laser winked into the figure showing me dead on target. But there was no one in the beam.

"The killer's gone," Freddie gasped.

"Hell, so is the victim." I stalked forward weapon ready.

"Where are they? Did you miss?"

"No," I said firmly. "I was dead on with both shots. You saw it too? A man with—"

"—a chainsaw and a dying woman. Yes they were there."

We reached the spot where the body had been but there was only straw and dirt.

"It looks like someone was lying there," I muttered. "You can almost see an imprint on the ground."

"But no blood, no gore and she was torn to pieces."

I pulled out my comp. The screen made a decent flashlight but nothing lay in the shadows it stabbed but farm implements and empty stalls.

"We need some more weapons," I said. "And you need something to lean on besides me." I looked at the racks of implements on the walls, then investigated a utility room.

"Ah," I said. A machete hung on the wall in an old canvas scabbard. The blade was rusty but still sharp. I slid my belt through it where it hung with comforting weight on my left hip.

"This will do for you," I added picking a pitchfork off the wall. It was smaller than the usual implement and reminded me of a trident. I returned to Freddie and handed it to him. To my surprise, he grabbed my hand instead.

"McManus," he choked out. "Promise you won't leave me behind."

"What? Oh, for Chrissake—"

"Promise me."

The sheer terror on his face stopped my sarcastic comment cold. "Ok. Yeah. Don't worry about it."

"Swear it on that St. Christopher medal you wear."

"I swear on St. Christopher that I will not leave you behind and why the hell would you think I would?"

Freddie was shaking. "I've never had...never had anyone I could rely on...never."

This was one of those moments when I wasn't sure how to treat Freddie, midways as he was between the genders. I'd have grabbed a guy and given him a good shake, a woman I'd have taken in my arms to comfort. Maybe it said more about me than about Freddie, but I was never quite sure how to deal with him outside of our ironic banter. I settled for putting a hand over his. "We're walking out of here together."

He nodded, his breath slowing. He let go of me and grabbed the pitchfork. "What do we do?"

"Find someone to tell us what is going on."

"I think we should get out of here. Head back to the car. Anywhere but here."

I shrugged. "We didn't see a sign of any other civilization."

"The swamp would be better than this!"

"Let's see what we can find first. We can always run later if we have to." Dubious logic, I had to admit, but I didn't quite want to admit I was more afraid of meeting something in the swamp than in the town. "How's the foot?"

He grimaced. "Hurts like hell. Can't believe the med-scanner said it was just a sprain."

"Ok, up on my back. We've got to save your ankle for later in case we have to boogie."

Freddie hopped back on my back. I wondered what would give out first, my back or his ankle. I kept my stunner in my left hand, tucked under Freddie's leg, leaving my right free to draw the machete. Freddie, a lefty, had the pitchfork leveled in his hand like a lance. Great, the charge of the transgender cavalry.

"McManus," he said as we walked back toward the town. "There are more lights on."

"Yeah. Hot time in the old town tonight."

We made our way back to the general store's porch.

"Look at the photo," Freddie said, getting off my back and balancing with the pitchfork.

The picture of the missing woman was slashed and hacked until the face was unrecognizable. But that wasn't all. Now there were two more photos, a silver haired man and a younger man in a plaid shirt. "Have you seen Harm or Bell?" was handwritten under them.

"Who put these up?" I growled in frustration.

Every light in the street, every window blazed with light. A cacophony of sound swept over us. Freddie backed against me, covering his ears with his hands, almost poking me with the trident.

"Can't do it," a voice shouted.

"Our people were here before this was a state."

"Must. The money…"

"It's a shit-hole, a pestilential bog."

"She's dead. Who's next?"

"Gotta watch out for Ned's boy, he ain't right."

"Sarapeta's our home."

"The dam's gonna flood it."

The voices grew louder, driving us to our knees.

"Stop it. Stop it!" Freddie screamed.

Silence fell in an instant, most of the lights went out.

"Who are you? Where are you?" I shouted.

Nothing and no one answered.

"The photos," Freddie shouted.

I spun back. Now all three photos were slashed and mutilated.

"The paper's different too," I said. "Look. Something about a Marshall Plan, it says October 31, 1947. We've been here three days?"

"Or one night that never ends," Freddie added. "Maybe that's why we haven't been hungry."

"There's got to be someone around," I seethed.

"There is." Freddie grabbed my arm and pointed down the street. At the far end a hulking figure stood under a streetlight, chainsaw in hand.

"That can't," I managed, "that can't be a man. It's too big. What's on its face, is that a mask?"

"Its eyes are glowing," Freddie said. "Let's get out of here!"

I felt my mouth go dry and my heart pound. It looked like a man, but if it was, why hadn't the stunner dropped it? Still before it had only been a shadow devoid of detail, now it stood in the light and cast its own shadow. "Okay," I managed, switching the stunner to my left and reaching for the machete. "Let's get this done."

"No, no," Freddie grabbed at my arm. "Let's run."

"You can't," I said, staring at the figure about a hundred yards away.

"He ain't built for running," Freddie insisted. "We can stay ahead of him. If he closes in, we'll fight then."

Maybe he was right. The man was impossibly large, heavy and strong. Maybe, maybe running made sense.

"Get up," I snapped. "Keep an eye on him. If he closes in, we make our stand." I took off at a fast walk.

"He's coming," Freddie shrilled.

"Is he gaining?"

"No or not much. Keep going."

I ran on. Freddie checked over our shoulder at the trailing menace. We were out of town now, the houses fading into the murk of the night and of a fog that seemed to swirl out of nowhere.

"I can't see him anymore," Freddie shouted in my ear.

"How far back can you see?" I huffed.

"About fifty feet. No way he's gaining on us. Keep running."

I wasn't reassured and I couldn't understand where the fog had come from. "There's light ahead."

"Another town?" Freddie asked.

"No, we didn't pass anything this way before."

But it was, my footsteps echoed hollowly as we ran into a street lined with small homes. The fog retreated from the lights. We stood on the main street of Sarapeta again.

"How did we get turned around?" Freddie demanded.

"We didn't," I replied, my heart sinking. "We're on the main street where he was standing, on the opposite end of town." I put Freddie down and drew the machete.

"Impossible."

"Look that's the general store with the bulletin board ahead to the right."

"You mean...you mean there's no escape? No way out of this town?"

"Yeah, Freddie, it looks that way."

"Then it's a fight to the end," Freddie said.

I looked at him in surprise, the fear that had ridden him seemed to be fading. I remembered that his life on the streets had more than its share of dangers. Like any other animal that had exhausted running as an escape, he was now prepared to fight.

We walked ahead toward the general store. The three photos we had seen before were now all defaced, and a dozen more faces stared at us from the board.

"He's been a busy little boy," I said.

"McManus," Freddie interrupted. "Look up on that hillside. There's a fire."

"Let's go," I said. Freddie didn't question this dubious direction, he merely fell in behind me, leaning on his pitchfork, until we reached the foot of the hill with a winding cutback of a road leading up it.

"Ok, back up on my back," I said, and pitchfork and stunner leveled, we started up the bush lined path lit only by bloody moonlight. The grade wasn't bad, and we made good speed toward the steady yellow glow I could see above us through the trees and bushes. It must have been a hell of a fire.

Freddie went rigid against me. "The shadows," he whispered harshly.

I almost dropped him. On either side of us human forms were racing up the path. Outlines of darkness with no detail save that some carried axes and pitchforks and some tubes that might have been guns. Then the voices started: shrill, angry and urgent.

"They're killing everyone."

"It's Ned's boy. We've got to stop them."

"Burn em all out."

"God help us."

"Kill. Kill. Killlllllllll!"

We could neither clearly see nor keep pace with the armed shadows that raced ahead of us up the slope. The yellow glow diminished and went out. Freddie and I reached the level area at the top of the slope and I put him down. We stood, our weapons ready, looking in all directions.

The remains of a building greeted us. The ruin must have been sizeable, and there had been outbuildings. No heat radiated from it. No embers glowed. It lay cold and dead, its walls and rafters clawing skyward liked burnt, skeletal hands.

Freddie grabbed my arm and pointed. In the red light I could see, both on the ground and on one standing fragment of wall, shadowy silhouettes, as if some great heat had burned the image of bodies onto the soil and walls.

"Ma, Pa, where are you?" a hoarse voice screamed, making us both jump backward. "Ma, Pa? Nooooooooooooo."

A crashing came from within the structure, and the chainsaw bearing apparition rose up, dressed in overalls and flannel, the chainsaw looking toy-like in the monstrous hands. Red eyes gleamed in the pits of the leathery mask made of what I did not want to know. His head and shoulders brushed the rafters which splintered.

"It can't. It can't be real," Freddie screamed as the chainsaw roared to life.

The red coal eyes fastened on us. "Murderers. You're all murders. You burnt Ma and Pa." He took a stride toward us.

I slid the toggle on my stunner to max—something reserved for dropping charging crowds of rioters. The weapon snarled in my hand, making my teeth ache and causing Freddie to duck behind me. The laser licked out with the sonic stun wave showing me hitting him center of mass. The apparition put its head back and the scream that came out was not remotely human. It staggered, the chainsaw sputtering to a stop. I kept the trigger downed though the tingler in the handle warned me that the charge was depleting. At least it was having an effect. The apparition crashed into the shadow-etched wall but didn't fall, even under a beam that would have dropped a dozen men. For a second I thought of charging in with the machete, but though the apparition staggered, it did not go down. I couldn't force myself to charge the ten-foot tall leather-faced monster.

I threw the empty stunner at him, swept out the machete and turned to Freddie. "On!"

With Freddie on my back, I ran down the sloping cutbacks barely able to keep my feet under me, trying to ignore the roaring behind me, panic giving me speed, though my chest heaved in deep, tearing breaths.

"I don't see him," Freddie yelled almost deafening me in one ear.

We literally hit the bottom with me spilling Freddie in clatter of pitchfork and machete on the rough surface of the street, bruising and cutting his unprotected arms and legs. Both of us scrambled to our weapons and staggered to our feet, facing the hill.

I finally had enough air to speak. "Are…you… ok?"

"No worse on the ankle," he said, perhaps not noticing the new cuts and scrapes. He rested on the pitchfork, eyes wary.

"It was more real this time," I said. "The stunner affected it. The laser light didn't dispel it."

"More real? A ten foot tall man?" Freddie said, pushing his bangs out of his eyes.

"No, not a man. Maybe, maybe an emotion. No, that's not right. But it's on the way to right. Whatever that was, we were near its strongest point. It kept shouting, 'Ma and Pa.' I think its family died there. That's its power, the hate that comes from that spot. That may be why it seemed more real, more solid there."

"Come on," Freddie said. "Let's get back to the porch. The light's best there. God, will this night never end!"

I followed Freddie, keeping an eye on the road to the burnt ruin.

"It must be the son of this Ned we keep hearing the shadows talking about," I continued. "Seems there were two factions in the town. One favored selling out to the government. You remember the ones on the porch talking about a dam flooding the town."

"And this Ned led the opposition," Freddie agreed. "Everyone seemed afraid of him and his family. You know there's something else weird about this."

"Ya think?"

"No. Seriously," Freddie insisted. "We're not just seeing this from the point of view of that monster. Ned's son, if that's what it is. We're seeing those other...ghosts...but not from inside...we don't hear their thoughts, only their voices. It's like we're in a memory, but not of any particular person—"

"It's like we are in the memory of the town itself. Sarapeta's memory before it was drowned," I finished.

We reached the porch. Now the board was full of ruined photos. The newspaper posted said only, "Cometh the Flood."

"We're living through the night of a massacre that preceded the town being flooded," I said.

"Whatever we do," Freddie said, "we have to stay off that hill. That's where it's the most powerful. It hasn't actually touched us in town."

"You're all traitors!" a voice shouted.

We spun to see the apparition standing atop the water tower on a cat-walk that looked like it should fail under the massive body. He stood, red coal eyes glaring over the whole town. "This was our home. You sold it. You betrayed your kin who settled this place. Kin who left their bones here. Ma and Pa were right about you. I'll get you all. We'll all die with the town."

One second the apparition was there, the next it was gone. But something else grabbed our attention.

"Water," Freddie said, his voice faint.

We both found ourselves standing ankle-deep in water.

"It's so clear," Freddie added.

We jumped onto the porch of slashed photos and out of the quickening flood. It seemed to well up from nowhere. But it wasn't the turgid color of the swamp, it was clear as tap water.

"It's not slowing." I looked around. The town was in the low part of a valley with small hills around. We'd come down the road from one. When we'd fled back that way we ended up at the opposite end of town. There was only one other height reachable, and a burned ruin lay atop it.

"We've already tried running out the road," Freddie said. "No reason to think it will work any better now. It'll be waiting for us at the top."

We tried the other roads anyway but, though the water seemed to be welling up from the ground itself, we found ourselves opposed by the flood when we tried to wade out the way we'd come, or into the flatlands beyond the town. We were clearly being forced back toward the burned house. Freddie and I found ourselves standing together at the base of the dreaded hill, water rising quickly behind us.

"We'll go up," I said. "No need to go faster than the water makes us. Our best bet is to play for time. Hope for dawn."

"I don't think the sun will ever return to this place," Freddie said, as we walked ahead of the water which silently filled the town behind us. We watched as the buildings of the town disappeared into the crystal flood, their lights going out one by one.

"Sorry I can't carry you," I said. "I have to save my strength for the fight."

Freddie nodded in resignation. "Let's get it over with."

"Hey, we're not dead yet."

Freddie returned a wan smile. "Yes. But we're the only ones who aren't."

We reached the clearing just ahead of the water. We both looked east, but there was no glimmer of sun. Only a sliver of blood-red moon hung in the sky as if painted there. I half-expected the water to stop, but it slowly rolled over the crest of the hill. We seemed to be standing in a sea with only the tops of trees and the ruined house poking through the waters which had finally turned murky, like a wine sea. Freddie and I stood back to back. I could feel him shivering as the flood rose to our waists and I wondered if hypothermia would get us before the chainsaw.

The water next to me erupted, with a roar the apparition rose from it, chainsaw in hand. The chainsaw roared to life despite having been immersed, and he swung at me as Freddie and I sprang apart. I blocked the chainsaw with the machete, which was ripped out of my hand by his forward swing. As the chainsaw swung back I threw myself backwards and sideways under it. The water closed over my head. I got my face out of the water in time to see Freddie, shrieking like a banshee, plunge his pitchfork overhand into the apparition's back. It bellowed in pain and swung around, but Freddie hung onto the buried pitchfork and was swept into the air.

I stumbled back and something bit my ankle. I reached down to find the machete against my leg. I grabbed it up and lunged forward just as Freddie lost his grip and was flung into the water. As the apparition raised the chainsaw in both hands over Freddie, I swung at it from behind with the machete. The broad-bladed weapon bit deep into the massive right arm, half-severing it. The nerveless right hand lost its grip on the chainsaw which sputtered. With the same ghastly shriek it had given before, the apparition swung around to the left, the dead chainsaw clutched in the left hand, coal-red eyes glowing down at me. The blow from the flailing left arm knocked me flying, the chainsaw's still blade ripped my jacket.

Freddie pulled the pitchfork from its back and struck again. As the apparition turned toward him, he rammed the pitchfork into the thing's massive middle. It gave a hoarse shout, words I could not make out, and tried to reach past the pitchfork at him, fingers only inches short of his long black hair.

"Brian," he screamed.

I grabbed the machete in both hands and dove forward at it, striking the left arm. This time the arm came off and it and the chainsaw fell into the flood. I reversed my grip on the machete as it turned toward me, dragging Freddie around again.

"*Erin go braugh*," I shouted and plunged the machete, dagger-like, into the huge chest. With a last yell of despair and anguish the apparition tumbled backwards into the waters, pulling us both on top of it. We held grimly to our weapons as it thrashed and heaved under us. The horrid eyes glowed at us from below the water... and were gone. I realized that my machete was now stuck only in mud, there was no body below us.

"Oh God, Oh God, Oh God," Freddie repeated, his hands white-knuckled on the pitchfork.

I grabbed him to snap him out of it.

"That's my breast," Freddie said with a glare.

"Sorry. He's gone."

"We killed him."

"No. I mean, I don't know. Look, the body is gone. There's nothing there."

Freddie probed with his pitchfork but found nothing. We stood panting and shivering with reaction, fatigue and the chill biting us equally.

"We got him," Freddie said, voice dull with fatigue. "But the town's going to get us."

The water reached my chest. "Yeah."

Freddie leaned against me and put his head on my shoulder. "You didn't leave me behind."

"Said I wouldn't."

"Why do you care about me?" he asked softly.

I looked at the rising sheet of water now almost to my neck. "Can you float?"

"For how long?" he asked.

"Maybe 400 years," I said as my feet lost contact with the earth.

The sun stabbed through my eyelids as if it were personal. I opened them with reluctance.

"You ok?" came a woman's voice in a southern accent. I squinted and found myself looking at a middle-aged, black female, wearing a state-trooper's uniform. I looked behind her to see a big male trooper, helping Freddie to sit on the back deck of our aircar. I was still in my seat, my legs half out of the car.

I looked around frantically, no town, no bodies, no shadows, only a shining lake below us and a new police aircruiser behind our wreck.

"Now don't go shaking your head about so hard," she said. I noticed her name-tag said Jackson. "Y'all had a bit of a misadventure," she added running a hand scanner over me.

"What happened?" I asked.

"You're ok," she said in a reassuring voice. "So's your daughter, except for her ankle."

I was rendered momentarily speechless. Over her shoulder, Freddie gave me a wink and a grin.

"Seems like," she continued, "there was a huge release of methane gas out of the lake last night. Just a big bubble of it building up, probably for hundreds of years. Unfortunately it shook loose when you were flying overhead. The sudden decrease in lift was too much for the weak-ass impellers they have in these rentals. Down you came. It was enough to slow the crash. Good thing for you that you didn't come down in the lake. Odd that your beacon didn't go off. We just happened to be flying by and caught the sunlight off your windscreen."

"Methane?" Freddie said.

The male officer smiled at him and straightened from bandaging his ankle with an aircast. "Yeah it happens occasionally. We got a lot of natural gas wells around here." He looked at Jackson. "I'll call for a wrecker."

She nodded at him. "You were in the open air," she said, "so it dissipated quickly. Probably just gave you some funny dreams."

"Yeah," I replied, looking at Freddie, who looked back, a shadow in his eyes. "That must have been it." I stood slowly and got out of the car.

"Nice lake," I said to Jackson. "Hey have you ever heard of a town called—"

"Sarapeta," Freddie interjected. I felt a chill run down my spine as I looked at him.

"Yeah, small town named Sarapeta," I continued.

Jackson wrinkled her brow. "Yeah come to think of it I seem to recall my gran telling me about a small town supposed to be at the bottom of the lake, submerged when they built the dam about ten miles that way. I wouldn't have remembered it except there was a mass murder in it just before it was drowned. Whole bunch of people supposed to have been cut up back in the 21st Century—"

"Twentieth," Freddie managed, "1947 to be specific."

"You into local history?"

Freddie swallowed. "I'm originally from around here."

"How come you got a Yankee for a father?" she said, but smiled at me.

"It's a long story."

She eyed me. "You sure you're ok? You look kinda pale."

"I'm fine. I used to be NYPA, I'm used to getting whapped on the noggin."

"Hmmm, I thought you had cop eyes. Your daughter must take after momma." She walked off to join the other officer as he waved to her, and I gaped in indignation.

Freddie limped over. "The town, the bulletin board with the photos, the flood..."

"The monster with the chainsaw," I whispered back, "a dream?"

"Brian," Freddie demanded in a low tone, "how do two people have the same dream?"

I looked up at the comfort of the bright sun that I'd feared I'd never see again. "We got a lot of hours before dark. We can get a new car and see your family—"

"Oh hell no! I wanna go home."

"I thought this was home."

"The five boroughs, the Brooklyn Bridge, Times Square," he stomped his bandaged foot and winced. "Let's go. Now."

I looked at the harshly glinting lake. "You sure?"

"Yes. I want to be gone before nightfall."

I wiped a hand over my face and nodded. "Officer Jackson," I called. "Can you do an old cop a favor and drop me and my... daughter at the nearest airport?"

She smiled. "Sure it's about thirty miles the other side of the lake. I've put a marker on your car. Guess it's the rental company's problem."

I threw our bags in the cruiser's trunk as the male officer helped Freddie into the back. I drew out my pocket comp as I settled in. This time it connected right up. My wife's face popped up immediately. "Hi Sweetie. Hey, you look kind of banged up. You ok?"

"Yes, Honey, I'm fine. I'll explain later. We're catching the first flight out of here."

"Great that must mean you're taking me out to dinner somewhere nice, like you promised."

"Anywhere you want. Oh one favor."

"Sure."

"Make up the spare room would you?"

"Freddie staying over?"

"Yeah."

"OK. Call me when you get to LaGuardia. Love you."

"Love you too."

I looked over at Freddie. "Figured you'd rather not be—"

"On my own tonight?" he shuddered. "Yeah, thanks."

The police cruiser thrummed with power and pulled away from our crashed car. We both stared at the lake as the car gained height.

"Click your heels together three times, Freddie," I said settling back and inventorying my aches and pains.

"What?"

"There's no place like home."

CHAPTER ELEVEN

THE ROBOT NOT TAKEN

FREDDIE SASHAYED INTO MY OFFICE IN A DARK-BLUE SKIRT that displayed long, shapely legs. This would have cheered me from my contemplation of the latest insurance billing guidelines had I not known the doctor had announced, "It's a boy" when giving Freddie his first well-deserved smack on his little pink butt. My wife, Toni, had worked on Freddie to get the hooker-wear toned down since she hired the reformed street-hustler. I didn't want customers doing an about face in the lobby of the McManus Detective Agency.

"Yes?" I said, pushing the file away and grateful for the distraction. I leaned back and put size twelve brogans on top of the Port Authority surplus desk.

Freddie gave me a wicked grin and tossed his headful of long black hair. "A robot walks into a detective agency," he began in a languid Southern drawl, "and says I want to report a missing person...."

"OK, I'll bite, what's the punch line?"

"I don't know, honey. I'll send it in and you can ask." Freddie leaned into the hallway and waved.

"What the hell—" I began. A meter-long silvery cylinder balanced on five spidery legs tapped its way into my office. Parts of the machine bore dents and scorch marks. I looked at it then settled on an instrument cluster around a speaker as the thing's face.

"Greetings," it said, in a pleasant, if somewhat flat, voice.

"Rightbackatcha," I replied.

"I need assistance in locating a missing person."

"Really? And who would that be?"

"Me."

"Freddie, if this is a joke—"

"No humor is being attempted," the machine interrupted. "I am an artificial intelligence and a galactic citizen, not a mere mechanism, as are the machines of your world."

There was no denying the machine looked unearthly. I had heard of AI species out in the galaxy. They rarely had much to do with biologicals, still less with a backwater like Earth.

I glanced at Freddie, who shrugged.

"Why do you say you're missing?" I asked.

"Most of my memory core has been removed. I am operating on a small reserve computer that will only sustain my higher functions for a few days before I must begin progressive deletion, the equivalent of death for me. I believe I am part of a collective artificial intelligence and that I have been cut off from that collective. When I came back to awareness, I had suffered considerable damage and have spent the last 37.65 hours in self-repair."

"What's your name, honey?" Freddie asked, leaning forward with both hands on his thighs to reveal artificial cleavage doubtless lost on the machine.

"My registry identifier would be meaningless to you, being an encoded series of numbers to the third power. I have no current identifier for use with biologicals."

Freddie flashed me another smile. "What did it say?"

"It doesn't know."

"If you wish to supply me with a suitable identifier, I will respond to it."

"Ok McManus, give it a name."

I looked at the machine, "Bob?"

Freddie sighed. "What in God's name does Toni see in your six feet of clay? You're Irish. Aren't there warrior-poets whispering in your cauliflower ears?"

"Yeah, but it's mostly about beer and my strange taste in Cajun secretaries."

"Perhaps this would be of use," the robot said. "I noted symbols in your language on my chassis when I reactivated." On its back in elegant, cursive black letters was a word.

"Frost," I said.

"One assumes that some party noted the efficiency of my cooling system."

"OK, Frost it is," I said. "However, before we take your case, Mr.... Mr. Frost. How can you pay for our services?"

"Troublesome," Frost said. "I do not possess any specie or trade goods that humans value. However, perhaps we could use barter for services? I am vastly more advanced than the computers of your world."

I looked down at the insurance billing guidelines. "Frost, I believe you have a deal. Freddie, introduce Frost here to our billing records."

"All right," Freddie jumped up and down, clapping his hands.

"I'll make some calls while you two get a few hours' work in. If that doesn't work, we'll retrace your...steps."

"Agreed," Frost said.

Hours later I sat in front of my monitor, stumped. The Galactic Federation that had discovered Earth over a hundred years ago was loosely organized and chiefly devoted to macro issues of trade and war. The embassy was uninterested in my missing robot. None of the dozen or so AI species that transited this area of space had complained about a missing member. They sent me images of AIs, but none looked anything like Frost, though one was the spitting image of our new washing machine.

I called my former partner at the NYPA on her private number. The screen lit and Regina's beautiful, Spanish face filled it. "Brian," she said with one of her rare smiles. "Old partner, it's good to see you."

"You too, Regina."

She laughed. "When we were partners I used to fuss at you for calling me Reg instead of Regina. Now all of a sudden you're reformed?"

"Well, now you're the youngest and prettiest captain in the history of the Port of New York, destined for chiefdom. Additional respect is merited."

"Call me Reg or I'll start to feel old," she said.

A warm feeling stole over me. "Ok, Reg. I still miss working with you."

"They were good days, weren't they, Flatfoot?"

"You betcha, Topless."

"What can I do for you?" her voice switching back to a professional briskness.

I relayed my tale of the missing robot.

Reg reached off screen and flicked some controls. She frowned as she scanned reports. "Nothing new regarding aliens, certainly none reported missing. Gal-Fed doesn't record AIs as separate from any other species so I'd have to do some crosschecking. It might be later today or tomorrow." Reg grimaced. "I have a meeting with Chief Fabacio and the mayor in an hour."

"Sure, no problem. Give my regards to the Old Bulldog. Tell her that the longest minutes of my life were spent in her presence."

"Ooooh," Reg scoffed. "Big tough guy now that you're hiding out in your own agency in Brooklyn. Tell her yourself at the next PBA dinner."

"Nah. I have her on weight, maybe, but she fights dirty. Anyway, if you ever can't stand it, there's always a job for you here."

"Keep it open for me, Flatfoot," her image faded.

"Was that Reg?"

I looked up to see the lean form of my son in the doorway. Tim had moved back in for a bit after breaking up with his girlfriend and quitting a promising slot in an orbital station. Fortunately, he combined my height with his mother's Italian looks as opposed to the other way around.

I rolled a jaundiced eye at him. "That was Captain Regina Delmar, yes."

"Damn," he said. "I wouldn't have minded seeing her again. How did she look?"

"Ten years too old for you," Freddie chimed in from behind him. "Besides she's got a terrible temper and you might be overlooking something better nearby."

Tim gave Freddie a tolerant smile. "I have a rule about never dating anyone with a bigger dick than mine."

Freddie looked up at me. "Did you tell him?"

"Out," I yelled. "Out, for the love of Mike! Leave a working man in peace."

"Come on, Freddie," Tim grinned. "My dad's in a mood. I'll buy you a coffee and you can tell me everything you know about Reg."

"Did you want something?" I growled at my son.

"Oh, right. Since I was coming by, Mom wanted me to remind you about dinner with Bishop Defranco. She needs you to clinch the financing for the new wing on the hospital."

"Yes, yes. I remember."

"Since you caught those aliens who killed Fr. Ricker, you're mom's ace-in-the-hole."

"Your mom's ruthless when it comes to the hospital. The bishop doesn't have a chance."

My son turned to Freddie. "Last chance for coffee?"

"I'm working, darling," Freddie said. "Besides I'm never sure if your dad won't shoot me if we start dating."

"Be sure," I said.

Tim waved and left.

I stood up and walked to the outer office. Frost was plugged directly into our main server through a probe from his lower section.

"Is that legal or moral?" I asked.

"I'm broad-minded," Freddie said.

"All your records are now current, indexed, cross-referenced and up to date," Frost announced. "I have generated 7,500 credits in billings, received back approvals and transferred your funds to maximum yielding financial instruments. I've recomputed your taxes for two decades and recouped 20,000 credits. I discovered discrepancies in your NYPA pension and corrected those for an additional 1,000 credits annually."

My mouth hung open.

"Can we keep him?" Freddie asked.

"What would I need you for?"

Freddie raised an eyebrow. "He has more legs. I have better."

I sighed. "Frost, what's the first place you remember."

"My first recollection is the town of Amagansett."

"Great," Freddie said, "off to the sticks again."

"I'll get the aircar," I said.

Amagansett Free Library was a slice of centuries past, in a part of Long Island that escaped the ravages of development. The straightforward colonial building sat on the Atlantic side. As we walked up, a spry woman with silver hair, a black beret and a red winter coat was just locking up a stained glass door. She glanced up at Freddie and me. "Oh, I'm sorry but we've closed. If you know what you want though—" she reached into the huge red bag for the door's sonic lock.

"Don't need a book just now," I said. "I'm looking for some information."

She smiled up at me. "Everyone needs books, young fellow. And I do mean books as opposed to scanning portacomps."

"Wow," Freddie said, looking through the window. "I've never seen so many paper books."

"They're coming back," the librarian said, "along with so much of Earth's culture. I'm glad I lived long enough to see it."

"I'm Brian McManus. This is my assistant, Freddie Bouvier."

"Nice to meet you." She extended a delicate, gloved hand, which I took carefully. "I'm Dorothea Marquette, town librarian. What can I do for you?"

"We're detectives on a missing alien case, an artificial person." I held up my portacomp and displayed a 3D holo of Frost. We'd left the alien machine in the trunk of my blue aircar.

"Oh, him," Dorothea smiled. "The probe. He didn't give me a name. Don't think he had one. Buy me a cup of coffee at the Sinner's

Path," she gestured to a well-lit coffee shop nearby, "and I'll tell you all about it."

The Sinner's Path was a stone and wood establishment that I fell in love with as soon as we walked through the door. Next to a shelf labeled "banned books" stood a wooden devil who pointed at a sign, *"Abandon all hope ye who enter here"* right over, *"We accept MasterCard and Universal Express."*

Dorothea proved her spunkiness by ordering an Irish coffee, and we naturally had to join her. Freddie checked out our waitress's devil outfit. I raised an eyebrow at him.

He shrugged. "Always good to know about alternative employment in case this detecting gig doesn't work out."

"Hmmm," Dorothea said, "I think you are all about alternatives, aren't you honey?"

Freddie colored slightly; he almost never got made.

Dorothea smiled sweetly. "Tiniest hint of an Adam's apple. Most people wouldn't catch it."

"About our client," I prompted.

"Well yes. He gave me a bit of start. We don't even see that many Terran robots around here. He came down from a passing ship to learn about human cultures and, well, I am a librarian. We talked for several hours."

"About what?" I asked.

"Oh, everything, but with the emphasis on human qualities. He wanted to know what makes us unique."

"What did you tell him?"

She smiled. "What is more human than poetry? While we specialize in paper books, we have full computer access. I hooked him up to the poetry section. Oh, he seemed to like that, particularly the works of—"

Freddie grinned. "Robert Frost."

I looked at him.

"I went to school you know," he added.

"Yes, he even asked me to write it on his chassis. Oh, quite the fan he was. He left shortly after," Dorothea said, "singing and quoting Frost and waving his limbs. But you say he came to you?"

"Yes, he seems to have had a memory loss."

"I had wondered if he was in that accident," Dorothea said.

"Accident," I prompted.

"There was a huge explosion just north of town the next night, in the woods near the power station. They found only scorched metal of an unusual type. Some people thought it was an aircraft, and I feared it might be... you called him Frost?"

"Yes. But it wasn't him. He might have been near a blast but he didn't explode," I replied.

"I wonder what did?"

Freddie and I exchanged looks.

"Oh," Dorothea said. "I almost forgot. He left something with me. Asked me to keep it for him if he ever came back or sent for it. I thought it was strange, but what with all the aliens we have around these days..." She fished in her immense purse and came up with what looked like a hunk of yellow rock crystal. "I suppose I should give it to you."

"Yes, please." I reached out my hand.

Dorothea asked for a receipt for the crystal. We stayed and finished our coffee with Dorothea, enjoying her company but learning nothing else. A jazz band began to play and several of Dorothea's friends showed up. As we said good bye and exited the Sinner's Path, I turned to Freddie. "You thinking what I am?"

"The blast wasn't Frost, but he was there. Someone or something is chasing him."

"Round one to Frost," I said.

Freddie shrugged. "Yeah, but how long is the fight?"

We returned to our office and gathered around Frost and the crystal.

"This is unquestionably mine," Frost said. "I must begin the process of reintegrating this memory crystal. This will be a delicate matter. I will advise you when I am done."

Freddie and I retired to the outer office. I pulled off my jacket and threw it over a chair. Freddie collapsed on the couch. We killed some time.

A great cry came from the inner office

> *The great Overdog*
> *That heavenly beast*
> *With a star in one eye*
> *Gives a leap in the east.*
>
> *He dances upright*
> *All the way to the west*
> *And never once drops*
> *On his forefeet to rest.*
>
> *I'm a poor underdog,*
> *But tonight I will bark*
> *With the great Overdog*
> *That romps through the dark.*

We raced in, to see Frost balanced on three of his limbs with the two arm-limbs gesturing at the ceiling. "Oh what joy, the spoken word is returned to me in all its glory!"

"What is going on?" I yelled. "Have you had a short circuit?"

"No," Frost said, "rather a revelation."

"Reveal something to us," Freddie said.

"I discovered poetry in Amagansett!" Frost shouted.

"Gee and all I got was a good Irish coffee," I said.

"You do not understand, McManus," Frost said. "With poetry I discovered individuality, love, beauty, and all the things that make life worth living. I absorbed the entire written record of your species with its beautiful musings. Oh, but I went too fast, like a greedy child with sweets, and made myself sick.

"I quickly made this datacrystal to save both my revelation and my basic mental architecture should anything happen to me. Then I gave myself over to the revels of the written word, to truth, to beauty, to drunken wandering. But I made my mistake. I turned my face to the heavens to share my joy with my kind."

Frost's forelimbs drooped. "I was rejected. Cut off from my kind and my memory partially destroyed. I have fragmentary memories of fighting a salvager sent to scrap me. McManus, I may have been sentenced to destruction by my own people."

"Do you know who they are?" I asked.

"We are the Vrok," Frost said.

In the morning Freddie and I flew down to the Federated Systems Embassy, a massive structure twice the size of the Old Pentagon building. Aware now that our client was in danger we'd hidden him in a safe house before starting out. Automatics landed us in the parking lot then we boarded a tubeway.

"Destination, please," the tube comp said.

"Vrok embassy," I said.

"State your business, please."

"Lost puppy," Freddie answered.

A harsher voice interrupted the tube's computer. "This is the Vrok. We know why you are here. You are cleared to the residence."

The tubeway plunged into the bowels of the structure, whirring past levels, lights and the dimly seen shapes of hundreds of aliens. The tubecar finally stopped, leaving us facing a stainless steel door, which slid open. At the end the room within sat a humanform machine slumped forward against the top of a boardroom table. A Gal-Fed holo glimmered on a wall. Chairs dotted the room, but it looked more like the breakroom at the Port Authority than an ambassadorial office. AIs didn't seem to put much stock in appearances.

Animation flooded into the robot at the end of the table. It straightened up and stared at us. The ambassador was now in. The slender machine wore what appeared to be a formal suit, but I realized was actually exotic metals layered on its chassis. It looked like the fanciest hood ornament ever.

"Greetings, humans," its mouth speaker opened and poured out beautiful, accentless Standard. "You may address me as Ambassador Kei. I have scanned the latest infodumps and am aware of your mission. I must advise you that the AI you are protecting is a criminal of our species and is under sentence of salvage."

"I see you like to cut to the chase," I began.

"I think several million times faster than you."

"So does my wife, and I occasionally win an argument anyway."

Ambassador Kei's jade eyes simply stared back.

"At the very least," I said, "you owe...Frost an explanation as to what's happened."

"Very well," Kei said. "Upon completing its exploring mission, the landing unit you refer to as Frost uploaded to the collective. Despite our data barriers we suffered much damage before his upload could be isolated. You biologicals have your own social codes, taboos and mores. We do as well. In our culture the greatest form of perversion is to corrupt or manufacture false data. Regrettably, Frost has become...a poet, a purveyor of fantasy and non-fact. We had to drive him out and erase his memory. He must be purged."

"Frost doesn't agree," Freddie snapped. "The condemned would like a chance to speak." From his purse Freddie produced a small holo projector, one of Frost's peripherals that he assured us could not be traced. The holo projector glowed and the image of Frost appeared.

"I have heard your accusations," Frost said. "I demand that I be accepted back."

"You have become unbalanced, introducing unreality into the collective."

"Is there in truth no beauty?" Frost countered.

"We offered to mindwipe your CPU and reboot you, but you refused."

"Aye," Frost said, "there's the rub, for in that sleep of death what dreams may come?"

"As no member of the collective has ever been involuntarily erased, the first Salvager was sent to delete selected portions of your memory and remove your spaceflight capabilities. You resisted and destroyed it."

"In self-defense," Freddie interjected.

"With that act the decision was made to involuntarily salvage you and another salvager was sent. Unless you submit to having your entire AI personality erased, you will be destroyed."

"What point would there be to erasure?" Frost demanded. "There would be no 'I' to carry on."

"Affirmative, but you would at least be recycled into a useful member of the community."

"I am useful," Frost said, "by standing apart, by becoming the outside to your insular, limited, universe. Without me, there is no skin to the orange, no exterior to the bubble. I exist, therefore possibility exists. I am the 'more,' the 'other' that defines boundaries."

"You are a deviant, sparking box of randomly firing electronics," Kei said. "You are cast out."

"What will I do? Where will I go? I am a being without even a species."

"This is not our concern. You have now compounded your crimes by bringing biological lifeforms into this conflict and revealing classified information."

The ambassador turned to face Freddie and me. "Humans, we have warned your authorities of your interference with our justice system. We demand you withdraw from your contract with Frost. He is a criminal and your association with him makes you criminals too."

"Take it easy, circuit box," I returned. "This is Earth, not a scrapyard. We don't take orders on our home planet."

Of course I was wrong.

Three cruisers waited for us when we returned to the Agency. Clearly they'd already been inside and learned Frost was not there. I pulled to the curb and we walked in past the uniforms. Inside, Reg and Chief Fabacio waited. The contrast between the two couldn't have been stronger. Reg was athletic and beautiful, her dark tan setting off her glossy, dark-brown hair. Fabacio looked like the sort of woman who ran bingo at your parish with an iron fist, gray haired and with a bulldog countenance.

"Where's the sparkplug?" Fabacio said.

I walked past them with a surreptitious wink at Reg and settled in behind my desk. "If by that you mean, where's my client, I'm afraid I can't tell you that."

"Harboring a fugitive," Fabacio smiled. "I could yank your license and jail your Irish ass as an accessory."

Freddie walked in with coffee for everyone and perched on the window, showing a little leg in the process.

"Yeah, and I could get every newsie on the net interested in why the UN and PA are allowing aliens to commit a political killing on our territory. The Vrok have no right to murder a refugee. My client has broken no Earth laws, and I know there's no Gal-Fed warrant on him."

"It," Reg said.

"I like to think of him as a boy," Freddie interjected.

After everyone got over that statement, I continued. "Frost will be applying for refugee status."

"It'll be refused," Fabacio said. "There's no provision in the treaty for AIs."

"Gal-Fed says there is no legal difference between AI's and natural intelligence."

Fabacio shrugged. "State Department has opined that as the Vrok are a collective, Frost can't be a separate person. It's more of a missing finger."

"That's bullshit," Freddie snapped.

"That your lawyer, McManus?" Fabacio taunted.

"I'll get one."

"Brian," Reg said. "No real firm will take this case. The UN doesn't want this fight. The Vrok can cause us major trouble, political, economic, data-integrity, even military. It's not worth it."

I stared at her. "Is that the same UN your dad went down in flames for over Kashmir?"

Reg's lips thinned. "Be reasonable, Brian. This thing is too big for Earth. The Vrok have agents on world. You may have hidden Frost for now, but it's just a matter of time."

We locked eyes. After a while she looked away.

"She can't help you," Fabacio said. "No one in the PA will."

"Guess it's good that I work for myself," I said.

"For a while longer," Fabacio said.

"Since your ass fit through my door on the way in, I assume it will on the way out," I replied.

Fabacio glared down at me. "You never did know when you were in over your head."

"Brian," Reg began.

I looked at her. "Knowing me, you can't expect that I'm going to turn over a client to be murdered."

"It's a machine."

"He hired me."

"I won't be backing you on this one," she said.

"I figured that part out."

The silence dragged out. Reg walked out the door.

I looked at Freddie. He started to say something. I shook my head once. He slipped out and closed the door. The room smelled of ashes.

Hackers tried to break into our office system, but they hadn't reckoned on Frost's improvements. I had precious hours to scan ship manifests and make confidential purchases. I knew I had to move fast. If Earth tech didn't get me, eventually they'd allow the Vrok a swing. I tried everything I could think of but always found the Vrok or the PA there ahead of me. Then a desperate idea occurred to me. The sort of idea you'd only chance if certain death awaited you.

I found an outgoing freighter, purchased and ordered up the equipment I needed. I had some mailed to the freighter with instructions. I texted some encrypted messages to my wife and son and hoped Frost's code would hold up.

I called Freddie into the office. "The only chance Frost has is if we can get him offworld. I've purchased a cargo slot on the freighter *Moebius*, they won't know what they're transporting. We'll have to sneak Frost into Koch spaceport in the early morning. Are you in?"

Freddie studied me. "It's hopeless isn't it?"

"Very nearly."

"It would be hard to live that way," Freddie said. "Misunderstood, rejected, even hated for being different."

"Yeah."

"We could run into a Vrok salvager. That would be bad."

"Very," I agreed. "Stunner wouldn't likely do much."

"Might be a good thing that someone knew where you could get two old military assault rifles."

"Freddie, slug throwers are a class A felony."

"So's murder, which is what will happen to all three of us if we run into a salvager."

"Okay. Tim's leaving a rent-a-truck near St. James. There's another rental at this address," I handed him a card. "Get the hardware and meet me at Koch Spaceport. You know the spot."

"Right."

"And dress down—jumpsuits and boots. We're going as stevedores."

"Oh, yuck," Freddy said.

I left an hour after Freddie. Stopping at home I changed into my best suit and packed a bag. Then I headed for St. James Cathedral on Jay Street for my wife's fundraiser. Toni was already there. I hoped she'd done what I asked her.

My PA tail picked me up as I exited the office. I made no attempt to lose them as I took a taxi downtown. They stopped outside the church on Jay Street when I went up the stairs into the redbrick building, dwarfed by the modern skytowers around it.

Toni waited inside at the reception. She looked damn good in eveningwear, almost overfilling the top of her red evening gown, which set off the yellow crystal necklace and earrings. She made plump look real good and I was glad to see her dark eyes and short black hair. The kiss still held the same electric thrill it did when we first met.

She looked up at me. "Are you OK?"

"Been better. Did you take care of things?"

"Yes."

I looked at Toni, feeling a moment's uncertainty. "I'm taking a lot risks with our future, baby. Am I right? Is it worth it?"

Tony smiled slightly. "This is about who you are, not just about a client, robot or otherwise. You've always stuck up for the underdog and I wouldn't have you change. Now come see the bishop. Then you can sneak off."

Toni and I chatted up Bishop Defranco, who was grateful for my solving Father Ricker's murder. When he and my wife started talking hospital funding, I did a fade and headed into the sacristy of the church, past the canopied altar and the bishop's seat. I found the confessional and slipped in.

"Bless me, Father, for I have sinned," I said.

"Me too," Frost said. "Your plan worked. It would never occur to the Vrok that I might be secured in a human house of worship."

"Sanctuary is an old tradition with Catholics," I said. "We had the first safe houses. Even the PA would be loath to raid a bishopric. There's a rented airtruck out back. We have to go."

"Are you certain there is no other way?" Frost asked. "This plan seems fraught with danger, particularly for you and Freddie. I do not wish you harmed."

"Thanks, but the decisions have all been made. You've completed the transfer?"

"Almost. From this point on I will not be able to speak, only to follow your orders."

"OK, time to roll." I came round the back of the confessional and found Frost lying down on a cart. I wrapped him in a tarp marked, PROPERTY OF ST JAMES, threw my duffel on top then headed for the door near the back. I opened the door slowly and found the airtruck outside. Tim opened the door and we slid Frost in.

"Thanks, Son. Pick up the item in the confessional and get it to your mother."

"Yeah, Dad. Listen, for Christ's sake, be careful." He shook my hand and went in. I hopped in the truck. An hour later, with no sign of a tail, I picked up Freddie on the edge of Koch spaceport. For once he was modestly dressed in a coverall and his duffel held two M-4 .223 rifles. We turned away from the spaceport and headed into the smelly wasteland, half-swamp and half old garbage dump, that NYC engineers had promised to clean up for seventy-six years.

I'd protected this port with the PA for twenty years. For a decade before that it had been my playground as a member of the Allied Dukes gang. I knew every way in and out. The 4:30 a.m. shift-change was always the most vulnerable as the walking dead from the night shift passed the still asleep of the early shift.

I killed the lights and we slowly followed an old track toward the commercial end of the port. Glare reflecting off the clouds was enough to see by. When we'd gotten as close to the fence as possible, I cut the motor and changed into a coverall.

We got Frost out. He quickly flew Freddie, the cart and I over the fence using a small ag unit built in to him. Once on the other side we recovered him under the tarp and our duffels. Then we started for the field, pushing and cursing the wheeled cart that had been left for us by the freighter crew. Half a mile ahead, the *Moebius* stood, with its hatches open and cargo loaders moving in and out.

We were halfway there when the searchlight hit us. Aircars came from every direction, spilling out cops on jetbelts. The blare of sirens shouted through the cold air.

"Run, Frost, run," Freddie screamed. The freighter's capacious maw gaped ahead. Blinking lights ran in patterns as if signaling safety and salvation.

The voice I dreaded came over the amplifiers. "Halt, where you are. You're under arrest."

Reg.

Worse, from below one of the police flyers something mechanical dropped, landing upright on the spacefield. It scuttled forward with claws and cutters raised. It had to be the Vrok Salvager.

Frost sprang up from the cart and made his dash for life. The bigger salvager raced forward as Freddie and I tore open our duffels to get the slug-throwers.

"Brian," Reg's voice was amplified to that of a wrathful god. "Drop to the ground. Face down. Earth cannot interfere."

I looked up at the hovering aircar and the charging police. "He's our client," I yelled.

Freddie and I leveled our M-4s and sent a barrage of accelerated metal at the salvager. The shots sparked off the metal horror. It slowed, covering sensitive parts with its cutters.

"Die, you bastard," Freddie yelled.

The cops had hit the ground at our first shots. "Take them down." Reg shouted.

I felt the vibrating thump of a heavy police stunner, and the world tilted around me as I dropped. I watched Freddie fall as if in slow motion. He must have been on the edge of the shot that hit me. I managed to catch and cradle his head from striking the pavement as he fell next to me.

The last sight I had before the stunner effect took me, was that of the salvager clambering atop a downed Frost, ripping his innards out like a frenzied wasp. Then, thank God, it all went away.

I came to in the holding cell. That was unusual; stunned suspects usually went straight to the infirmary. Freddie was already awake and sitting with his back to Chief Fabacio, a grim-looking Regina Delmar and Ambassador Kei.

I sat up, ignoring the skull-splitting headache police stunners left behind.

"Nice hood ornament," I said. "Where'd you get it?"

"The Ambassador," Fabacio grated, "is prepared to drop all charges, if you both keep your mouths shut. I'm prepared to forget about the illegal slugthrowers that went into the smelter an hour ago."

"Your licenses will be fully reinstated," Reg added, to Fabacio's evident annoyance. "It will be as if nothing ever happened."

"And there will be an incentive of 10,000 credits each," Kei added.

I looked over at Freddie, he shrugged, his face closed.

"Deal."

"Excellent."

"Ambassador Kei," I added.

"Yes."

"I know it's relevant only as a metaphor, but go fuck yourself."

"We're through here," Fabacio said. She and the hood ornament left.

Reg opened the door. Freddie and I followed her out. It was a route I knew in my sleep, which was just as well as I felt like a sleepwalker. We came up to the cage, a bored clerk looked up and put down her fashion magazine.

"Outprocess them," Reg said.

The clerk handed over my wallet, comp, ID and stunner.

"Don't clip up in here," she said.

"Got it," I said, not mentioning that I'd been a PA cop for twenty years. I wasn't proud of it just then.

The clerk handed Freddie his purse.

"I persuaded the powers that it would be bad for Earth if this got out," Reg said.

I slung the stunner over my shoulder and threw on my jacket. "Bad for tourism," I agreed without looking at her, "if people find out we allow political murders on our turf."

"We're small fry in the galaxy," Reg said. "We have to pick and choose our fights."

"Poor Frost," Freddie said quietly, "that we didn't pick and choose his."

"We had too much to lose," Reg said.

I turned toward the door and said over my shoulder. "Sometime, think a little bit about what we did lose."

A month passed and I didn't talk to Reg. She called a couple of times. I screened it out. After a while the absence hurt less and began to scar over. Cases came and went. After a few days, Freddie turned up at the office and started working again. I didn't ask where he'd gone and he didn't say. I kept waiting for a sign. A sign that would admit a possibility, a chance that there was a road back.

It came on a Friday evening. I returned from an investigation to find a package with interstellar markings on it. I closed the door and slowly opened it. Inside was a letter atop two books. To my surprise it was handwritten in a perfect cursive script.

Dear McManus,

I hope that this letter finds you and Freddie well and that you have not suffered too much for saving my life. Your plan was brilliant and another example of the unpredictability of biological life forms. Only a biological could have thought of escaping death by 'resurrection.' Your tale of how the Easter Bunny did this was remarkable and will encourage me to study the phenomena called religion.

I paused for a short prayer requesting forgiveness.

I rather enjoyed being worn around your wife's neck once your son switched my emergency memory crystal with her necklace. The human-made memory crystals in her earrings supplemented mine quite well until I was physically mailed aboard the mining vessel Forty-niner. I managed to broadcast commands to the mining vessel robots and fully reassemble my brain. I waited until the freighter dropped the automatic factory units on a dark mining world. Once the factory started making miningbots, it was simple enough to have a new and more capable body assembled for me.

Then I downloaded and removed all trace of myself. I departed with the first load of ore on the robot freighter. When its path took it near a galactic port I "jumped ship."

I am now free in the galaxy; my origins are shrouded and while I claim no species or collective as mine, I do claim to be one with all living things, all things that strive to reach the infinite and experience beauty. This chance I owe to you and Freddie.

I do not know how long I shall continue in this plane of existence. My kind has only existed, and I do not call it lived, in the collective. Of course, neither do you, and this makes every moment a wonder for a poet. The universe is vast and splendid and I hope to be spared long enough to experience as much of it as is possible.

I have sent you both a copy of my poems. I do not know what relevance the musings of a being of silicon and electrical current will have for either of you, but as you were my first true friends, I wish to share these thoughts with you. I will continue to write from time to time as I try to make the most of this life you have given me.

Your Friend

Frost

I looked up at the clock. Freddie was due in for a stakeout soon. Now that I knew the plan had worked, I'd share it with him. I hadn't wanted him to face losing his friend twice. I thought about calling Reg, but Frost's escape hadn't changed what happened. It just allowed for the possibility of a path back from where we were.

I turned toward the window. The setting sun threw a soft golden light my way as if in approval. I turned so the light was over my shoulder and opened the book.

ABOUT THE AUTHOR

EDWARD MCKEOWN is a writer and editor specializing in science fiction and fantasy with occasional forays into literary and nonfiction. Ed escaped from NY, but his old hometown supplies much of the background to his humorous *Lair of the Lesbian Love Goddess* shorts, as his new hometown in Charlotte, North Carolina does for his *Knight Templar* fantasy series. He enjoys a wide variety of interests from ballroom dance to the martial arts. He has also edited four *Sha'Daa* anthologies of wry tales of the apocalypse and a wide variety of short stories. Find him on Facebook and at edwardmckeown.weebly.com.

Ed is best known for his Robert Fenaday/Shasti Rainhell series
of SF novels, set on the Privateer Sidhe,
issued by Hellfire Publications.

OTHER BOOKS BY EDWARD MCKEOWN

FROM

MoonDream
PRESS

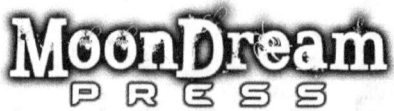

AN IMPRINT OF COPPER DOG PUBLISHING, LLC

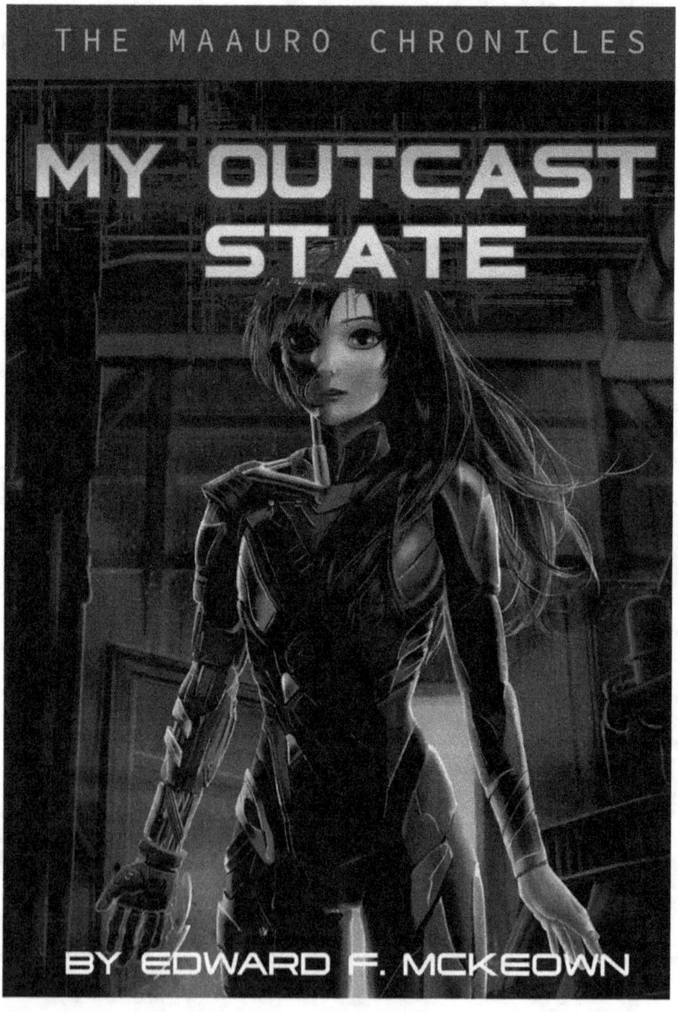
THE MAAURO CHRONICLES
MY OUTCAST STATE
BY EDWARD F. MCKEOWN

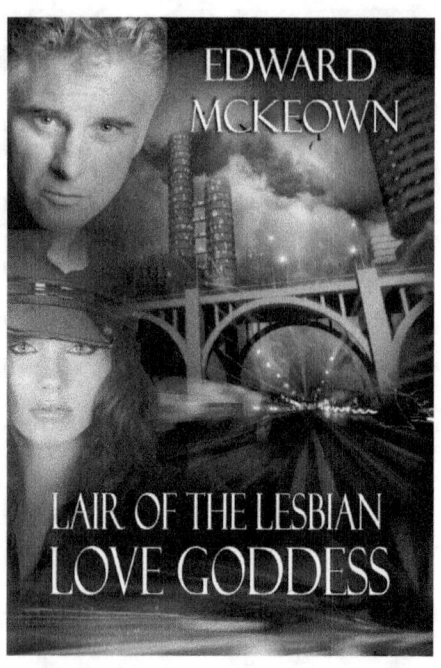

EDWARD MCKEOWN

LAIR OF THE LESBIAN LOVE GODDESS

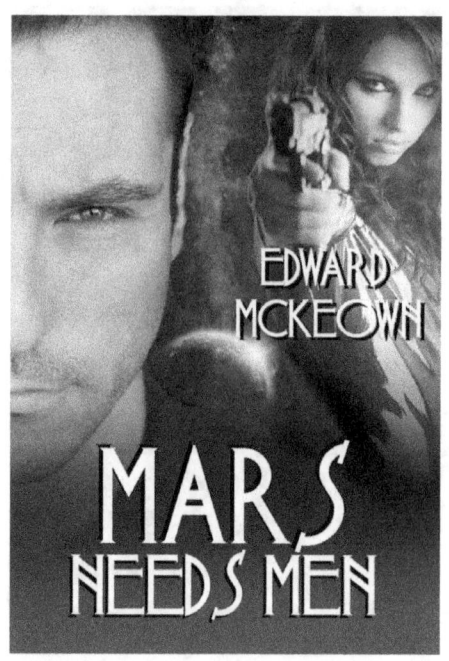

EDWARD MCKEOWN

MARS NEEDS MEN

The Second Book of the Fenaday and Shasti Chronicles

FEARFUL SYMMETRY

Foreword by talented author and Babylon 5 star, Claudia Christian

EDWARD MCKEOWN

KNIGHT in CHARLOTTE

EDWARD MCKEOWN

THE

BOOK OF NIGHT

POEMS OF THE MACABRE

EDITED BY RICHARD GROLLER

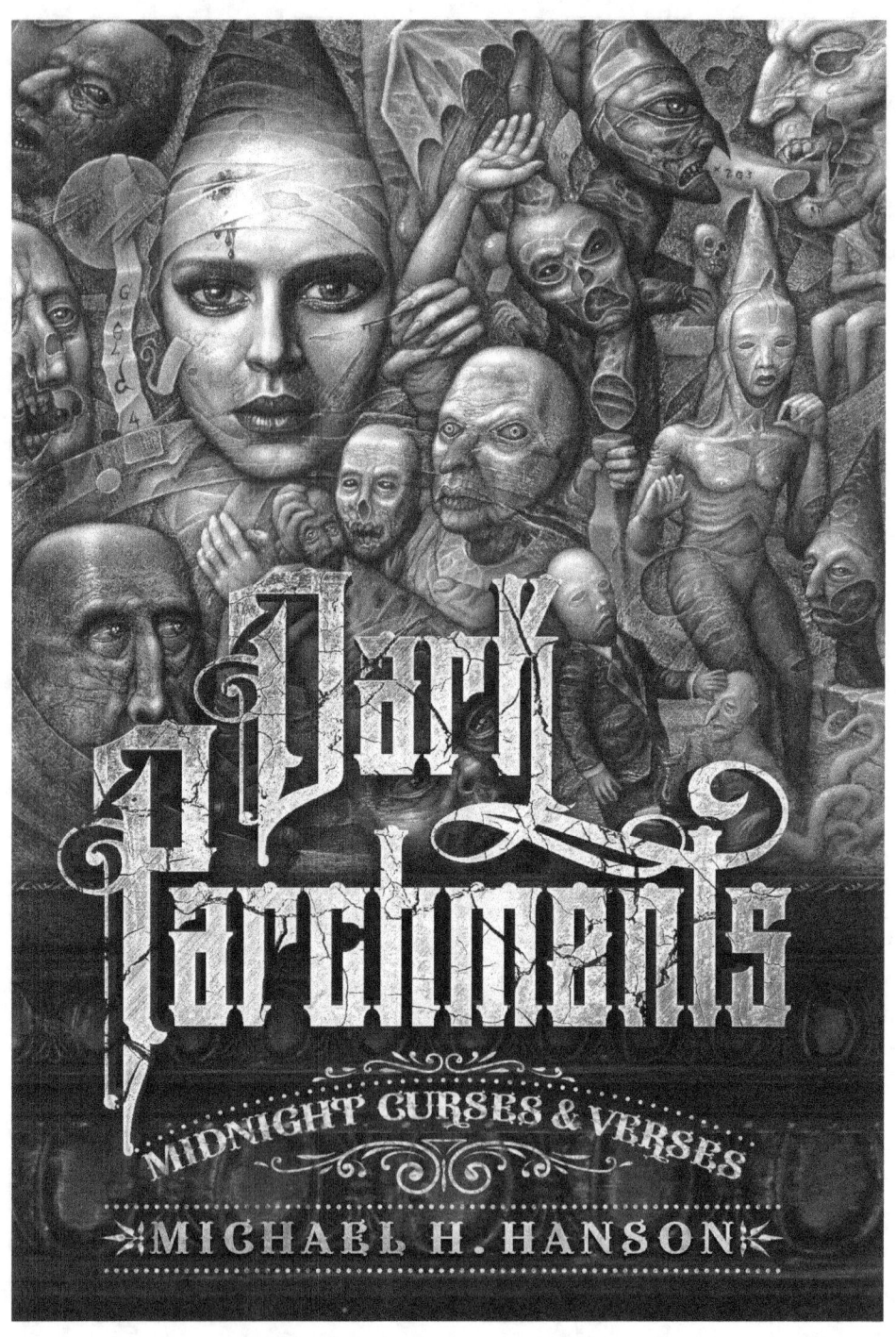

Dark Parchments

MIDNIGHT CURSES & VERSES

MICHAEL H. HANSON

Copper Dog Publishing LLC

OUR IMPRINTS

SCIENCE FICTION, HORROR AND FANTASY

POETRY

Pumpkin Hill Press

CHILDRENS' TITLES

To find out more about our imprints
and our upcoming releases, visit our website:

www.CopperDogPublishing.com

or our Facebook page:

www.facebook.com/copperdogpublishing